Faith Change

A Nina Bannister Mystery

by

T'Gracie and Joe Reese

Copyright © 2018 by T'Gracie and Joe Reese

For information, email Cozy Cat Press, cozycatpress@aol.com or visit our website at: www.cozycatpress.com

COZY CAT
P R E S S

ISBN: 978-1-946063-62-5
Printed in the United States of America

10 9 8 7 6 5 4 3 2 1

Glory be to God for Dappled Things
For skies of coupled color as a brinded cow;
For rose-moles all in stipple upon trout that swim;
Fresh-firecoal chestnut-falls; finches' wings;
Landscape plotted and pieced—fold, fallow and plow;
And all trades, their gear, tackle and trim.

All things counter, original, spare, strange;
Whatever is fickle, freckled (who knows how?)
With swift, slow; sweet, sour; adazzle, dim;
He fathers forth whose beauty is past change:
Praise him.

Gerard Manley Hopkins

For the Barbers, whose faith never changes

PROLOGUE

The creek drew her on, as she knew it would.

She had slipped down into it a mile or so back, at Milepost Three of the old Northern Mississippi logging trail. Now she was approaching Tombigbee Park itself, and watching for the signpost or marker that would announce her passing.

She could sense the coming change.

She was approaching her people's land now.

As for the creek itself, it was so different from the fir and evergreen forests that topped and surrounded it. It was a multitudinous thing, a camouflage of colors and textures, of shale rocks and speckles of iron ore and maple leaves and, here and there in the dark pools, the splash of gold and orange from perches' gills or bream flanks.

She made her way along slowly, carefully, reverently, as though she were in church.

Which, of course, she was.

How far was it now, the place she was looking for?

Not far, not far.

She could hear coming from the very rocks and trees themselves the words that had stolen this land from her people:

"Your father the President proposes to give his Chickasaw children a fine tract of country on the other side of the Mississippi River, of equal extent in exchange for their present lands..."

The other side of the Mississippi River.

A barren wilderness which would eventually become the Oklahoma where she herself had grown up.

The Trail of Tears.

And the stories she and all her people knew by heart.

Chickasaw that they were.

An "equal exchange" for their real home—these lands, this Mississippi, these forests where she now would begin work as a park ranger.

She made her way carefully out into the middle of the creek, white limestone rocks slippery beneath her boots.

Now she could peer up between the branches of oak and pecan and fir, up into the blue summer sky.

Three things she and all tribal children learned first, sitting on their fathers' knees as she had done: the creation, how they had been made, the migration, or the story of their original wandering so many centuries before, the story of the pole—and the nature of Ababinili, the one word for Four Beloved Things Above: Sun, Clouds, Clear Sky, and He That Lives in the Clear Sky.

And the greatest power of them all, the sun, the Great Holy Power above.

She could not look directly at it, of course, because divinity cannot be confronted in that way; blindness would follow.

But she felt its heat, its power.

In the old times, the real times, it was represented in each village by a sacred fire. Guardian priests watched over this fire and gave out coals for each household. This had the effect of bringing the sun into each home.

She moved on.

The banks closed in upon her, and she had to climb up out of the creek itself, which had become deeper.

The trees lowered themselves down over her, darkening the world.

Which became quieter too, all noises subsumed into dark-mossed green pools.

There before her in a patch of thorn and thistle sat a rabbit, deathly still, watching her as she approached, too frightened to move, almost invisible, save for its dime-shining eye that tracked her while, reflecting the sun, it gave itself away.

She would not bother it.

Other things would, of course, for the existence of this gray-furred and paw-furtive creature was both plagued and blessed by higher forces, benevolent, dangerous, merciful, cruel: the Hottuck Ishtohoolo, who were good spirits inhabiting higher regions, and the Hottuck Ookproose, or Evil Ones residing in the dark regions of the West.

All of them hiding among this stunning variety of trees, which, as a park ranger, she had been forced to learn and identify: Pumpkin, White and Blue Ash, Eastern Red Cedar, Shortleaf Pine, Pond Cypress, Eastern Hemlock, Pecan, Water Hickory, Winged Elm

And on and on.

There before her, almost obscured by undergrowth, was a brown wooden signpost upon which, in yellow letters was carved in yellow-painted letters, the words:

YOU ARE NOW ENTERING THE TOMBIGBEE STATE PARK

A park surrounding the Tombigbee River, which had been the heart-vein of the old lands.

After another quarter mile, she began to hear voices, campers, parents and children hiking on the trails which surrounded the creek. She made her way up the slippery bank and out into the forest itself, tipping her hat as she met various campers, who spoke joyfully to her:

"Beautiful day, Officer!"

"It certainly is. You folks have a good time."

She walked on, the trails becoming more crowded now.

Finally Tombigbee Lake spread itself out before her.

Not a very big lake—she could easily have swum across it. So could many of the teenagers who now were splashing and horse playing near the bank, warned not to go beyond the rope barrier making the rest of the lake a no swimming zone.

Because, had the rope not been there, for every hundred swimmers who made it, one would not.

She let her eye flirt across the blue surface.

A few boats out toward the center, and several fishing piers extending sixty or so feet out into the water.

A solitary man sat out toward its end, rod held loosely in his lap as he stared at the red bobber floating motionless.

"Good afternoon," she heard herself saying.

He half turned, smiled, laid the pole carefully on the pier beside him, and returned her greeting.

"Good afternoon yourself, Officer!"

"Having any luck?"

A large grin spread through his brown, rather unkempt, beard.

"Only a couple of bream. I've got a license you know. My name's Tamp Neufeld. I'm a preacher; you can trust me."

"I'm sure I can," she said, approaching him. "I would never suspect a man of God of violating the fishing laws of The State of Mississippi."

He shook his head:

"Well, I wouldn't be too certain. We preachers aren't all that trustworthy. We're taught, 'Render unto Caesar that which is Caesar's, and to God that which is God's.'"

"How do you tell the difference when it comes to fishing"

"Anything under a pound is Caesar's and we cut it loose. Bigger than that, we thank God and eat it."

She nodded, making her way out upon the rickety pier.

"That clears up the problem," she said.

He nodded, reeling in the bobber a turn or two, and said:

"Sound theology has a way of doing that."

She sat, crossed her legs, and peered out across the lake.

"What is your denomination?"

"Methodist. And yours?"

She smiled and shook her head:

"I'm kind of in between,"

"Between what?" he asked.

"Two traditions, I guess you might say."

"Meaning?"

"I'm a full blood Chickasaw Indian. Still, my parents took me to a Christian church. A Baptist church. Felt like they needed to, I guess. The modern world and all. I got baptized. And I know all the hymns."

"Well, that's a beginning."

"Yes. Except I can't sing."

"We all have our limitations."

"The other limitation I have, at least as far as Christianity goes, is my dad."

"I thought he was the one who made you go to church."

"Yes, and he went too, as well as my mother and sister. They bought into it."

"Your father didn't?"

She shook her head, remembering.

"Not really. He never forgot the old ways. The Chickasaw ways. He had been taught them by his father before him, and on back and on back. Even though we were in Oklahoma, where the government made us move at the turn of the century, his heart was still here on the Tombigbee River, where the tribe was from who knows when up to the coming of the Spanish."

"And your heart?"

"Like I say, I'm kind of caught in the middle."

They were quiet for a time, listening to music coming from radios on the opposite shore.

"So," she said, finally, "are you here on vacation?"

He shook his head:

"No, I'm just up here on an advance scouting mission."

"How's that?"

"I'm from down at Bay St. Lucy."

"On the coast?"

"Yes."

"You're a long way from home."

"I know, but...well, you're new to the park service I suppose."

"Third year, but first week here at Tombigbee. They've asked me to come as a kind of Native American Cultural Ambassador. I'm to give lectures on Chickasaw culture. I'm also putting together a small museum near the main camp building. But this 'scouting mission' you're on?"

He smiled.

"The First Methodist Church of Bay St. Lucy comes here every summer, first week in June, as a kind of all church retreat. It's like the old Tabernacle meetings for us. Adults, kids, everyone comes."

"How many?"

"There'll be between fifty and sixty of us."

"When will you start arriving?"

"Next Sunday after church. It seems like a long way to come, I know. But a good many years ago one of our members—a wealthy man—made a large donation, stipulating that we use a major part of it to come here summers. He had grown up in the area and loved the park. So now it's a tradition. We have to pay out of the church budget, of course—the donation has long since run dry. But our congregation thinks it's worth it. And, this year, too, there's going to be something a bit special. We're going to be joined by The Bethel African Methodist Episcopal Church. We've thought about doing it for some time, and this year it's finally going to happen."

"That's exciting."

"We think so."

"How will you all get up here?"

"Cars, buses—we're like the children of Israel heading up to the Promised Land. Anyway, I'm one of the church's two pastors. Technically I'm an assistant. I always come up a couple of days before the others arrive, just to check everything out. I'll be going back to Bay St. Lucy in an hour or so. But this trip up to the park is bittersweet for me."

"How so?"

"It's my last one, at least I think so. We may not be here next year."

"I'm sorry to hear that."

"Well, we have a fine young pastor—Brother Aaron Rockman—been with us about a year. He thinks we're wasting money doing this every year. He hasn't brought up the matter with the congregation yet, but he will. I know the Bishop in Jackson agrees with him. We'll just have to wait and see what happens."

"I hope it all works out."

"I do too. Miss?"

"Smallwood. Barbara Smallwood."

"Nice to meet you, Barbara. But now if you will excuse me, I'd better pack up this rod and head back to the main building. A few things to do before driving back."

She watched him reel the sinker and bait in. While he did so, she said:

"You may or may not know. In 1737 a Chickasaw delegation met with John Wesley in Savannah. They talked, I'm told, about all things the Chickasaw shared with the Methodists."

He smiled as he threw away the worm and put the bobber and hook in a green tackle box.

"Perhaps you will talk to us about similar things in the days to come."

"I'd be honored."

"Well then—until we meet again."

"Yes. Until then. Go with God."

"You too, Barbara Smallwood."

And, so saying, he made his way over the rickety pier and onto the shore.

She watched him disappear into one of the trails that led back to the main camp building.

Then she turned, looked back over the lake, closed her eyes, and allowed herself to feel one with her people.

CHAPTER ONE: HOMAGE TO CHARLES DICKENS

It was the best of times, it was the worst of times.

And had Charles Dickens himself been in Bay St. Lucy on June 2—especially in the late morning or early afternoon—he could not have put it better.

It was the best of times because people were everywhere. They were running on the beaches, splashing in the surf, cavorting on the sand dunes, hang-gliding over the cabanas, renting the floats, buying the hot dogs and cotton candy, perusing the gift shops, filling all available tables in the snack shops and restaurants, and spending money spending money spending money and spending money.

So in that sense it was the best of times.

It was the worst of times because the people of Bay St. Lucy—the real people, the winter and spring people, the people who actually lived in the town, went to Bay St. Lucy High School, sat on the town council, and endured winter temperatures that sometimes plunged into the high thirties—hated the summer people with a passion and wished they all would leave.

Leave their money, of course.

But still, leave.

As for Nina Bannister, she dealt with the situation by spending her time in one of two ways: during most of the daylight hours she worked in Elementals: Treasures from the Land and Sea, where she dealt with mostly sane people who were not getting drunk on pina colladas, were not getting fatally sunburned, were not stepping on jellyfish, and were not poking with long sticks the occasional Portuguese Man of War that had just washed ashore on the beach and did in all actuality look like the most beautiful and filmy-transparent football ever inflated by God, who, having made both the oceans and the beaches, would never have allowed in either one of them anything that could cause pain.

No, she sold the latest seascapes by Ramoula Peters; Havilland Dinner Service in the Wheat Pattern; Limoges: Hinged Chef Hat; Pickle Casters; Meridian Baskets; and Hermann Traditional Mohair Bears.

True, she did not sell a great many of these things, but the fact that Elementals was empty for a large portion of the day allowed her to read Dorothy Sayers or Janet Evanovitch or Sara Paretski.

During the day, that is.

Evenings she did precisely the same thing.

She closed Elementals at five, made her way through the small parking area to the metal pole around which was tied the chain to her Vespa, climbed aboard, started the little blue cycle, put on her helmet, and turned on the key to the ignition.

Vroom.

Good old Vespa; never had failed her yet.

She then pulled the vehicle slowly out into the street, Breakers Boulevard, and looked around her, behind her, over her, beside her—at all the antics that were going on in what was getting to be the cool part of the day. Skateboards careening illegally down a major thoroughfare, hang gliders hanging and gliding, their pilots wearing outlandish costumes reminiscent of Superman or The Three Stooges, little children screaming, bigger children screaming, everybody, when one really noticed it, screaming about something or other, and all beings on or around the bicycle lane bordering Breakers Boulevard—dogs included—splotched with various flavors of ice cream.

Through this madhouse she putt putted her way home, to the beach shack which nine or even ten months of the year afforded her a somewhat quiet retreat—if one did not count the arrrrgggh of the incoming or outgoing tides—but which in June, July or August, lay open and exposed like the high ground of a battlefield.

She could always see, as she pulled into her own driveway, the fishermen and swimmers and sunbathers and wave riders and athletes and bathing beauties and beachcombers and poets and sketch artists and drunks—all of them passing between her shack and the sea, all of them looking up at the stilt-riding porch and the big picture behind it, and all of them thinking:

"I wonder who lives there."

So that there was nothing to do but pull the Vespa into the garage area under the shack, secure it with chains as heavy as Marley's ghost might have worn, take off her helmet, revolving slowly as she did so in such a way as to allow her to use it as a weapon if necessary, hide it under a huge blanket which she hoped smelled strongly enough of urine to keep away those who might wish to urinate on it—and run fast up the rickety stairs.

Then open the door, squirt quickly into the entrance hall then living room—

—and lock herself inside.

Close the curtains!

Turn out the lights!

Nobody home!

This was her routine on those gentle summer nights when, elsewhere in the country, normal people might be starting their barbeque grills and pondering the orbed moon.

And this had been her routine tonight.

Except that this night was special for Nina Bannister.

So that this particular evening, rather than making herself a little supper—probably frozen tamales as well as anything else—reading for four hours in the bedroom, putting cotton wads in her ears, and attempting to go to sleep a ten o'clock—this particular evening she went immediately to sleep at six o'clock.

It was a superhuman feat, given, but two glasses of wine purchased the day before at Baggatelli's Bakery and Delicatessen did not hurt the process.

And she woke up at midnight.

A kind of witching hour for everyone else in the universe.

The opposite for Nina.

For when she got out of bed and made her way to the picture window, when she pulled back the curtain and looked out over the sea, she could tell that everything had worked out the way she expected.

Everything had changed as it had been supposed to change.

The moon was hanging, huge and white, out over the middle of the ocean.

"And the moon like a flower," she heard herself whispering, "in heaven's high bower, in secret delight, sits and smiles on the night."

A few people still remained scattered on the beach, but they were wrapped in blankets—even though the night was warm, midnight meant blankets and these were lovers and dreamers, not wild-eyed thrill seeking infants.

They made little or no noise, nor any movement that rivaled the coming in and going out of the growling white laced waves.

This being the new world that surrounded her, she could do what she had to do, and had done for some years now.

Her pilgrimage.

She pulled on a baggy sweater, made a cold cut sandwich, ate quickly, and slipped from the shack and down the stairs.

The bag containing the things she needed was waiting for her beside the Vespa where she had left it.

She stowed it in the little compartment behind the seat, unchained and started the Vespa, and headed out.

The warm sea air washed over her, and within a minute or so she was quietly chugging past the darkening businesses of slumbering Bay St. Lucy:

The Blue Crab Gifts Gallery

Clay Creatures

Maggie May's

The Social Chair

Mike's Treasures

Aloha Gallery and Frame Shop

Jayne's Novelties and Gifts

And on and on.

Until, turning carefully from Jackson Boulevard onto Sea Pine Way, she viewed, and slowly approached, the building she was headed for, steepled, soft golden lighted, and sitting on the slight hill that allowed it to look down on its town:

The Bay St. Lucy First United Methodist Church

She stopped the Vespa, killed the engine, and propped the cycle against a white picket fence that surrounded the church and the graveyard behind it.

No chain, no keys.

This was sacrosanct ground.

Anyone stealing anything from this place would be instantly struck by lightning and disintegrated.

This she fervently believed.

Entering the building was no problem for her, since, named a lay-leader three years earlier, she had been entrusted with keys to front and side doors, as well as to the fence surrounding the cemetery.

A quick rasp of metal, a tug on the tall and ponderous white doors, and she was within the sanctuary.

Moonlight filtered through the stained glass windows and bathed the pews in ghostly shapes of revered figures.

Mary Magdalene at the Tomb of Christ.

Peter Denying Jesus.

The Entry into Jerusalem.

She made her way down the center aisle.

She knelt at the altar.

The cross loomed before her.

"Heavenly father..."

And she prayed.

There were times—many times in the last weeks—that Frank was with her, talked to her, advised her, as he had when he was her husband and still alive.

But he was not here now, nor did she talk to him.

It would not be right. It would be selfish.

For she was talking not to Frank but to God.

And this she did for several minutes, while tears ran down her cheeks and made her eyes glimmer.

When she had stopped (for one never "finishes" praying), she got to her feet and made her way to the left of the altar and outside, into the cemetery. The stones were familiar to her, and the names chiseled in their gray limestone.

Elders of the city.

Barker

Jackson

Duvall

She turned left, then right, always aware both of the town sounds faintly intruding themselves (a siren here, a wispy strain of radio music there) and the grave sounds (a cricket, a cicada in one of the oaks spreading above)—until she came to Frank.

Frank Bannister
1940-2010
From Your Loving Wife Nina:
'"The Music in My Heart I bore
Long After It Was Heard No More"

She knelt; from the small bag she had brought she took a white candle and a red rose.

The rose she laid carefully at the base; the candle she placed in a brass ring that had been attached to the stone.

She lit it, saying to the flickering flame:

"We'll go to camp in a week, Frank. And we'll have your fishing contest. And I know you'll be watching."

She watched the candle throw its light on the rose.

And she watched the moon throw its light on everything.

Then she got to her feet and left.

INTERLUDE: NINA'S DIARY

I'm a bit surprised that I'm writing like this, because I've never done so before. Strange. I love writing, love to write, and am constantly writing to various friends. I also know so many people in my situation—basically alone, widowed or divorced—who get great pleasure out of communicating with their diaries. But I have never done so.

Why now, then?

I don't know.

It may be because I feel that something is changing, but exactly what it may be, I just don't know.

It's five thirty in the morning as I sit here writing this. I'm outside on the deck. The sky is just beginning to turn a lighter blue in the East, and it will continue to get lighter until it turns silver, then yellow, then red. Sunrise, I read in the paper, will be at 6:20. Then the tourists will begin to appear down on the beach.

I slept only a little last night—or this morning rather.

I took Frank his flowers and candle at midnight as I always do this time of year. When I got back here I just didn't feel like going to bed so I sat in the living room just thinking about things, life in general I suppose, for a couple of hours. I guess people tend to do that as they get older. You know you are actually getting older— have gotten older, have become aged—when your memories outnumber your hopes.

I read that somewhere, I don't know where.

But anyway, that's how it's gotten for me.

It's all like a movie that I've seen, and now the movie is almost over. Lights will go up in the theater and it will be time for all of us to go home.

Except, I guess the lights will go down and not up.

Anyway, I just feel the need to communicate with somebody.

In a week the church goes on Retreat. I don't know why we've come to call it that. It seems like in some ways the church has been retreating all year, backing away from this or running scared away from that. Maybe we don't need to do a retreat; maybe we need to do a 'charge' instead.

But anyway, retreat it is.

The Retreat Committee will have a big meeting in one of the upper rooms of the church tonight, just to hammer everything out, to be sure all the details are finalized, the food provided for, singing and skits and theatricals arranged.

Anyway, there's always a nice feeling about the day before Summer Retreat. It's a cleaning out time.

Furl will be with the Giusti's—John will pick him up Thursday morning before we leave.

He usually stays with Jackson Bennet—he likes their kids so much. But the Bennets will be at the retreat with me next week.

Yes, that's right. The Bethel AME congregation will be joining us!

That's never happened before.

I think it will be wonderful, I really do.

But I can write more about that later.

Oh look! Some red streaks in the sky!

And there, there are my two porpoises swimming by from north to south, just enough light out there to see their black bodies glistening. Wonder where they're going?

Doesn't matter, as long as they know.

Which I guess they do.

Anyway though, Furl is out of the shack this week and the next, and is being well taken care of by the Giusti's.

And as for the rest, it's a time of, as I wrote before, cleaning out and starting over.

I'll use up all the food in the house, so that the refrigerator will be empty while we're gone and the pantry will be bare.

I'll go to the grocery store the Sunday afternoon after we all return and set in a new supply of groceries.

I love the routine of Retreat.

It's always the same, and means it's always something I can depend on.

I hate the summer tourist crowds that spill out on the beach after Memorial Day weekend. It's like I'm living beside a Midway. It will be nice to be away for a week.

No surprises.

And that's the best thing about it all: no surprises.

CHAPTER TWO: THE   CHURCH   OF   NO
SURPRISES

No surprises.

Church always began at the same time on Sunday morning, ten o'clock sharp.

No surprises.

There was always the painful ceremony of making her way through the outer vestibule, painful because all of the smiling—broadly smiling—men and women who were her long term neighbors in Bay St. Lucy, insisted on greeting her:

"Nina!"

"Good morning, Nina!"

"SO nice that you could make it this morning, Nina!"

"How are you feeling today, Nina?"

"What a joy to see you today, Nina!"

"How is Furl coming along these days, Nina?"

"You're looking good these days, Nina!"

And why was this painful?

It was painful for two reasons: first, all of the people who greeted her with such enthusiasm were bigger than she was. Worse, their hands were bigger.

Especially the men's. So that their handshakes simply enclosed her tiny little fingers and crushed them together, holding and holding and holding until she first acknowledged the seemingly unexpected joy of this unexpected—even though it happened every Sunday—meeting, and second she almost screamed out in pain the words "LET ME GO YOU'RE KILLING ME!"

rather than the more obligatory words, "Fine, doing well, Furl's good, so nice to see you too, it is wonderful weather, isn't it? Fine, really fine, just...just so fine I can't tell you..."

And on and on until she had personally greeted every one of the fifty-eight people who were her fellow parishioners, and made her way through the vestibule.

And there before her lay the sanctuary.

About two-thirds full.

She never failed to stand a moment before taking her eternal and unchanging seat on the end of the eleventh pew from the front, and examine the OLD DEPENDABLES who had already arrived and were watching the altar and beyond as the white-robed choir filed in.

She always brought to mind one of her favorite literary passages, the opening of a particular chapter of Victor Hugo's *The Hunchback of Notre Dame*, in which Quasimodo, The Bell Ringer of Notre Dame, is being introduced:

"There seemed to emanate from him a mysterious influence which animated the stones of Notre Dame and made the ancient church thrill to her deepest depths. He was everywhere. He multiplied himself at every point of the structure. Now the terrified beholder would descry, on the topmost pinnacle of a tower, a fantastic, dwarfish figure climbing, twisting, crawling on all-fours, hanging over the abyss, leaping from projection to projection to thrust his arm down the throat of some sculptured gorgon; it was Quasimodo crow's-nesting. Again, in some dim corner of the church one would stumble against a sort of living chimera crouching low, with sullen, furrowed brow: it was Quasimodo musing. Or again, in a steeple you caught sight of an enormous head and a bundle of confused limbs swinging furiously at the end of a rope: it was Quasimodo ringing for vespers.

Egypt would have declared him the heart of the temple; The Middle Ages took him for its demon; he was in fact its soul."

Those equally familiar with the First United Methodist Church of Bay St. Lucy would have recognized the creature's successors in people such as Inez Whittaker, Maybelle Simpson, Lannie Baker, his wife Cindy, and their daughter Allison.

They were everywhere, and they multiplied themselves at every point in the institution.

When pies were needed to be supplied for the 4th of July bake sale to be held at the town armory, with proceeds split equally between The Veterans of Foreign Wars and the church's committee to Feed the Indigent? Inez, of course, would arrive no later than ten a.m. with the back of her station wagon overflowing with two apple, three chocolate, two raspberry, and five lemon custards (her specialty), all of which would be snapped up within the first hour of the evening.

A member of the congregation was found to have been admitted to Bay St. Lucy Hospital, from any sickness or infirmity ranging from severe flu symptoms to strep throat to incurable pancreatic cancer? Maybelle would be in the room of the afflicted even before the attending physician, with flowers, solace, any food that might be allowed under the circumstances, and a heartfelt promise that either the sickness would be weathered within a matter of days, or that, such being impossible, the patient would be in heaven with prior deceased loved ones and ecstatically happy for the rest of eternity.

Someone needed to preside over Children's Church (which meant taking all young members under the age of twelve to room 42G and riding herd over them, even over Bobby Thornapple, whom not even the town's toughest first grade teachers could deal with) for the duration of the real service? There was Cindy, leading twelve scruffy bodies up the aisle, soon to disappear into the outer vestibule, then to disappear completely, none of those involved to be heard from at all during the regular service, except for a few muffled screams.

The Presbyterian Church would have taken these people to be the PW in the Presbytery (or Presbyterian Women in the Presbytery); The Baptist Church would have taken them to be the WMUSBC (Women's Missionary Union of the Southern Baptist Convention); but they were, in fact, heartfelt members of the UMW, or United Methodist Women—or in other words—the church's very soul.

A man was needed (for some challenges did require a man, feminism notwithstanding) to supply a pick-up truck or come and fix the toilet without charging anything like what a plumber would have charged or take over running the fishing contest, the same one Frank had invented? Here was Lannie, large, multi-skilled, ever willing, and versed in all skills ever developed through millennia of human existence. Lannie always with his subtle smile which indicated that at the basis of human existence there lay not only hope, but, even more remarkably, humor.

After noting these things, she took her seat.

The service began with Allison Baker, now permanent acolyte, coming forward and with a long golden wand—she could have been a creature out of a fairy tale—carefully lighting the altar candles, an act which prompted her father to note that she was actually performing an "Act-o-Light," which prompted her mother to say in mock disgust, 'Oh Lannie, honestly!' and Allison herself to say, 'Oh, Daddy!'

Then came the two pastors, Brother Tamp and Aaron Rockman.

Then came the first song.

The nature of which depended on whether the rather elderly Margery Peterson or the young university music student Gregory Huffman was playing organ on that particular day,

Nina always hoped for Margery, whose presence at the instrument boded "Blessed be the Tie that Binds," or "Tell me the Stories of Jesus," rather than Gregory, who meant "Buxtahold, Prelude #21 in D-Minor."

Today was Buxtahold.

Oh well.

Then came joys and concerns.

This part of the service had become a bit of a problem.

At one point, several years earlier, joys had equaled concerns in numbers, as they generally do in life.

But as the congregation aged, the latter had taken precedence over the former.

Also, the reporting process itself had changed.

It had in the old days been simply:

"Lanelle Davis has been admitted to the hospital."

But now the ladies doing the reporting had become much more specific, and they spoke more slowly, enjoying the dramatic pauses surrounding certain organs and symptoms:

"Dawson Lewis' brother Richard, who as you know lives in northern Oregon, has been diagnosed with non-recurring empfairinaitis, which has begun to produce malignant tumors on the anterior lobes of both his descending pineal glands and his median femoral artery."

This announcement being generally followed by a long and sustained:

"Oooooohhhh!"

Nina had ceased to be certain of whether the moan was a sincere expression of grief or a show of respect for the anatomical knowledge of the speaker.

After a time, of course, all of these preliminaries ended, and it was time for Pastor Tamp to do the morning prayer and for Rockman, the head pastor, to preach the sermon.

Making Nina say to herself:

Concentrate of the morning prayer, Nina!

And:

Concentrate on the sermon, Nina!

But, of course, she could do neither.

Perhaps because she was thinking mainly about the two pastors and about how different they were.

Tamp had been in Bay St. Lucy forever, weathering the coming and going of at least five other ministers, each of whom had ranked as his superior. He was always, in Nina's mind, more a character from old black and white cowboy movies than from theology school. Long and lean, a bit scrabble-bearded even on Sunday morning when he was at his most fastidious, blue eyes flashing out at the congregation, he always seemed ready to shout out:

"Now let's us have some dern good dancing!"

He was, in short, though possibly a bit Billy Graham, much more Gabby Hayes.

And she loved him.

Everybody loved him.

As for Aaron Rockman…

…well, what could she say about Brother Rockman?

He was young, probably in his early thirties.

But no one held that against him.

He was from the North—probably they had all been told where in the North but it did not matter because the North was the North.

And not everyone held that against him.

He was known to be ambitious, rising in the hierarchy of the church, and probably hoping to leave Bay St. Lucy fairly soon to be posted in, if one gave him the benefit of the doubt, Jackson, if one did not, Boston.

He was unmarried.

Which meant either that he saw the Church as his first love and Jesus as his spiritual spouse as nuns do, or that he was not somebody a woman could love.

Nina tried to withhold judgment on that issue.

She did not succeed of course.

And he was conservative.

Conservative, and sent to Bay St. Lucy to keep the church in line.

For, in fact, the church of Bay St. Lucy was two churches. One church was an institution to be found in any small Mississippi town, composed of country people, Southerners, good neighbors, eaters of and makers of, cornbread made in skillets and coming out with blackened bottoms on each of the slices.

The other church reflected the fact that Bay St. Lucy was an artists' community.

Painters and sculptors, some of whom were sitting in the congregation today.

Some of whom did not always accept the pronouncements of The Book of Discipline.

And some of whom, like Meg and Jennifer, sitting over to the left in the far back pew, were gay.

So these were all things that intruded into Nina's mind and pushed out the ideas and possible inspirations to be found in First Philippians, 2-6. There was something else, though.

For today she realized the service would not end with the usual offering and the singing of the Doxology.

There was another pastor still to be heard from.

A Black one!

This was a man she had seen on the Streets of Bay St. Lucy often, and a man whose name she knew:

Reverend Abraham Goforth.

But now here he was in her own pulpit, in her own church.

Did she mind?

A small wiry man with iron gray hair.

Quick, darting eyes.

He smiled.

Wonderful smile.

Tamp smile.

"My brothers and sisters in Christ, I bring you greetings in the name of Jesus Christ our Risen Lord, who has a question to ask you all. And that question? That question is, when, in this great nation of ours, comes the most segregated hour of the week?"

Pause.

He looked at everyone in the audience.

One by one.

Of course, they all knew the answer.

Sunday Night, Eleven O'clock
Home from the Planning Meeting

I like it that we meet in an upper room.

I like to think we've just had a last supper. I can go around the table and substitute disciples for the committee. Lannie Baker is Peter. That would fit, big tough Lannie being a fisherman. Marvin and Bill Thomas are James and John. I never could keep James and John separated in my head (except that they're the sons of Zebedee, who I can't keep straight in my head either.), but Marvin and Bill are twins, and I can't keep them straight either. I don't know who Judas Iscariot is, but I guess that's fitting. He wouldn't be Judas Iscariot if you knew who he was.

Inez Whittaker and Maybelle Simpson are Martha and Mary of course.

Do all the work, get little of the credit.

Cindy Baker is Mary Magdalene.

Okay, okay, I know Mary Magdalene wasn't at the last supper, but I don't know any other Bible women to make Cindy right now, except for the real Mary, and I'm pretty sure, because of Allison, that Cindy isn't a virgin.

The meeting went about as expected. There are a thousand little details—food, who's bringing what and for what day, what meal—all the stuff that has to be in place for the fishing contest, all the stuff that has to be in place for five evening vesper services, all the arts and crafts stuff (last year we ran out of paste, and there was you know what to pay for that!), and on and on.

Except that, about forty minutes into the meeting a bombshell was dropped.

You have to understand that this particular meeting was different from the start. Five members from Bethel were there.

One of them was Alanna Delafosse.

You would know Alanna if I had been writing in you every day, because I see Alanna almost every day.

And even if I saw her only once a week, she would still be unforgettable.

The cultural maven of Bay St. Lucy.

Her bombshell?

Well, to get ready for it you need to realize that the song leader position is very important at summer camp. We do a great deal of hymn singing, from the little ones to the old ones.

Except this summer was going to be a problem.

Our song leader had some health problems, and theirs was on a trip that couldn't be postponed.

So Alanna had volunteered to find a song leader.

If I had done that, I would have looked here in Bay St. Lucy.

Alanna looked in New York and Los Angeles.

And who did she find?

I'm going to paste into your pages, diary, an article from the Entertainment section of last Sunday's New York Times.

Here, Diary—see if you can digest THIS:

"The most startling, least promoted segment of the Hollywood Pop Award Evening opened the show. It was a verbal barrage and choreographed massacre by Jack Fontenot, who dominated all hip-hop categories and won Album of the Year. He started with a giant video of an American flag behind him and, around him, a formation of marching soldiers in camouflage and ski masks, as he rapped about poverty and revenge in 'XXX.' There was also an excerpt from 'DNA'— thoughts like 'Dodging Bullets, Reaping What You Sow'–with Mr. Fontenot flanked by fist pumping soldiers. It seemed to have ended with a gunshot and a blackout—but there was more. Soon Mr. Fontenot turned to verses he had recorded as guest raps for Poor the Kid and Black Rock, refusing all conciliatory roles: 'Who am I? Not your father nor your brother, not your reason, not your future, not your comfort, not your rebel, not your glory. 'The soldiers had turned into red-hooded figures: one by one, with rhythmic gunshots and flames behind them, they fell to the stage. And, with syllables flying at machine-gun speed, Mr. Fontenot had created a pop-culture moment of almost complete social destabilization."

A rap singer!

A famous rap singer even! And the article goes on:

"The music industry is undergoing changes unlike any in its history, and Mr. Fontenot, almost unique among performers, has capitalized on the rise of

streaming, realizing how digital multi-consuming has sub-created an advanced rubric for a nouveau, at times resurgent and at others bordering on disingenuous, deactivation of power re-generation."

So, when I told you I liked Retreat because it was always the same, with no surprises?

Forget that.

Here is one huge surprise already!

I wonder if there will be more.

CHAPTER THREE: AND ON THIS ROCK I BUILD MY CHURCH

There are two ships which carry great importance in the Methodist Church. One is stewardship, which means money. The other is fellowship, which means food.

Pies of all kinds.

Salads.

Rolls.

Loaves of homemade bread.

On certain occasions barbeque. On others ham. On others chicken.

And on all occasions for Nina Bannister, potato salad.

She was good with deviled eggs, too, and the eggs she brought to no matter what occasions almost immediately disappeared.

And so was it certain to be, she was sure, this particular Wednesday night when the women of the church met for their mid-week fellowship.

They met in a large room down the hall from the sanctuary, a room perfect for the occasion. It was a room adorned with few or no religious artifacts—a bare brown cross hung on this wall, a small framed map of the holy land on that wall—but filled otherwise with bridge tables that sat four apiece, and longer tables upon which the platters and bowls and jars and other kinds of food and drink containers could be placed.

Nina loved the occasions.

For during them she had learned years earlier to become something other than a high school principal, and now something other than a retired/widowed high school principal. Just as Margery Thompson there on the far side of the room had become something other than the wife of the president of the First National Bank, and Susan Watkins had become something other than the manager of the local supermarket, and Dierdra McKenzie had become other than the owner of the town's leading clothing store.

No, during these evenings they put aside educational backgrounds, marriage successes or failures, monthly or yearly income—even religious questions or beliefs— and became simply The Women of the Church.

Politics were never discussed.

This is not to say they had no political insights or stances, for there in the large room, one now helping herself to a helping of Nina's potato salad, one third of which was now gone, was the town's assistant mayor, and there choosing between sweetened and unsweetened ice tea, the town's district attorney—but that they had entered a different and higher realm.

They were not gossiping.

They had simply entered a world which men would probably never know.

The meeting lasted an hour and a half, during which time Nina found herself seated at four different tables, talking with at least eight different people.

Talking about what?

Half an hour afterwards she herself had forgotten.

There was, of course, one topic which did tend to recur.

The rap singer who was to be their song leader in the summer camp.

Is it true that he had won a major Hollywood award?

"Would he," Ramoula Peters had asked, "wear sunglasses and a long black leather coat, and would he wear his hair in deadlocks?"

Dreadlocks, someone had corrected.

Whatever.

And would he sing without any melody at all and just say words—street words, whatever those were?

Would the entire congregation of the First United Methodist Church of Bay St. Lucy be asked to go to a five day camp in which they never sang "Tell Me the Stories of Jesus, Write on My Heart Every Word?"

And Nina wondered about Alanna.

This was her best friend, of course—aside perhaps from Margot—and, perhaps it should have fallen to her to approach Alanna and let her know, subtly, that certain members of the congregation, not the painters nor the poets nor the sculptors, of course, but the more conservative members, had a few questions about this appointment.

Perhaps she should have taken her friend aside and asked simply something such as:

"Have you taken leave of your senses?"

Or:

"Have you gone insane or what?"

Maybe, maybe she should have done that.

Maybe she still should.

And so she left the meeting pondering those questions, and letting them rob from her the more normal pleasure of picking up her potato salad bowl and noting that it was completely empty, scraped clean by a group of people who probably counted among the potato connoisseurs of the world.

She had tucked the bowl under one arm and, her purse held securely beneath the other, was beginning to make her way toward the basement exit, when she was aware of a noise behind her.

She turned.

A door had opened.

The Pastor's office.

And here was now the Pastor himself, Reverend Rockman, all smiles, stepping out into the hallway.

"Ms. Bannister!"

She was, for a second or so, somewhat at a loss for words.

In the first place she had no idea that Reverend Rockman was in the church at all that evening. He always seemed to step out and surprise her.

In the second place she was surprised that he addressed her with such cordiality, since the two of them had enjoyed little personal contact in the past months since his arrival.

No tension between them, of course.

But there had not been a kind of—well, it was surprising to see him here and smiling so broadly.

That was all she could say about it.

But to him she did find some words, after all.

"You're working late, Pastor."

The smile broadened as he took a step toward her:

"Too much work! It never gets done!"

"I'm sure that's true. Any head Pastor must have a thousand things on his plate, from preparing sermons to visiting the sick to dealing with budgets—most of us out in the pews have no idea, I'm sure."

He was quiet of a second, then nodded and said:

"Well, actually, since you said that…"

"Yes?"

"It's all of you out in the pews that make my job possible in the first place. Ms. Bannister…"

"Nina."

"Yes, good, Nina. It's a shame we're taking this long to get on a first name basis."

"You've had a lot of people to get acquainted with."

"Yes, that's true. But you should have been one of my first. I wonder—do you have a couple of minutes to spare?"

"Of course."

"Then… perhaps you could join me in the office for a time?"

"Glad to."

"Good. Come on in then."

She did so, and in a short time the two of them were seated at a large round table.

She looked around; she remembered being in this office before for pastoral conferences of one kind or another.

It looked somewhat different now though.

Had he changed the books?

"Would you like a cup of coffee?"

"No, no thank you. It sounds good, but I could never get to sleep."

"I understand."

"I wanted to let you know: I enjoyed your sermon on Sunday. We all did. That's what we were talking about upstairs in Women's Fellowship."

This was a lie, of course. What they had been talking about in women's fellowship was the rap singer, and whether they were all going to have to sing dirty words.

"Thank you. I love Philippians. Always have, since theology school."

"I do too."

Another lie. She had no idea who the Philippians were, or even what they were.

What was she lying so much?

Of course it would hardly do to say: "I have never read one word of Philippians, and I spent your entire sermon today daydreaming about completely other things."

No, rather than do that, just go on lying.

He went on:

"I appreciate the compliment, I really do. But I need to compliment you, too, Nina."

"Why? What have I done?"

"More than you know. Not just you of course. Inez, Maybelle, Lannie, Cindy—there are always stalwarts in any congregation. They are the glue that holds the church together. And all of you have held this church together very well, during some, well let's say, difficult times."

He leaned forward and put more of his weight on the table.

He was a compact man, built like a rock as well as named for one. He could have been, she mused, not too many years ago a football player. He had black piercing sparkling eyes that went with his black piercing sparkling hair and his black piercing sparkling shoes—and as he leaned toward her she had the feeling he was preparing to run a play rather than merely express a point.

"The truth of the matter is, Nina…"

Uh-oh, she found herself thinking.

She hated hearing sentences that began, "The truth of the matter is…"

Such sentences made her ask the speaker—in her mind of course—why bring up the matter at all of if you're NOT planning to tell the truth of it?

And what the speaker inevitably meant to say was, "I'm going to tell you something you don't much want to hear."

But there was no help for it here.

She was trapped in the basement of the church with a Philippian-loving running back.

"The truth of the matter is, the church has gone through some difficult times in the last few months."

She wished now for coffee.

If she had coffee in front of her she could sip and not have to speak.

As it was, she did have to speak, and so she said:

"Oh, I don't know."

Billy Graham could hardly have topped that one.

Good job, Nina!

"Yes, you've all dealt with the problems well, internally—but it could not have been easy. The truth of the matter is, you had to go through a period of almost eight months without a head pastor. These things happen, of course. Your previous pastor passed away unexpectedly. A new appointment cannot always be made on the spur of the moment. And so a great deal of pressure was placed on you, your congregation, and, of course, Brother Tamp."

"And I might add," she said, "that Tamp did an incredible job. He was everywhere. And you know—I'm sure the Bishop knows—he isn't really paid. His compensation is a dollar a month. And has been for years."

"Yes, we're certainly aware of that. But Reverend Neufeld, as I'm certain you are aware of, does not hold a degree in Theology."

"That's true."

And who cares? she found herself thinking.

"It shouldn't matter a great deal, of course. It isn't necessary in the course of leading a church day by day to know Greek or Aramaic. But there are other matters that tend to be more pressing."

"Such as?"

"Well, as you yourself pointed out, there are budgetary concerns."

"Are we in debt? More than we were eight months ago? Did Tamp go off to Las Vegas and gamble all our money away?"

He laughed.

"I've been told often about your sense of humor. I'm now enjoying it firsthand."

Enjoy, enjoy, she thought.

But she said:

"I really wasn't aware we were in financial trouble. I don't think anyone in the congregation knows that."

"It's not as acute a problem as I may be making it out; but it could get to be one."

"How?"

He took a deep breath.

Now he's going to get, she realized, to the heart of the matter.

"I'm sure there are rumors going around about my concerns."

"Which concerns?"

"The summer Retreat."

"I may have heard some things. I didn't pay them much mind."

"Nina, I think it may be necessary to pay them a great deal of mind."

"Necessary why? The Retreat is a part of the church heritage. We've been going up to Tombigbee for years."

"I know."

"And we pay for it with our money. Money that goes into the collection plate every Sunday."

"Instead of what?"

She looked at him.

"I don't understand your question."

"I'll put it as callously as I can. Too large a percentage of the congregation's offering is going every year to rent these cabins and defray the other expenses of a week in the wilderness."

"I'm still not sure I…"

"Our main building here in Bay St. Lucy is getting old, and it's not being kept in proper repair. There are five toilets. Two of them are currently not working."

"But Lannie Baker has promised that next week…"

"Lannie Baker is a dedicated Christian and a jack of all trades. But he is not a professional plumber. And the people who are professional plumbers cost money."

"I'm sure if there were a special offering we could come up with the money to fix two toilets, even if we had to hire a professional."

"But it's worse than that."

"How?"

"There are major structural problems that must be dealt with."

"We didn't know that."

"Because Tamp didn't tell you. Brother Tamp likes to see people happy. He likes to make people happy. But sometimes there's bad news, and it has to be addressed. There is the news, for example, that the church here at Bay St. Lucy is contributing far less to the UMCOR relief program than other churches of similar size around the country."

"Again, we didn't…"

"You didn't know, and, again, it's because Tamp failed to tell you."

Silence for a time.

Finally, Nina:

"Are you telling me this may be our last summer Retreat?"

He massaged his temples for a time, sighed, and then said, softly:

"I'm driving to Jackson tomorrow to meet with the Bishop and several other men. Financial people mostly."

"You won't go with us to the camp?"

"I'll join you on Monday or Tuesday, depending on how the meetings go."

"I hope they go well. But you must believe me: if this is just a question of money, then I know the community can…"

"It's not just a question of money."

He took a deep breath, then he told her what else:

"Nina, this entire co-operative venture with the Black church…"

The 'Black' church? she found herself thinking.

"It was done entirely by Tamp and Brother Abe."

"Yes. They're friends. Have been for a long time."

"But no one in the hierarchy of the church was apprised of it."

"Why should they have been?"

Now he had changed somewhat; it appeared that he was talking to a child:

"You must understand. This is not like two Methodist churches on opposite sides of town getting together for a softball game. No, the Bethel Church is entirely different from us."

"Because of their color?"

"Of course not! Because of their theology. They do not believe the same things we do. We take our policies and doctrines from the Book of Discipline. Their authority comes from…oh, it doesn't matter. It's just…well, we all need to make the best of this. And Nina, please, don't look at me as the bad guy in all of this."

"No. I won't."

"No one loves Tamp more than I do."

Except everybody in the church.

"I realize that."

"I know you do. And, thank you for listening to me."

And so it was time for good-byes to be made.

CHAPTER FOUR: WHY THESE TWO SHOULD NOT BE JOINED…

The drive home was difficult. Not so much because of the fireworks that continued to send yellow or green tracers across what should have been a calm and moonlit Mississippi sea-night sky, but because of the nagging suspicion that things were not going to turn out well. Tamp was an institution, but he was now working for a man who did not honor institutions. He was working for an ambitious cleric who saw Bay St. Lucy as a stepping stone.

Frank appeared on the passenger seat behind her; she could feel his arms encircling her. He was deceased, of course, but much more alive to her than most of the people she knew.

"What do you think?" she thought.

The answer came clearly, as it always did.

"I think it's pretty obvious."

"How can you say that?"

"Because I'm dead."

"And that makes it easier?"

"Much easier."

"So what's the answer? How is this thing going to be resolved?"

"Somebody needs to shoot him."

And then Frank disappeared.

She had more questions for him, but he was gone into the night and into the recesses of her mind.

And there would not have been much time for chat anyway, first because she was almost home, and second because, when she did take the final turn that brought her coastline shack into view, she saw a jeep parked in her driveway.

What did this portend?

Trouble.

No, Nina, she told herself. *Don't be such a pessimist.*

So there's a jeep parked in your driveway. Why does this automatically mean that something bad is about to happen?

Mystery novels. That's it. You read too many mysteries, Nina. And whenever something new and different happens in a mystery novel, it has to be bad. Who would want to read about somebody who kept having good things happen?

This thing, on the other hand, was actually a good thing, as she realized when she cruised the Vespa past the parked jeep, braked, and dismounted.

"Hello, the Vespa!"

Two jeep doors opened simultaneously and two strikingly different figures emerged: one tall and willowy, the other short and thick-oak-like.

"Meg! Jennifer!"

For the visitors were in fact Meg Brennan and Jennifer Warren, each smiling as they stepped toward Nina.

"We know it's late, Nina, and we hate to bother you."

Nina smiled as she hung the helmet on the handle bars and locked the Vespa to the metal pole that was its home.

"There are no two people," she said, "that I'd rather be bothered by."

The three of them met at the base of the stairway which led up to Nina's shack, and they embraced the way only Mississippi people could embrace, unless one counted Alabama.

"We got here about twenty minutes ago," said Jennifer, "and you weren't here—but then we realized that you were probably at the Wednesday night social, and would be home directly after it, so we decided to wait."

"I'm glad you did," said Nina, starting up the stairs. "Actually the evening ran a little later than normal. I wound up talking to Brother Rockman."

Meg:

"How did that go?"

Nina, now at the top of the stairs, shook her head.

"I'm not sure. He's an odd duck. He thinks this might be...well, let's not talk about that now. Here, wait until I unlock the door. There we go; come on in."

It was strange, she thought, not having Furl to sidle up against her as she entered. Strange not to feel him rubbing up against her ankles and saying in Cat, 'Where the hell have you been?'

But he was at the Giusti's and thus all right.

Except for what they might do to him if he kept swearing.

Who knows? Maybe they could cure him.

"Sit down anywhere, you two. I think I've got some cheese balls already put out on a platter, and there's some mandarin orange slices, too. Want coffee?"

Both of the women shook their heads:

"Couldn't sleep. Thanks for offering though."

"No bother. Here, let me get this stuff out of the refrigerator."

She did, and in a little over two minutes they were parked, two on the couch, one on the large green chair facing it.

Cheese balls and mandarin orange slices sat decoratively on the coffee table between them.

The food did not disappear as quickly as possible though, and it did not take Nina long to realize that this was a 'cheese triste.'

A sad cheese.

No, Nina decided. Hardly the poetic value of the French 'vin triste.'

But then one was doing without wine, and without the French.

What could one expect?

Her first instinct had been correct though. There was trouble involved here. And there was nothing to do but wait for it, through a few more pleasantries, a few we're doing all rights, and the store's business is okay.

But then it came, just as Nina was beginning to regret the fact that she did not have anything stronger to offer the two of them than coffee.

Like scotch.

"Nina, we've come to ask a favor of you. And we realize this might be…well, difficult. If you don't want to do it, we'll understand."

Or rum.

Maybe gin.

A big bottle, whichever.

"Tell me. If I can do it, I will."

"Something, well, difficult may be about to happen in our lives."

Oh God, were the words that came into Nina's mind.

Sickness.

Cancer.

She thought of last Sunday's joys and concerns.

Tubular cancer of the distending dithrobya.

"What is it?"

"Marriage."

She was silent for a time, and then riposted wittily, imagining gin if not actually tasting it:

"What?"

"We're going to get married. We think."

"You already are married. I think."

"That was a civil marriage. Done a year and a half ago in New Mexico, where gay marriages are legal."

"Yes, I remember it. The trip cost you your coaching job, Meg."

"Well, there's no point in talking about that now. Jennifer and I are perfectly happy running the shop, and the bills get paid."

"All right, but I still don't understand…"

"We want a church wedding."

Aha.

The gorilla in the room.

It wasn't cancer, but even Nina, lay person Nina, knew immediately that this might be, in some ways, more complicated.

"You want to be married," she asked, "in the Methodist Church?"

Duuuh, Nina.

What did you think, The Great Buddhist Shrine of Sri Lanka?

Get on board here, girl.

"Yes."

Well, at least that eliminated the Temple.

And who wanted to go to Sri Lanka anyway?

"Meg, Jennifer—I didn't think that Methodist pastors were allowed to perform gay marriages."

Both seemed to answer at once:

"They weren't. Not up until a year ago, anyway."

The two of them now seemed to have merged into one speaker:

"But now there are demonstrations going on in churches all over the country. Here: we printed this off. We got it from the internet:"

Nina took the piece of typing paper that was offered to her and read:

Only the General Conference speaks for The United Methodist Church. When the lay and clergy delegates to General Conference approve a statement, it is published in the *Book of Discipline* and/or the *Book of Resolutions*. These words come from the people of The United Methodist Church.

341.6: Ceremonies that celebrate homosexual unions shall not be conducted by our ministers and shall not be conducted in our churches.

"All right," Nina said. "That seems pretty clear to me. You can't do it."

"That's what we thought. But look at this. Also from the internet."

Another sheet of paper:

Rejecting the denomination's stance on gay rights and same-sex marriage were important issues for at least 15 United Methodist annual (regional) conferences this summer.

United Methodists from Washington and the northern panhandle of Idaho approved legislation supporting the Marriage Equality Act.

The law was signed by the governor in February and would have made Washington the seventh state to allow same-sex marriage. The law was set to go into effect June 7 but Referendum 74, an anti-gay marriage measure, got enough signatures to put the initiative on the November ballot and put the law on hold.

During the June 21-24 meeting, delegates also approved a resolution to address 'a lack of congruence between the denomination's hardened stance against homosexuality and its historic affirmations of the rights for all people.'

The Rev. Sandy Brown, pastor at Seattle First United Methodist Church, said the *church's stance is "wrong, stupid and evil."*

Both Jennifer and Meg were beaming as Nina putdown the article.

"Do you see, Nina? We're not alone anymore. The Seattle First United Methodist Church. To prohibit a gay couple from being married by a pastor, in the church, is "wrong, stupid, and evil.""

"Wow."

There was not much more she could say, so she said it again:

"Wow."

"Nina, this issue is splitting the church apart."

Finally, Nina asked: "But do you want to split the church apart?"

"No. But we also don't want it to remain medieval because its members refuse to think. And we want our rights."

There would have been silence in the little shack living room except that a repeat of World War II was being played out on the beach below.

"When is this wedding going to happen?"

"At the Retreat. We don't know yet which night. Now it looks like Wednesday. And, Nina, here's the big favor: we want you to stand up with us."

"You want me to be your best man?"

"Well, the terminology gets a little difficult. Best Man, Maid of Honor—let's just say we want you and Alanna to be down there with us."

"I'd love to. And I'm sure she would too."

"Yes. We were over at the Auberge des Arts this afternoon. She's agreed to take part."

"Not surprising. It will be a great honor for both of us."

Boom boom boom. Fireworks. Rock music.

All sounded the same.

Finally, Nina spoke, saying what the entire little room knew had to be said:

"Meg, Jennifer—who's going to perform the wedding?"

"Brother Tamp."

"Of course. You contacted him and he said yes?"

"No. He contacted us."

"What? Just out of the clear blue sky?"

"No, of course not. We had talked to him a little more than a year ago and he said he would need time to think about it. We never heard back. Yesterday he called. He had been up to Tombigbee getting things together and doing a little fishing."

"Yes, he always does that."

"He said that, while he was there he came to a decision. He said marrying us was the right, honorable, and Christian thing to do. And so he was obliged to do it."

"What if he performs the ceremony and the Bishop in Jackson refuses to recognize it?"

"That's the beauty of the thing, Nina. A church wedding, we learned, is not like a civil wedding. There is no law involved to be broken. It's only that, a ceremony, and it can no more be taken back or made not to exist after it has been done, than a song can be unsung. The only thing that can happen is…"

"Yes?"

"Tamp can be removed as an Associate Pastor."

"He knows this?"

"Yes."

"And it's all right with him?"

"He said, 'it's time.' Then he said, 'If this is the last thing I do as a pastor—well, it's probably the best thing."

"Tamp would say that, but..."

"But what?"

She looked at them.

"I think you both know 'but what?'."

"You mean Brother Rockman?"

"Yes. What if he doesn't allow it?"

"We asked Brother Tamp that question."

"And he said?"

"He said, 'Let me worry about Brother Rockman'."

And that was that.

Fifteen minutes later, Nina, best man to be, was sitting on the deck ignoring the tourists she had only hours ago found so distasteful.

She wished for Furl but Furl wasn't there and nothing remained of him but his familiar yowl.

And she wished for Frank but he was not needed now, having told her all she needed to know about Brother Rockman:

"Somebody needs to shoot him."

CHAPTER FIVE: DRIVING TO THE CAMP

Saturday morning.

The Baker's red Ford Crew cab crunched on the shells paving the parking area in front of Nina's house.

"Hop on out, Allison, and see if Ms. Nina's ready," said Lannie.

Allison opened the back door of the four-door cab, hopped down on the step then to the ground and scampered up the shaking steps, to Nina's door, her two braids flapping up and down as she ran.

Knock, knock, knock.

She turned back and waved at her parents. As she twirled back to face the door, it opened.

"Hi, Ms. Nina!"

"Good morning, Allison! Are you ready to go?" Let me grab my bags." Nina picked up the small, green roller bag by the handle. *This must be 30 years old*, thought Nina, doing the math in her head. *Someday soon the zipper or the wheels are going to fail. Oh, well, maybe one more trip.* Nina reached back through the door and grabbed a plastic grocery sack, its contents bulging. She handed the plastic bag to Allison, closed her door, locked it and pocketed the key.

Nina followed Allison down the stairs. Lannie had gotten out of the truck, and, taking Nina's bag, placed it in the well-packed back of the truck.

"Got everything?" Nina asked him.

"Yep! Two sizes of fishing poles, your box of trophies and ribbons, three plastic buckets—"

"Here, Lannie, can you find a place for this?" Nina took the plastic grocery sack from Allison and handed it to Lannie. "I got some extra sunscreen and bug spray to use during the fishing times." Lannie used his left hand to open the top of one of the boxes and placed the sack on top, folding the flaps back down.

"Allison, you and Ms. Nina hop in the back seat and we'll take off."

He opened the back seat door. Nina, aware that Allison had caught up to her in height, waited to see how she maneuvered into the high cab.

"Ah, there's a step up—and handle to grab." Nina slid herself onto the seat as smoothly as she could. Snapping her seat belt, she greeted Cindy, who was turning around in the front seat to look at her.

"Good morning!"

"Good morning, Ms. Nina! Are we ready to go?"

Lannie backed the truck around and pulled out onto the road. Nina looked back one last time and thought *Good-bye, old shack*, as she mentally checked through her departure tasks: "lights out, check! Patio door locked and curtains pulled shut, check…"

Nina looked through the windshield at the first car with MayBelle, Jane and Helen riding with Tom Simpson. She looked back to check on the other pickup truck carrying Brother Abe Goforth and Alanna from Bethel. The vehicles had been traveling a little above the speed limit, and had gotten through the speed trap outside of Hattiesburg with no problem. *They should be at the park in about an hour and half,* thought Nina. Suddenly, she heard a siren in the distance. She looked back. "Lannie, slow up a bit," said Cindy, also looking back. The siren grew closer and closer. "Lannie! Where is it?" Allison started to giggle.

"Daddy!" she chortled.

"Lannie Baker! You stop that!" cried Cindy. The siren abruptly stopped and Lannie grinned, looking back at Nina in the reflection of the mirror.

"Lannie, was that you?" asked Nina.

"Daddy can whistle like a siren!"

Lannie and Allison laughed together, and Nina joined them.

"Honestly, Lannie!" Cindy, too, had a smile on her face. "He can be quite a trickster, Ms. Nina."

"I remember," said Nina, thinking back on Lannie in middle school, and some of the pranks he'd played on people in high school. Always good natured, no one ever seemed to be very upset when they were the target of his pranks.

When they were about an hour from the park, Allison wanted to go to the bathroom. Lannie flicked his lights off and on to let the lead car know he was getting off and pulled up to a gas station. He pulled over to a parking area away from the lanes getting gas.

"Come on, Allison, I'll go in with you," said Cindy, opening her door. Allison opened the door on her side and the two of them went into the station.

"I think I'll just stretch my legs," said Nina, remembering back to what Dr. Singh had told her once she finished her Coumadin course. "Always remember to wirgle your ankle and feet. Never sit too long in an airplane or car. Every 30 minutes or so, wirgle." It took Nina a little while to realize Dr. Singh probably meant "wiggle" or maybe "waggle". Having been seated about two hours, and tired of "wirgling," Nina got out of the truck and walked around it. Cindy and Allison came back out, Allison bearing Doritos, beef jerky, and a Snickers bar. Cindy opened the front passenger door for Allison. "Why don't you ride up here with Dad the rest of the way and I'll sit and chat with Ms. Nina."

Soon they were on the way again. Allison flipped on the radio and found a station that she liked.

Cindy leaned closer to Nina and lowered her voice. "I wish we had a different preacher than Rockman."

Nina raised her eyebrows and whispered back, "What's the problem?" Cindy and Lannie had been stalwarts in the church. They had been youth leaders for fifteen years, starting with their older two, Britton and Emily, and planning to finish when Allison graduated from high school, in six more years. Never in all those years had Nina heard either of them speak badly of a church leader.

Cindy sighed. "He's such a dictator. And a money cruncher. He told me that we couldn't take our youth on the mission trip this year. Can you imagine that? Our church has always managed to raise the money for them to go to Houston and work on houses. I know the seniors are going to be very disappointed. With him, it's always "No". Is that anyway for a pastor to act?"

No, she thought. But then she banished thoughts about Rockman and let her mind wander to other times she and Frank had driven up to the park. Now down a hill and around a curve, the road on both sides filled with forests of trees. The sunlight broke through and dappled the road. "Welcome to Tombigbee State Park". Lannie braked at the guard house.

"We're from the Bay St. Lucy church and the Bethel church coming up a day early to get everything ready for when all of the others arrive tomorrow."

The woman ranger handed a parking pass through the window to Lannie. "Welcome! You can use this pass to go in and out if you need to as long as you're here."

Lannie put the parking pass on the rear view mirror, and leaving his window down, drove slowly toward the lodge where they would be staying. One more curve in the road, and there it was. A feeling of joy washed over Nina.

The lodge was in front of them. One part of the lodge was stucco, with a red roof and an entrance at street level that looked like a hobbit door. This was the older section, built in the 1930's. The newer section, added on in brick and adding another story of rooms. The older section was like staying in an old inn, and the newer section was like staying in the Holiday Inn. The newer entrance, with a circular drive for unloading vehicles, and an accessible entrance for people in wheel chairs was at a ninety degree angle to the old entrance. All three vehicles in the caravan pulled around the circular drive and parked. The three drivers got out and stretched. Nina got out and ran back to greet Alanna and Brother Abe. She grabbed Alanna and gave her a big hug. "I'm so glad you're all with us here this year!" She was enveloped in the scent that Alanna always seemed to be wearing—jasmine? Coconut? Something both earthy and sweet followed Alanna wherever she went.

"Lannie, after you check us in, can you drive your truck around to the kitchen area? We need to start setting up the kitchen for the meals for the church. We've packed sandwiches and chips and drinks for a quick lunch, and then we can get the trucks unloaded," said Maybelle. "Tonight we'll eat from the restaurant buffet, but I want to be ready to cook when the church folk arrive on Sunday." She rubbed her hands together, as if anxious to begin cooking for dozens of people. Breakfasts for those staying in the lodge would be cold—donuts, cereals, yogurt, and hot coffee. Retreat breakfasts would be heftier with bacon and sausage and biscuits and pancakes. Lunch could be had in the dining room at a soup and salad bar or in the snack area if your tastes ran more to pizza and hot dogs. Dinner was what

Maybelle lived for. The lodge restaurant was theirs for the week, and Maybelle and her crew were ready: gumbo (prepared in Bay St. Lucy and frozen for transportation) and rice and hush puppies made on site for the first night; spaghetti and meat sauce—also prepared in Bay St. Lucy and frozen for the trip up. One night would be "breakfast for supper" with bacon and sausage and scrambled eggs and pancakes and toast, another would be ham and butterbeans and the crowning night would be the fish fry after the fishing contest. Janie always took care of desserts and had been baking cookies and brownies, and pies, and sheet cakes—never leaving her kitchen for at least a week before the Retreat.

The travelers grabbed their bags and entered to lodge to check into their rooms.

CHAPTER SIX: FIRST SATURDAY AT THE CAMP

Nina's eyes opened and her first thoughts were about how rested she felt and she rolled over in the bed to see what time it was by her watch. 5:55. She sighed. She always wanted to sleep a little later and after all the big muscle activity from yesterday she felt certain she would sleep until 9:00 or later. She flipped back over on her back, threw the top cover off and left only with a sheet in the warm room; she looked out into the room. It was a small room with a gabled ceiling slanting over the head of the bed. Sunlight streamed through the slats of half-opened blinds. After the hard work of yesterday, and the busy days of the Retreat itself, the Retreat Committee always took Saturday as a day to rest, refresh and do whatever they wanted to do. Nina thought she would head out to her favorite reflective area of the park and have breakfast after she returned. Slipping off her night gown, she headed to the little bathroom to begin her day.

Nina enjoyed the early morning cool air against her skin. *See, it was good to wake up early sometimes,* she thought. She headed west on the trail away from the lodge. Soon the branches of the trees overhead screened her from the bright light of the rising sun. She skirted around the path going down to the amphitheater and kept walking west, her steps thudding softly against the dirt of the trail. Ahead was a large meadow with posts embedded in the ground. Four posts set the corners of a rectangular area, and four more, and four more. Nina made her way to the center of the area and turned in a slow circle letting her eyes track and her mind imagine the walls of the barracks that these posts marked the corners of. A sign gave information about this area, but Nina didn't need to read it. During the Depression, in the 1930s, young men, some as young as some of her high school students, came to Tombigbee park. Out of work, in fact, they had no work in their home towns across the nation; they were hired by the government to do public works and came to northern Mississippi to build the lodge and outbuildings as part of a WPA work team. She walked over to a spot in the corner, away from the others. Here she knew was where the "trouble-makers" were housed. She always wondered what kind of trouble young men out in the middle of nowhere could get into. She smiled. These would be some of her students. Trouble, yes, but worth the trouble if she could catch the mind and inspire the learning. The barracks hadn't been much shelter to begin with, and over the years, the buildings had collapsed into themselves, until some state warden decided it would be better to remove them and leave this simple memorial to catch unsuspecting hikers and teach them a little U.S. History. Nina reached her hand up and padded the top of the post that was only a little shorter than she was. "Bye, boys, see you next year," she softly whispered.

Returning now into the rising sun on her back, she retraced her steps to the lodge. This time she noticed a young female park warden coming out of the door of a small frame building near the lodge.

"Good morning!" Nina paused and wiped the back of her hand across her brow. The day was beginning to heat up.

"Good morning," answered the young woman.

"I'm Nina Bannister, and I'm here as an advance team for the churches coming up tomorrow."

"Barbara Smallwood." The woman nodded. "I saw all the activity yesterday with boxes of food being unloaded back in the kitchen area. I met your pastor, Tamp, last week."

Nina nodded. "Brother Tamp has always come up the weekend before. He says it's to finalize the plans and the payment, but we all know he wants some extra fishing before the busy week with the church."

Barbara chuckled. "That's what he was doing when I met him!"

"What are you doing here?" Nina gestured to the open door to the small building.

"Come in and see," said Barbara, turning to reenter the building. "There's not much here right now, but I'm happy with the location and the size of the space."

She turned back in the center of the room to face Nina who had followed her in. The space had been lined on two sides with glass-topped display cases. The building was old, but she could also see it had been recently cleaned. A broom was leaned up against one corner.

"There's still a lot to do," Barbara offered. "But this is soon going to be the Chickasaw Nation Museum. I've been hired here to be part-time warden and part-time museum curator. You can't see it now, but there are at least twenty boxes of artifacts that I've been going through and cataloguing. Ten I brought with me from Oklahoma with the blessing of the Chickasaw leaders and the rest have been donated by locals who'd found artifacts over the years on their farms. This land used to belong to the Chickasaws. We were the ones who named it Tombigbee."

"That's amazing!" said Nina. She studied the young, dark-skinned woman in front of her. "Are you…?"

She stood a little straighter and said, "Yes, I am a full-blood Chickasaw woman." She smiled at Nina. "It has always been a dream of mine to teach people that come to this park about our presence here. When I went to college, I studied the Chickasaw history and minored in museum studies. I first worked in Oklahoma for the state park service, but when I saw on the website that Tombigbee State Park needed some extra help this summer, I knew I could do that job and get the museum up and running. The warden who hired me agreed to let me try. I almost have all the artifacts catalogued. Another day or two and I'll be ready to move the boxes down from the third floor where I've been working into the museum space."

"Do you need some help moving the boxes?" Nina offered, thinking of the high school students of the church and the service activities they were supposed to complete during the week. "I have some young, strong men and women arriving tomorrow who are always looking for something to do. I bet if you had a couple of them, we could move the boxes in no time."

"That would be great!" said Barbara. "Are you sure they wouldn't mind?"

"No," said Nina. "In fact, their youth leaders Lannie and Cindy are here now. Why don't I bring them by after breakfast to meet you to see what you need moved."

"I'll still be here for a while after breakfast. I'm waiting for a locksmith to come and put in a lock on that door and give me the keys. Some of these artifacts are quite valuable and some could be a little dangerous if stolen. I have one good example of a 19th century small ax that the Chickasaw traded for to use with wood needs. I don't want to move anything in until I'm certain I can secure it." She reached back and flipped the end of her long, black braid up and fanned the back of her neck with her other hand. "Whew, it's warm in here, too. I might have to see about a window unit or no one will ever want to come see it."

Maybe our church could help her with that, too, Nina thought.

"Well, I better be going while breakfast is still available in the snack area. It was nice to meet you, Warden Smallwood—"

"Please, call me Barbara, Nina."

"Okay, Barbara." Nina smiled. "I'll bring Lannie and Cindy by a little later this morning."

Barbara smiled and touched the brim of her hat in a small salute to Nina.

Nina walked back the lodge, her mind filled with ways to help her new friend, Barbara.

Sunday Evening
My Room:

Whew! Everybody's here—teams have set up tents in "their" area, families, wee ones and single adults are paired up in their rooms. The Koinonia Class members are napping—bless their white heads. I'm glad the noisy teens will be sleeping outside, far away enough so that their noise won't bother anyone in the inn. (And so happy that I have my favorite room in the old part of the building—complete with the best view of Lake Tombigbee!)

Everyone arrived safely. I better stop writing and get ready for Vespers. It will be the first time to hear our new choir director. I hope Alanna is right.

Tuesday is the kids' practice fishing before the big tournament—and I've got some new ones to get started.

Solo Deo Gloria

CHAPTER SEVEN: THE RAP MAN

She looked out across the amphitheater, now rapidly filling, The Bethel AME Church, the First United Methodist Church.

"Nina! Come here and sit with us!"

Alanna and the Bennets with a space between them.

She made her way along the row, hugging as many people as possible, finally inserting her little body into the narrow space still available for her.

Jackson Bennet's wife leaned over and said:

"Isn't this exciting?"

"Yes, it is!"

"Jack Fontenot right here, ready to lead us in singing!"

"It's hard to imagine!"

Of course, that, at least, was true.

"Do you like Beyonce, Nina?"

"I've never been there."

A slight silence for a moment; Jackson smiled, took her hand, and said:

"Well, maybe we can take you sometime."

Then the lights went down in the amphitheater and Jack Fontenot walked onto the stage.

She had seen a few pictures of him during the previous day, having gone online to research this strange phenomenon that was now to be the community's leader in song. What she had viewed was hardly encouraging. Dark sunglasses, golden fruit-loop earrings, African warrior garb—how was he ever going to relate to her church, a church of white and—let's face it—old men and women?

But the figure who now appeared before them was nothing like she had imagined.

He was a slight young man, caramel-colored skin and tight curls that showed his Creole heritage. He seemed to belong as much on Bourbon Street as Hollywood and Vine. As for dress, it was quite conservative. He wore a sky blue long sleeve shirt, khaki trousers, and brown hush puppies that were the same color as the guitar he carried with him.

Not an electric guitar, Nina found herself noting.

Just the plainest instrument imaginable.

The crowd had become one animal that was now holding its breath. The Youth, The Young Marrieds, the Seniors, and all the other appellations and sub through super appellations used by the church to divide its membership, peered down at the stage, upon which was nothing at all except the plainest of straight chairs.

Jack Fontenot down in it.

He cradled the guitar in his lap, and, for a short time, communed with it.

He seemed to whisper to the six strings, and, hearing their reply, used his left hand, now wrapped gently around the neck of the instrument, to turn and re-turn oh so carefully the tuning pegs.

Listen to the e-string listen to the d-string listen to the g-string...

And on and on for fifteen seconds.

Half a minute.

While the crowd-animal continued to be transfixed.

Until, finally, Jack Fontenot looked up at them.

It was as though the sun had come out.

There it was, the sun itself.

The man smiled at them with a facial ray-gun that made the night go away, so broad and white and welcoming and love-filled was it that it warmed the entire amphitheater an additional hundred degrees.

What was, Nina wondered, he going to say?

That question was answered immediately.

He wasn't going to say anything.

But how was he going to lead them in song?

There were no songbooks.

There had to be songbooks!

Didn't there?

And on the worn wooden benches encircling them—no books.

So how in heaven's name…

But then she began to realize.

It was, in fact, Heaven's name.

For he strummed, ever so softly, the most beautiful chord in the world.

The chord was accompanied by the most beautiful voice in the world.

Not exactly a tenor voice, nor was it capable of being categorized as any other human voice. It was The Archangel's voice and they had all died and they were now in Paradise where such chords and such voices happened all the time. Throughout eternity.

It had been worth waiting for all along.

He sang:

"Far away the noise of strife upon my ear is falling…"

Stop.

Look around the crowd.

Everyone here belong in Heaven?

Yes?

All right then, we'll strum a different chord, progressing from the first one as though it had grown naturally out of the hole in the center of the guitar. And that voice again that voice that voice that voice that…

"Then I know the sins of earth beset on every hand…"

The sins of earth, yes, there were sins of earth, of course there were. But they weren't going to win. This ethereal music had an answer for them, was going to beat them, yes it was yes it was….

Third chord.

Followed by:

"Doubt and fear and things of earth in vain to me are calling…"

YES they are calling in vain YES YES YES they are calling in vain I don't care about them will never care about them ever again EVER AGAIN BECAUSE…

BECAUSE BECAUSE BECAUSE..

"For I am dwelling—in Beulah Land!"

Ahhhhhhhh—from the crowd, which knew the song, of course, and which had always heard the song, and whose forefathers and foremothers Black or White or young or old had always known the song and the words of the song the words the words the words…

…and the rhythm.

For something had changed now within the guitar. And coming out of the guitar, out from that magic hole in the center of it.

Jack Fontenot was picking now.

Thumb on the bass string fingers on the higher strings thumb on the bass string fingers on the higher strings.

Bum bum bum bum bum bum..

The chorus.

THE CHORUS!

"I'm living—on the mountain—underneath a cloudless sky…

"I'm drinking—at the fountain—that never shall run dry!"

And everyone was clapping.

It was impossible not to clap.

"Oh yes I'm feasting—on the manna—from a bountiful supply

For I am dwelling in Beuuu—laaa—land!"

Silence.

For one split second.

That radiant smile spreading itself around the theater as Jack Fontenot turned his head.

Turned his head right...

Turned his head left...

Then stood up and played the chorus again, this time louder:

"I'm living on the mountain, underneath a cloudless sky...

"I'm drinking at the fountain that never shall run dry!"

Everyone is standing now, everyone is clapping, and everyone is singing along.

Loud.

"Oh yes I'm feasting, on the manna, from a bountiful supply

For I am dwelling in Beu—lah—land!"

There was a tremendous urge to burst into applause, but, of course, that was impossible, first because one did not applaud in church and second because Jack Fontenot was going back to the slow pure strum that was to accompany the second verse:

Far below the storm of doubt upon the world is beating,

Sons of men in battle long the enemy withstand;

Safe am I within the castle of God's Word retreating;

Nothing then can reach me—'tis Beulah Land.

And now the rhythm again and now the clapping—joyous, full-throated song that made Nina wonder about earlier times. Tabernacle times, when wagons pulled up to what now were paved parking lots, when men in long full beards and women in bonnets came together after long days in the cotton fields to be a community.

Pickbing pickbing pickbing pickbing...

...living on the mountain, underneath a cloudless sky,

I'm drinking at the fountain that never shall run dry;

Oh, yes! I'm feasting on the manna from a bountiful supply,

For I am dwelling in Beulah Land.

Pickbing pickbing pickbing pickbing..,

Slower now, working up to big finish...

Oh, yes! I'm feasting on the manna from a bountiful supply,

For I am dwelling—in Beuuuu-laaa-Land!

Pandemonium now, everyone hugging each other.

But the music continued!

It went from Beulah Land straight into:

What a fellowship, what a joy divine,
Leaning on the everlasting arms;
What a blessedness, what a peace is mine,
Leaning on the everlasting arms.

Leaning, leaning,
Safe and secure from all alarms;
Leaning, leaning,
Leaning on the everlasting arms.

And they were leaning! Arms around each others' shoulders, all smiles big as Jack's now, the wooden floor rocking while the congregation all responded to the heavenly command to:

SING IT AGAIN SING IT AGAIN SING IT AGAIN SING—

Leeeeeening!

Leeeeeening!

Safe and secure from all alarm!
Leeeeeeening!
Leeeeeeening!
Leaning on the Everlasting arms!

So that finally Nina, somehow getting her voice up into Jackson's hearing range, standing on her tiptoes and bellowing loud enough that he might possibly hear, screamed her question:

"Is this what it's like in Beyonce?"

He grinned down at her and started to answer.

But he could not, of course.

Another song was starting.

CHAPTER EIGHT: FIRES AND MYTHS

After the hymns were sung, various groups gathered in different parts of the park. They built campfires and recited myths.

Barbara Smallwood's Myth:

"A big part of our belief is what the old ones called 'the migration legend." The story tells about how we came here to Mississippi, to our homelands. All Chickasaw children learn it, just as I did. Anyway, the search began long, long ago, when the tribe lived in the land of the setting sun. The gods told the old and wise tribal leaders that we were destined to move to the lands meant for us. The guide to these lands was a pole, carried on each day's march by the tribe's holy men. At night, as the tribe rested after its march through the wilderness, the priests placed the pole upright in the ground. During the night the gods, invisible as the wind, came and moved the pole. The direction it pointed to by dawn served as a compass to guide the day's march. Almost every day it told the people to move toward the rising sun. Eventually my ancestors crossed the Mississippi River. The sacred pole continued to direct them East until they came to this place, the land where we're camping now. Next morning the pole was as erect as the holy men had placed it the night before. It hadn't moved. The people celebrated. This was their new home."

Cindy's Myth

Cindy looked around at the high school kids ringed around the campfire.

"And what about that one, Ms. Baker?"

"Which one?"

"Over there, just beyond the tip of our roof? The one that makes a 'w.'"

"That's Cassiopeia."

"Tell."

"All right then. Well, Queen Cassiopeia, wife of King Cephas and mother of Andromeda, was very beautiful. She bragged that she was the most beautiful woman in the kingdom. As time went by she began to say that she was the most beautiful woman in the world."

"That wasn't very smart, was it?"

"No, honey."

"So what happened to her?"

"What always happens to people who brag too much?"

"Bad things."

"Exactly."

"So what things happened?"

"Well, eventually she even bragged that she was more beautiful than the goddesses themselves. Poseidon, god of the ocean, heard about how vain she was and got mad, because he thought he had created the most beautiful creatures ever in the form of his sea nymphs. He was so angry, that he created a terrible sea monster, Cetus, to ravage the seas. Cetus sank ships, killed sailors, and destroyed whole towns and villages along the sea coast. The people of Cassiopeia's country were terrified. They asked Poseidon what could be done to stop the monster. Poseidon said that it was simple. All Cassiopeia had to do was say the sea nymphs were more beautiful than she was."

"That was simple,"

"It would be simple, but Cassiopeia was too vain. She refused. So the people asked if there was some other way to stop the destruction. He told them yes. Cassiopeia would have to sacrifice her only daughter, Andromeda."

"How?"

"The people chained Andromeda to a rock in the ocean to be sacrificed to Cetus."

"Would he eat her?"

"I don't know. I do know that Perseus saved her and turned Cetus into stone. Poseidon and his brother Zeus commanded that Cassiopeia become a constellation in the sky for being so conceited about her looks. Her punishment is that she is upside down in the sky, just like we see her now."

Brother Tamp's Myth

In the main building of the Tombigbee Park was a larger meeting room, where a fire burned in the fireplace.

In this room the Koinonia Class was meeting.

Requisite: members must be seventy five years old, or older.

They had asked Brother Tamp to read for them, and he was doing so.

They loved to listen to Tamp read.

They loved the quality of his voice, and the way he looked, with hair as silver as theirs, as he stood behind the podium.

And they loved the way he scorned new biblical translations such as the Twenty First Century Our World Translation or the Bible for Busies Translation.

No, Tamp read only from the *King James Bible*.

As he was doing now.

He had read for some minutes, telling them a story they had heard innumerable times. But that did not matter. It was always fresh, and it always gained in power as it neared its end. And as they, as was undeniable, neared their end.

"And God said, Let the waters bring forth abundantly the moving creatures that hath life, and fowl that may fly above the earth in the open firmament of heaven.

And God created great whales, and every living creature that moveth, which the waters brought forth abundantly, after their kind, and every winged fowl after his kind: and God saw that it was good.

And God blessed them, saying, Be fruitful, and multiply, and fill the waters in the seas, and let fowl multiply in the earth.

And the evening and the morning were the fifth day.

And God said, Let the earth bring forth the living creatures after his kind, cattle, and creeping thing, and beast of the earth after his kind: and it was so.

And God made the beast of the earth after his kind, and cattle after their kind, and everything that creepeth upon the earth after his kind: and God saw that it was good.

And God said, Let us make man in our image, after our likeness: and let them have dominion over the fish of the sea, and over the fowl of the air, and over the cattle, and over all the earth, and over every creeping thing that creepeth upon the earth.

So God created man in his own image, in the image of God created he him; male and female created he them.

And God blessed them, and God said unto them, Be fruitful, and multiply, and replenish the earth, and subdue it: and have dominion over the fish of the sea, and over the fowl of the air, and over every living thing that moveth upon the earth.

And God said, Behold, I have given you every herb bearing seed, which is upon the face of all the earth, and every tree, in the which is the fruit of a tree yielding seed; to you it shall be for meat.

And to every beast of the earth, and to every fowl of the air, and to everything that creepeth upon the earth, wherein there is life, I have given every green herb for meat: and it was so.

And God saw everything that he had made, and, behold, it was very good. And the evening and the morning were the sixth day.

Thus the heavens and the earth were finished, and all the host of them.

And on the seventh day God ended his work which he had made; and he rested on the seventh day from all his work which he had made.

And God blessed the seventh day, and sanctified it: because that in it he had rested from all his work which God created and made.

These are the generations of the heavens and of the earth when they were created, in the day that the LORD God made the earth and the heavens,

When Brother Tamp finished, he put down the Bible on the lectern in front of him.

"Let us pray," he said quietly.

And they did.

Yet Another Myth

In a pasture ten miles or so from Tombigbee State Park, a larger fire was burning.

Approximately fifty men sat around it.

One man stood, paced back and forth, and gestured flamboyantly.

His stentorian voice carried easily over the crackling of the flames:

"Why are so many people bent on promoting race-mixing and racial equality? Because, it is Satan's goal to have us violate our Heavenly Father's law on mixing our seed with the other people of the world. What used to be wrong is now right. What used to be bad is now good. Our world has been turned upside down!

The Federal Government promotes the destruction of our race through its many programs. They require that businesses hire based on race rather than qualifications, they call this Affirmative Action. The Government supports mass Non-White integration. When the hordes of Third Worlders that enter our country cannot work, they go on Welfare. The Welfare Program allows the White people to pay for the Non-White people of the Country to eat and live, while at the same time causing the White people to lack in necessary funds to have children of their own. Our race, through the Government's power, now has the lowest birth rate. White Men and Women cannot have children because they pay 'mandatory child support' in the name of TAXES. Our Government promotes Race-Mixing through integration. Our Children are forced to go to school with every race under the sun. They are being taught that the races are equal. When did race-relations become part of educational curriculum? Our Children are being brainwashed all in the name of 'Humanity'

How Fires Go Out

It was later in the evening now. The younger children had been put to bed. But one of the college students, Kayla Morgen, had stayed behind.

Nina had long since retired as principal when Kayla graduated last year.

But somehow they had met.

And Kayla knew that Nina had read a great deal.

So for some months they had taken long walks on the beach.

Now Kayla, fresh off her first year at the great modern university, wanted to talk again.

"It was different than I thought it would be, Ms. Bannister."

"How? Was it harder?"

"No. But yes. In some ways. Not in the ways I expected."

"In what ways then?"

"We read things that…well that we never read in high school."

"Things like?"

"Voltaire. He hated Christianity, you know."

"Yes."

"He said it was dangerous. That it needed to be crushed."

"I know that he said that."

"But… somehow he makes sense. And when I'm here with all these people tonight…I'm not really with them, not the way I was. And I wonder if I ever can be again. Maybe I have to go on my own for a while. Can you be a Christian, on your own?"

She was interrupted by the sound of footsteps.

It was a bit scary, Nina found herself thinking.

Someone coming through the woods.

But then the someone actually appeared, and it was a smiling Brother Abraham Goforth, who bowed ceremoniously and said:

"Good evening young ladies!"

Nina answered:

"Thank you, Brother Abe!"

"Why, for what, may I ask, am I to be thanked?"

"For calling me young."

"It was my pleasure."

There was silence for a time. Silence except for the dull small beginning roar of a night breeze and the crackling of the fire.

"What have the two of you been talking of?" asked Abe. "I hope I haven't interrupted anything too personal."

Nina shook her head.

"No. It was just. Kayla just...well, it's not anything vital."

Abe looked at Kayla and asked:

"Is that true, Ms. Kayla?"

Kayla seemed to ponder this for a second, then replied:

"Well, it is kind of vital."

"Can you talk of it to me?"

"Yes. I can try to."

"Then by all means do so."

More thinking, then Kayla:

"I don't think there will ever be a time when I'm not a Christian."

"That's good to hear."

"But...I'm changing. And the church, the people here... it doesn't change, they don't seem to change. I don't think I'm like them anymore. I feel like I'm off on my own, somehow. So I wonder: can't I be on my own and still be a good Christian? Why do I need to belong to a church? Why do I need to belong to any community at all?"

Brother Abe merely nodded.

He looked at the fire for a time.

Then he reached behind himself, found a stick of wood around two feet long, and reached with it into the fire.

Carefully he succeeded in pushing and prodding out from the blaze a glowing coal the size of a human fist.

This coal he kept on shoving over the ground until it sat isolated, perhaps three feet from the fire.

"I…" Nina began to say.

But he put a finger on his lips and merely shook his head.

They watched the coal for a half minute, while its glow grew fainter.

Within a minute it was simply a grey mass of ash.

He poked it.

It fell apart.

Then he simply rubbed the ash until nothing was visible where the coal had been save bare ground.

He rose.

And he left, without saying anything more.

Finally Nina said, whispering:

"Let's go back to the camp."

And they did.

END OF PART ONE

CHAPTER NINE: FISHERS OF MEN

Monday dawned beautifully of course, as she knew it would.

It was THE FIRST FULL DAY OF RETREAT!

How could it not be a beautiful morning?

She was up at first light, and was not the only one. Having slipped on a bulky sweater (for the air outside was still a bit cool), she made her way down to the lake.

The lake—where preparations already were being made as the huge red sun rose, rivaling, she imagined, those made decades earlier for the Invasion of Normandy.

It was the first practice of the fishing tournament!

It began officially as it had for years, more years than she could remember.

That is, with Brother Tamp chugging out into the lake with a small motor boat, stopping the craft around fifty yards from shore, looking back in towards the children getting their poles ready and the adults helping them—lifting a bullhorn that had become official paraphernalia for the occasion, smiling the way only Tamp could smile, and saying simply in words that echoed over the green lawn leading up to the main building:

"And he saith unto them: Follow me, and I will make you fishers of men."

Nina cried, of course.

But that lasted only a short time, and then she watched.

She saw that:

Three pickup trucks, eleven small children, six male parents, four female parents, two dogs (where had they come from?), ten big white buckets of earth in which burrowed—blissfully unaware of the awful fate that awaited them, eleven thousand four hundred and sixty three red slimy earthworms, twenty six cane poles, forty eight hooks of various sizes with rubber safety caps on them, two hooks from which the safety caps had somehow come loose, thirty eight red and white plastic bobbers, sixty one lead sinkers, fourteen chains which, securely fastened to pier posts, were to hold captive the captured bream and whatever else might be caught and six first aid kits...

...were there.

Farther back toward the main camp building, halfway up the dark and lush green slope that led down to the lake, seven long tables, six silver platters of scrambled eggs, five silver platters of sausage patties, five silver platters of link sausages, three silver platters (why only three? Who knew?) of crisp just fried and smelling to die for bacon slices, a hundred various sized containers of rolls and biscuits and toast slices and cinnamon buns and bagels with cream cheese and coffee cakes and plain croissants and chocolate croissants and almond croissants, and five huge platters of pancakes, and beside them vats of butter and maple syrup and sixty three hundred forks knives spoons and napkins, and thirty vast urns filled with caffeinated and non-caffeinated coffee with innumerable little bags of sugar and Splenda...

...were there.

And also there, under scattered green canvas tents being hastily erected by Methodist-Marines who had learned their jobs through years of training, were the locations where various activities essential to summer spiritual growth were to take place. Arts. Crafts (Nina had never been certain which were which). Sunday school lessons now being done on Monday. Paint by number classes now being done by adults. Quilting sessions.

Organizing all of these activities were Inez, of course, and Maybelle, and Lannie and Cindy and Allison, who had somehow transformed themselves into Eisenhower, Patton, MacArthur, Montgomery, and Stonewall Jackson.

Nina stood on the pier nearest her, trying not to get speared by a hook, and marveling at the organizational ability of these people.

After a short time she was aware that Cindy had approached her.

"How's it all going, Cindy?"

Cindy shook her head:

Third army is in retreat.

"It's going all right so far, but…

As if foreordained, the 'but' appeared.

It was Inez.

Wringing her hands.

"We have a crisis in arts and crafts."

"Oh my God," hissed Cindy. "What's happening?"

"We're out of glitter glue."

"What? How could we be out of glitter glue?"

"Florence Merryweather thought the Parkers were bringing it."

Cindy simply shook her head:

"It doesn't matter. We have to get glitter glue now or we'll have nothing for the toddlers and the pre K's to do."

And, of course, they did get glitter glue.

In this case they got it by dispatching a teen-aged boy in one of the available pickup trucks to the Wal-Mart in Plantersville, five miles distant.

So went the morning, until ten thirty came around.

As did Brother Tamp.

"Hey Nina!"

"Hey Tamp!"

"Take a walk up the mountain with me? I feel a need to chat before the first big meeting at eleven."

"Sure."

And off they went.

CHAPTER TEN: A FEW THINGS YOU MIGHT WANT TO KNOW ABOUT

Monday morning, ten forty a.m.

The meeting took place in Ranger Headquarters, which was a small building designed to fit the rustic pattern of the other Tombigbee structures. Barbara Smallwood parked her jeep near two patrol vehicles, then got out and looked around her. Through several layers of yellow pine she saw the lake, sparkling and sun splotched, its surface ruffled a little by the morning breeze that had come up from the south.

As she opened the screen door and walked inside, a uniformed man seated behind a desk at the far end of the room smiled at her and asked:

"Captain Davis Starnes, Mississippi State Park Service."

She returned the handshake, feeling her own hand subsumed as she replied:

"Barbara Smallwood."

"I know. Glad I finally get to meet you. Welcome to Mississippi!"

"Thank you."

"We're happy to have you here at Tombigbee Park."

"It's good to be here."

"You come very highly recommended."

"That's good to know."

He was a big and square man, blonde behind his dark green uniform, clanking a bit as he leaned back and as the black leather paraphernalia he was wearing—service revolver, walkie-talkie, silver-plated handcuffs—all made their little complaining noises.

"Why'd you want to leave home and come here?"

"This is home."

"I see. You're Chickasaw, aren't you?"

"Yes, sir, I am."

"Been a long time since your people were here on the Tombigbee River."

"Yes. Well, we're back now."

His smile broadened:

"Indeed you are. You've forgiven us I hope for driving you out."

"Not really. We make the best of it though."

"I'm sure you do, I'm sure you do. It's good to have you here, Barbara Smallwood. You have a place to stay?"

She nodded.

"In the museum."

"How do you manage that?"

"There's an attic. I had a bed moved up there, a table, a couple of chairs."

"Don't you need a kitchen?"

"I've got a hotplate. And for that matter the main building of the park is only a couple of hundred yards away. My main work here for a while will be getting the museum ready, giving lectures there, that kind of thing. I didn't see the need to get an apartment in, say, Plantersville, pay rent, spend gas money driving over here every day."

He shook his head:

"I would have thought—you're single, right?"

"That's right."

"Well, I would have thought you might want to live in Tupelo. That's where all the action is."

"I didn't realize there was that much action in Tupelo."

"Regular Las Vegas."

"Probably be too fast for me then. No, I'm fine here in the park."

"That's good. Anything we can do to help you settle in, just let me know."

"I will."

He sat down and looked at her for a time, then said quietly:

"You're certified to carry a firearm?"

"Yes, sir."

"You realize I'm required to issue you one?"

"Yes."

He looked out the window for a time.

She allowed her gaze to follow his.

There was nothing to see through the open window except a branch full of oak leaves whispering to each other and to the wind.

"This job has gotten harder and harder in the last years. I'm sure they told you that in the academy in Oklahoma."

"Yes, sir. They did."

"Any point in asking why a woman might want to do it?"

"Same reason anyone might want to do it, I guess."

"That reason being?"

"You get to shoot people."

He smiled.

"You have a sense of humor."

"We had to develop one."

"It's not the way it was twenty—hell even ten years ago. Back then ninety percent of what we did was help people jump start their cars when the batteries went dead after sitting in the parking lot for seven days. That or tell the people in Cabin Ten to turn down their radio after ten at night."

"Well, that would get to be boring."

He shook his head, saying:

"I didn't find it so boring. Fact is, I kind of liked it. I wish we could go back to it."

"You don't think we will?"

He shook his head:

"No. Too much has changed. The world has changed. The timber industry, agriculture—the state's economy is dying. Kids are so depressed. It's as though they've got nothing more to live for. Barbara—it's all right if I call you Barbara, isn't it?"

"Of course it is."

"The small towns are where it's worse. Jackson, Vicksburg—those used to be the crime centers. But now it's towns around here with two thousand folks in them or fewer. Towns like Plantersville. In the past year alone eleven meth labs have been busted, all within a ten mile radius of this park."

"I understand. The same kind of thing is happening in Oklahoma. But does it involve the park here?"

The man sitting opposite her smiled, but it was a humorless smile, a tired smile.

"You think you can keep it out? They don't always make the drug deals in the center of town. Sometimes they go into the woods. Sometimes these woods. We don't have electronic fences. The dealers think that if they get in here they'll be safe from the police. And as for us, why, they don't think we are police. But we are. We've got to be. That's why all park rangers carry arms now. That and, well, other reasons. Worse reasons."

"What reasons?"

"There's a large church group up here. From Bay St. Lucy down on the coast."

"Yes, I know. I met one of their pastors a few days ago, and one of their members on Saturday. She offered to have some boys help get the heavier boxes brought

into the museum. Seem like nice people. What does that
have to do with me being armed?"

"He didn't tell you which churches were coming?"

"I think he said he was Methodist."

"Yes. But another Methodist Church is coming, too.
A Black Church. The Bethel African Methodist
Episcopal Church."

"Is that a problem?"

"Not for most people. Not for sane people. But not
everybody's sane, that's the trouble."

"Are you talking about…"

"I'm talking about the alt-right is what I'm talking
about. A kind of modern day Ku Klux Klan. They're
growing. Their membership is growing. And they let
you know who they are, they don't wear masks, they're
not ashamed. Five separate groups of them here in
Northeastern Mississippi. More than any other state. At
any rate, the head of one of them contacted me early
this morning."

"He contacted you?"

"Sure did. Like I say, they're not ashamed to identify
themselves. At eleven o'clock Wednesday morning
they're planning to have a rally by the lake in the
middle of the park. They've got Mason Baily coming."

"Who's Mason Baily?"

"He's a nationally known White Supremacist.
They're promising a peaceful protest, saying the white
and black churches shouldn't mix. They promise that
more than sixty members of the Aryan Nation will be
here."

"Jesus," she found herself whispering.

"He'll be here, too, I suppose. But he won't be
armed."

"Have you contacted the churches?"

"I called both of their pastors half an hour ago. I don't want them to be intimidated. But they have a right to know what's happening."

"Of course. Is there no way you can stop the rally?"

"That's debatable. I've called my superiors as well as a few lawyers I know in Jackson and Tupelo."

"So what should we do, as Rangers? What are the police going to do?"

He shook his head:

"We're going to have a meeting with all those folks I just told you about, plus maybe a few others."

"When?"

"Early this afternoon. You'll be where I can find you?"

"Sure. I'll be at the museum unloading boxes of artifacts."

"I'll send somebody by to get you when we've set a time and place."

"Good. I'll be easy to find."

Five minutes later she was back at the museum.

She unlocked the door, thought about going inside, but turned first to look out into the forests.

Her ancestors had peopled it with all kinds of supernatural beings: the Hottuk Ookproose, and the Hottuk Ishtohoolo for example. The Ishtohoolo were good and benign spirits who helped the Chickasaw in hunting and in war. The Ookproose on the other hand were evil spirits residing in the darker regions of the West. And the Lofas, monsters ten feet tall, who incited hatred and brought violence with them everywhere they went.

Now though, in modern and scientific times, educated people such as park administrators and rangers knew that such creatures did not exist.

Did not exist.

"Ha," she heard herself laughing into the forest.

Then she turned and went back into the museum.

CHAPTER ELEVEN: A SHORT TALK WITH BROTHER TAMP

Nina had followed Tamp upward through an obscure and narrow path. Finally the trail broadened into a clearing, from which they could look down upon the lake and the grassy lawn leading up from it to the main buildings of the camp.

The ghosts of people long dead were spread out far below them, even as she pictured family upon family of friends now gone, the Robertsons, "Chug" Peterson, Brother Baily, he of the eternal cigar stub, Florene Ohr, she of the wondrous smile that nothing was able to completely eradicate, not even the cruel cancer that, after a year and a half, had so withered and racked her body.

And the ghost of Frank, of course. Down there on the wooden platform that extended its arms out into the lake; down there smiling and gesturing and applauding as the children fished; Frank the Organizer, the Weigher of Lake Trout, the Counter of Catches, the Baiter of Lines, the Extricator of Hooks—the moving force behind THE GREAT FISHING CONTEST, BIGGEST AND BEST IN ALL METHODISM—and which would take place for real (no more practice sessions like the one this morning) beginning at 7 a.m. sharp tomorrow.

"Thanks for walking up here with me, Nina."

"My pleasure."

"I always like to trek up here on the first day of Retreat. The first morning actually."

"I can see why. It's a good place."

"You never came up here with Frank?"

She shook her head:

"He was always too busy with the fishing. We walked on a lot of the paths leading out from the main building. Just never got to this one, I suppose."

"You never stop missing him, do you?"

"No."

She was about to keep talking but she realized that she had nothing to say. Ordinarily, she mused, that would not have stopped her.

But it did this time.

Was she getting wiser in old age?

"Well, Nina, I love sitting up here. But I guess it's time to go back down. First big meeting. Announcements. I'm a little uneasy about one of them in particular."

They stood up and began to make their way down the mountain.

"You're going to make an announcement about the marriage?"

"I am."

"You know that's going to cause a great deal of controversy, Tamp. Half of the congregation will love you for doing it. The other half thinks all gays are going to hell. After you announce this wedding, that's all that will be talked about for the rest of the Retreat."

But Tamp merely shook his head, saying.

"No."

"Pardon?"

"No, that's where you're wrong."

"How am I wrong?"

"No one's going to be talking about it at all."

"Tamp, it's an issue that's tearing apart the Methodist churches!"

"I know."

"And you're telling me that you are going to perform the first gay wedding ever done by a Bay St. Lucy pastor and no one's going to be talking about it?"

"That's what I'm telling you."

"That doesn't make sense."

"Since when do things have to make sense in this world? Just take my word for it: now you see through a glass darkly. In half an hour or so—probably less actually—you'll see things more clearly. But we better part company now: I'll see you later.

They did part company, Tamp working his way toward the front of a crowd, Nina working to stay toward the back of it.

Within five minutes, the building that they had for some time called the Little Brown Church in the Vale was overflowing.

It had served, in the past, a crowd of fifty people.

Now twice as many wanted to get in.

Meaning that an overflow—including Nina—had spread to the lawn and was forced to watch through various doors and windows as Tamp made his way to the microphone and spoke, saying:

"Welcome to all of you. This is an historic occasion as you know. It has been widely written, and accurately written, that Sunday morning is the most segregated time of the week in the United States of America. Well, we're changing that."

Shouts of "amen,' and 'you tell it, Brother!'"

Silence restored.

Tamp:

"Normally this is a time for many announcements. The schedule of events for the next five days, things of that nature. But things are not normal now. Now I have only one or two announcements to make. The first one is that a White Supremacist group has announced that it plans to hold a rally in the center of this park on

Wednesday at eleven o'clock, in order to protest the mixing of white and black churches, which it takes to be a sin."

Stunned silence.

"I have been told by the head of the park ranger service that he does not know whether or not the meeting can be legally prohibited, or even moved. He has advised me also that he cannot rule out the possibility of violence breaking out. He has suggested that, for our own safety, we might want to pack up and go home in order to prevent bloodshed. I replied to him that all of us would meet at two o'clock this afternoon on the lawn leading down to the lake, to discuss what we as churches would do in the face of this threat. I believe we should disperse now, and discuss among ourselves just what our course of action should be. And that is all I have for right now."

He took two steps away from the podium, then caught himself and returned, saying:

"Oh and one other thing: this Saturday at ten a.m. either here in the park or back in our church at Bay St. Lucy, I will perform the wedding service of Meg Brennan and Jennifer Warren. Now all of you go with God."

He stepped away from the podium and into the crowd.

Which now, shocked and electrified, milled and flowed past Nina, embracing each other, crying, shouting, cursing, praying:

"They can't do this!"

"Will they have guns!"

"Our children are here, for God's sake!"

"We've got to go!"

"We've got to stay!"

"What do we do?"

And so on.

They said everything imaginable.

Except for one thing.

Brother Tamp had been right.

They did not talk about the wedding of Meg Brennan and Jennifer Warren.

CHAPTER TWELVE: MUSEUM IN HER HEAD

Barbara Smallwood, in another part of Tombigbee State Park, was succeeding in thinking neither about the Alt Right nor what its coming would mean for her as a park ranger.

Nor was she thinking about the Methodist churches that were now ensconced in the park, nor of their beliefs.

Rather, she was standing in the doorway of her museum, looking at twenty boxes and crates that had been unloaded by an athletic and cheerful group of teenagers, and which now sat adjacent to the far East wall, ready to be unpacked.

In her mind they were already unpacked.

The museum was sixty feet square, and every inch of it, from floor to walls to ceiling, was already occupied.

Unable to help herself, she entered the large room and began to make her way around it, occasionally touching a spot of spare wall space, as though consecrating it.

There, head high, looking sternly back at her, the painting of a Chickasaw warrior, top half of his bald-shaven head painted red, the color of war. White eagle feather—such feathers were only awarded to the best and bravest of warriors—protruding from long pitch-black hair that fell well below the shoulders.

And underneath the painting the words:

"Unconquered and unconquerable."

Her people had never lost a battle.

She moved on.

Two feet of wall space would be given to the illustrated time line:

1250-1300 Mississippi Residence, Woodpecker shell pottery

1400 Decline of Mound Builders' Society

1540 Battle with Hernando Desoto's men, Chickasaws victorious

And on until the great migration.

Farther still down the wall:

The Great Seal of the Chickasaw Nation, warrior with river in background encircled by purple ring.

And on and on.

The boxes emptied herself into her mind and she could see the whole thing so clearly:

"Chickasaw Trade Fair," painting by Tom Phillips

Pipe Tomahawk, made by Chickasaw Blacksmith, CA 1765

Display of arrowhead fragments, CA 1400

Beaded Sash, yellow red and green striped, CA 1500

Bear Efficacy Pot, CA 1600

Stompdance Vest and Hat, CA 1650

Red Princess Dress with Apron, CA 1550

Turtle Shells and Hatbands (Turtle shells were worn by women for stomp dancing)

And now, spread back along the floor, the ceremonial fire pit.

Our Fire.

A small sign and the words:

"For traditional Chickasaws there is no death, only another step in the spiritual journey that is life. The sacred fire used for stomp dance symbolizes this belief in constant renewal. Like life itself, it is impossible to kill the sacred fire. Its energy can be transformed or transferred, but never fully extinguished."

She could have gone on doing this for hours, so plentiful were the artifacts waiting for her to unpack and display them.

She was interrupted though by a young blonde park ranger—had she met him? Should she know his name?

Well, let it be. That would all come with time.

"Ranger Smallwood?"

"Yes?"

"There's a meeting…"

"Yes. Ranger Starnes told me about it a little while ago, earlier this morning. He didn't know where it would be, or exactly when."

"It's starting in five minutes, over in park headquarters. It's about—well, the Alt Right wants to have a meeting here in the park. There's a question about whether they should be allowed to do that."

She looked at the young man and asked him:

"Do you think they should be allowed to do it?"

"I don't know. There are reasons why they should be, I guess. First Amendment rights. It's America, and all that."

"And why shouldn't they be?"

"Lot of people could get killed."

"Well, that pretty much settles the issue, doesn't it? Look, why don't you go on over to the headquarters? I'll be there as soon as I can lock up."

"Yes, ma'am."

"You don't need to call me ma'am."

"What should I call you?"

"Call me Chief Eagle Claw."

"Really?"

"No, that's a joke. Call me Barbara."

"All right, Barbara. I'm Bob Lee."

"Nice to know you, Bob Lee. See you in a few minutes."

And he left.

It took her some time to make sure all museum windows and doors were locked. By the time she had done so and trekked the three hundred or so yards to park headquarters, the meeting had already started.

She sat in a corner of the room, right beside, as luck would have it, the young ranger—Bob Lee—who had just come to get her.

He leaned over and whispered in her ear:

"The big guy talking is Jackson Bennet. He used to be a running back for LSU. He's a lawyer now in Bay St. Lucy."

She listened as Bennet read from a document spread out on the table in front of him.

"This document establishes what's called the 'Imminent lawless action' criterion. That means that a man can come in here and advocate killing Black Folks, and there's nothing you can do about it unless you can prove that his speech has created an atmosphere in which a riot is imminent. And that's proven to be, in past cases, almost impossible to demonstrate."

"So what it boils down to is?"

"It means they can have the meeting."

"And if we deny their permit to meet?"

"They can sue the state of Mississippi."

Another comment from the pastor she had met earlier, whose name, she remembered, was 'Tamp.'

"But our two churches reserved the park for the week!"

Jackson Bennet shook his head:

"You reserved the cabins, and you reserved the right to use the grounds. You did not reserve, and cannot reserve, the right to exclude the rest of the public from coming in and setting foot on those grounds."

An African American man seated at the end of the table stood up, leaned toward Bennet, and said:

"Mr. Bennet, we're grateful for your legal advice."

"Thank you, Brother Abe."

"But now I must ask what I believe to be an even more important question."

"All right. Please go ahead. If I can answer it, I will."

"Mr. Bennet, are these people allowed to be armed?"

A pause.

Barbara Smallwood felt her heart beat a bit more unsteadily.

More than a hundred White Supremacists with guns…

…and what kind of guns?

Rifles?

Assault rifles?

The pause continued.

It became unendurable.

Then it ended.

With Jackson Bennet nodding his head:

"Yes, they can."

A huge sigh escaped into the room.

Brother Abe said quietly:

"That's insane."

"Nevertheless."

"Are you telling me, Mr. Bennet, that the presence of sixty men who hate African Americans and are armed to the teeth does not constitute a 'threat of imminent lawless action'"?

Bennet shook his head and gestured at the park ranger sitting beside him:

"Ranger Starnes?"

"Yes?"

"You're armed, are you not?"

"Yes, I am?"

"Does your presence here—even with your loaded sidearm—mean that lawless action is imminent?"

"No, but as a park ranger I am also a licensed law enforcement official. If I were just a private citizen..."

"You would still have the right to protect yourself, in or out of any state park. On Apr 27, 2015—Senate Bill 2862, signed by Gov. Phil Bryant in 2010, changed Mississippi law to allow people to carry guns in parks. "A concealed carry license holder should be able to have their firearm concealed, open or however they want to carry it in a public park."

And there was for a time silence in the room.

CHAPTER THIRTEEN: TWIN SERMONS

By two o'clock the lawn leading down to Tombigbee Lake was covered with people. There were the members of the two congregations, of course, but there were also more people who were arriving from Bay St. Lucy: family members and friends who had heard the news of the Alt Right's meeting on the twelve o'clock news and were just now completing the two hour drive up to the park. They had come, Nina supposed, to take their children (who had arrived Sunday afternoon on the bus driven by Moon Rivard) back home to safety as soon as possible.

Nina had seated herself—she had no idea why—on the wide porch of the lodge itself, and was now looking down on the milling crowd, and on Pastors Tamp and Goforth, who, microphones in hand, were preparing to address it.

She thought of two things: first, Milton, and his lines from Paradise Lost:

"They anon with hundreds and with thousands trooping came attended: all access was thronged, the gates and porches opened wide, but chief the spacious hall thick swarmed, as bees in springtime..."

Bees in springtime.

Yes, she thought of Milton but she also thought of Matthew.

For spread out below her was the mountainside, and beyond it The Sea of Galilee.

She could have been getting ready to hear the Sermon on the Mount.

Or in this case, twin sermons.

Goforth began, with a bit of microphone static crackling out over the grass, the crowd, and, on beyond, the lake:

"Brothers and Sisters in Christ…"

The crowd quieted itself and stared up at him.

"Brothers and Sisters, we must talk among ourselves about this thing that my Colleague Reverend Tamp has told you of some few hours ago. It is, we now know, true. This group of people is actually coming here for their rally. The time you heard about is correct: eleven o'clock Wednesday afternoon. So we have almost forty eight hours to make out plans. What those plans should be is up to you. Tamp and I have already talked the matter out between us, and we have decided not to make doctrinaire pronouncements about the issue. We do not, in short, intend to tell you what to do. You may in a figurative sense be our flock, but in a more real sense you are human beings and not sheep."

Some laughter filtered through the crowd, but the Reverend Goforth stilled it as he continued:

"The park service has been kind enough to set up three microphones up here, in addition to the hand held ones that Tamp and I are using. We see that several people have already lined up behind each of them. Let's start over here on my right: you may make a comment, or ask a question."

The first in line tapped the microphone gingerly, as though testing to see that it would not shock her.

It did not, so she spoke into it.

"I have a question for the two of you."

"Please ask the question," said Tamp.

"Are we certain that they cannot legally be blocked from staging this rally?"

Again Tamp:

"We are."

"Who says they can't be blocked?"

"The Supreme Court."

A few murmurs of discontent.

"Will they be armed?"

"If they want to be. Any person licensed to carry a gun in the state of Mississippi is also allowed to carry a gun in any Mississippi state park."

More murmurs. Louder this time.

The next person in line prepared to speak.

Nina let her gaze drift away from him though. This was not out of disrespect, although the man at the microphone was Robert Slater, insurance salesman whom she had taught years earlier and genuinely liked. No, it was nature that pulled her glance away. A large fish had jumped out of the water some two hundred yards out in the lake. Beyond the lake was the sky. A thunderhead had formed in the northeast above the trees, and, just beside it, the pale afternoon moon was setting, a far cry from the bright dime that had shined on them the night before.

"If we leave and go home," Slater was asking, "can we get our money back?"

Brother Abe shook his head:

"I talked to the people who run the inn. They say no."

"Why not?"

"The cabins are booked. There's no way they can be rented now for the rest of the week. It would be a terrible loss for them."

"But what about us? If all the plumbing went out and we had to leave, they'd give us our money back then, wouldn't they?"

Tamp stepped forward:

"But the plumbing isn't out. The park has done nothing wrong."

"No, except threaten our lives."

"No one has threatened our lives. Maybelle?"

Maybelle Witherspoon stepped to the microphone.

"Not in so many words. But we have all read about these groups and what happens when they demonstrate. People get hurt. Sometimes badly hurt."

"The people who run the park have guaranteed our safety."

"How can they make such a guarantee?"

"There will be police here."

"How many?"

"It's not certain yet. Officers from several of the local towns."

"I don't see," continued Maybelle, the microphone screeching with a defect in the sound system, "how we can stay. We have our children to think about. I think we should leave right now. As for the money, maybe we can bring suit against the park to get it back. But we have all come here, as we have every summer, trusting that we would be safe. Now we know we won't be safe. Even tonight. These people say they're coming on Wednesday; but what if some of them come tonight? What if some are on their way right now? Cars have already been arriving from Bay St. Lucy, rides to take the kids back. Let's fill those cars and start clearing out!"

There was some applause at this.

Nina could see people nodding their heads.

She could also see mothers holding their small sons and daughters close to them.

But there was something else to be seen.

There was the next speaker in line to be seen.

Lannie Baker, with his wife Cindy and their daughter Allison close behind him.

As he stepped to the microphone, Nina thought of the ride up with him, of his quiet humor, of his patience with the kids as they learned to fish, at his ability to fix the broken bathrooms at the church, his ability to fix broken windows at the church...

...at his quiet and solid ability to fix anything.

And he began.

Very quietly.

"I'm not good at speaking in front of this many people," he said.

The microphone screeched again.

He stepped away from it, looked at it, adjusted it...

...and fixed it.

No one in the crowd was moving.

Nina could now see lightning in the distant cloud, which had a cottony white and turbulent top, a dark blue bottom.

Another fish jumped.

Or maybe it was the same fish.

Park personnel, two teenagers, a boy and a girl, were bringing chairs out for the older members of the congregation.

These people sat down as the chairs appeared, forming a row in front of Tamp and Goforth.

As for the two of them, they also received furniture of a sort: one podium, dark and walnut color, for each of them.

There were folders on the stands.

Were they going to preach?

She was prevented in her thoughts on the subject by Lannie, who was not preaching, but simply talking— and what a difference between the two there was!

"I don't mean to tell anybody out there what to do. Mrs. Witherspoon, what you just said makes a lot of sense. I know we're all scared for our kids' sakes. Cindy and I are scared for Allison. As far as that's concerned, we're scared for ourselves."

Small ripples of laughter.

A few smiles.

Lannie continued:

"I've been in this church a long time. I still remember my own Sunday school lessons. I don't remember in exactly what room in our church I learned which important thing. I don't remember just where I was when I learned about The Last Supper, or The Prodigal Son, or The Woman at the Well. Somewhere I learned about them, though. And I learned one more thing. I do remember where I learned it. And when. It was Brother Tamp's first sermon."

He looked around, smiled briefly at Tamp—who gestured back at him—then faced the crowd again and said:

'Brother Tamp was talking about what the church is, the Christian Church. He was talking about the first Christians, those who had actually lived with Christ, talked with him. About those people who took their calling directly from Jesus. All they had to do was go out and fight the Roman Empire. Not just a few people with white robes and masks—but the Roman Empire. And Tamp said, talking about them and their church—and because of them our church—'If you want a safe and secure place, find a nursing home.'"

Laughter at this.

More laughter.

Which Lannie stilled by continuing:

"But the Christian Church is a dangerous place. Jesus told us to take a sword into the world. Not a real sword, not an assault rifle or an M16 or whatever—but a sword nevertheless. A sword that will change the world. We're supposed to turn the other cheek, but that doesn't mean we're meant to run away from danger. If Christians had done that, there'd be no church, in Bay St. Lucy or anywhere else."

Applause.

Lannie had fixed the microphone.

Now he was fixing the people.

And he kept on doing so:

"This place, this park, is our home. It's become a part of us. If these people can frighten us away from here just by showing up and hollering 'Boo!'—don't you think they can do the same thing down in Bay St. Lucy?"

"Tell it!"

"Speak out, Lannie Baker!"

"If they can demonstrate here, don't you think they can do the same thing in the park next to our church at home? Is the only way for us to keep our children, Allison and the rest, safe is to run away? Then what kind of Christians are we? What kind of people are we?"

There followed a kind of confused hubbub, with one man saying this and another saying that, and this went on for several minutes, with Lannie, Cindy, and Allison subsumed into the crowd.

Finally, Brother Abe stepped forward, leaned on the podium that had been brought out for him, and shouted into it:

"So what is the feeling of the congregation?"

There was, to Nina's great astonishment, only one feeling of the congregation:

"STAY!"

"STAY HERE!"

"WE'RE STAYING!"

Lannie, Nina found herself saying mentally, *you should have been president. You should have been a general. You should...*

She was interrupted in these musings however, by The Brothers Abe and Tamp, who were saying, almost simultaneously:

"We're proud of you, our Brethren. And we have some things to say to you. Which we're going to do now!"

The twin sermons, Nina found herself thinking, on the mount.

Tamp: Who shall separate us from the love of Christ?

Goforth: I have a dream!

Tamp: Shall tribulation, or distress, or persecution,,,

Goforth: It is a dream deeply rooted in the American dream.

Tamp: or famine, or nakedness, or peril, or sword?

Goforth: I have a dream that one day this nation will rise up and live out the true meaning of its creed, "We hold these truths to be self-evident, that *all* men are created equal."

Tamp: As it is written, for thy sake we are killed all the day long.

Goforth: I have a dream that one day on the red hills of Georgia, sons of former slaves and the sons of former slave owners will be able to sit down together at the table of brotherhood.

Tamp: We are accounted as sheep for the slaughter.

Goforth: I have a dream that one day every valley shall be exalted, and every hill and mountain shall be made low.

Tamp: Nay, in all these things we are more than conquerors through him that loved us.

Goforth: I HAVE A DREAM TODAY!

Tamp: For I am persuaded, that neither death, nor life, nor angels...

Goforth: "The rough places will be plain and the crooked places will be made straight, and the glory of the Lord shall be revealed, and all flesh shall see it together."

Tamp:...nor principalities, nor powers, nor things present, nor things to come...

Goforth: This is our hope. This is the faith that I go back to the South with. With this faith we will be able to hew out of the mountain of despair a stone of hope.

Tamp: nor height, nor depth, nor any other creature...

Goforth: With this faith we will be able to work together, to pray together, to struggle together, to go to jail together, to stand up for freedom together, knowing that we will be free one day.

Tamp:...shall be able to separate us...

Goforth: "From every mountainside, let freedom ring!"

Tamp:...from the love of God, which is in Christ Jesus our Lord!

Goforth: Free at last. Free at last. Thank God Almighty, we are free at last."

There was chaos in the crowd.

But it was joyous chaos.

CHAPTER FOURTEEN: THE CHURCH'S ONE FOUNDATION

The decision by the two congregations to stay for the entire week at Retreat was not unanimous, nor could it possibly be. The danger of violence was simply too great, and the memory of past headlines, faces filled with hatred, balloons filled with urine—all of these things were too indelible.

Still, by four o'clock p.m. it had become clear that more than 2/3 of the people who had arrived at Tombigbee Park on Sunday afternoon had resolved to stay until Friday, possible violence notwithstanding.

Nina, sitting on one of the piers, watching Tommy Fletcher catch and release bluegill, talked about it with Frank (who, of course, could not be seen by Tommy.)

You're staying?

Of course. Wouldn't you have stayed?

I don't know, Nina. There are some pretty scary people out there.

Yeah but you were a pretty scary guy yourself.

Well, since you put it that way…

And if it comes to that, you still can be. Being a ghost and all.

That's also true.

They have sheets. Why don't you put on a sheet?

You think I could scare the Alt Right?

I don't know. Maybe if you moaned and rattled some chains…

We don't have chains where I am.

Oh. Then we better forget it. Look! Here comes Lannie Baker!

He was great today, wasn't he Nina?

You saw his speech?

I see and hear everything you do.

Well then, you know. Yes, Frank, he was great.

Then maybe you had better tell him that. Bye for now.

And Frank disappeared.

Just as Lannie stepped onto the pier, smiling and shouting:

"That's a nice one, Tommy!"

The boy turned and beamed, as he held the rod out over the end of the pier and watched the wriggling gold red and purple fish sparkle in what was now beginning to be a setting sun.

"How much do you think he weighs, Mister Baker?"

"Sixty or seventy pounds at least."

"Really?"

"Sure. Either that or nine ounces."

"I think I'll choose seventy pounds."

"That's what he weighs then."

Happily the boy released the fish, whose weight had been determined to be seventy pounds.

Lannie squatted on the pier beside Nina, who said:

"Great job today."

He shook his head, saying softly:

"I don't know."

"What's not to know? You saved Retreat."

"You think that's the decision Frank would have made?"

"I know it is."

"How can you know that?"

"He just told me."

"Well. That makes me feel better."

"It should."

"I'm just not certain that we ought to…"

"Mr. Baker!!"

This scream from Tommy, who, having cast his line out again, had seen the bobber disappear and the line start to play out rapidly.

"What is that, Mr. Baker?"

"Don't know. Reel! Reel hard!"

The boy did so.

For a few moments it seemed a test of strength.

Finally, Tommy began to win though.

And within a few more seconds the bobber, hook, sinker, and unknown aquatic creature were being hauled toward the pier.

Finally, the battle ended, Tommy held his catch a squirming foot or so out of the lake.

Black and glistening, it looked like a foot-long section of living bark, except that it emitted a high pitched squeal.

"What is that thing, Mr. Baker?"

But Lannie had already gotten to his feet and was walking quickly toward the end of the pier, opening his pocket knife as he walked and spoke:

"That, Tommy my friend, is a baby alligator!"

"Oh wow! Can I keep him?"

"Nooo! That would be a very bad idea. Here, swing him over this way!"

Tommy did so; Lannie, as soon as the alligator was within his reach, cut the line, and the beast splashed into the water.

"Shouldn't we have tried to get the hook out?"

But Lannie merely shook his head:

"If we were dealing with a fish, yes. But this was not a fish."

"I know, but isn't it cruel to leave the hook in?"

"Maybe. But there's something else we have to consider."

"What?"

"Mama."

It took a while for this to sink in, but ultimately Tommy's eyes grew round."

"The mother's here?"

"She's not very far."

"What would she do?"

Lannie smiled faintly, the same smile, Nina remembered, that he always gave when he imitated a police siren.

"Well, I guess she might thank us for catching her kid."

And, of course, Tommy smiled too.

"Probably not," he said.

None of the three of them, despite themselves, could take their eyes off the lake, which remained placid.

They were still looking at it when another young boy strode up. Nina had seen him several times in his mother's shop: 'African Treasures.'

She smiled and stuck out her hand, saying:

"Darius Bailey! How are you, young man, and how is your mother?"

"She's fine, Ms. Bannister. But…"

"Yes?"

"I'm supposed to give you a message."

"All right. I'm here and waiting."

"There's a man in the lodge. It's, you know, the big room in the main building where they have all the canoes hanging from the ceiling."

"I know the room."

"He just said, if I could find you, he'd like for you to come there. I guess to talk with him."

"All right then! That's a clear message. Thank you so much for giving it to me."

With that she got to her feet, said good bye to Lannie and the two boys, took one more check of the lake, which was still calm, and walked toward the lodge.

When she got there and entered the main door, she noticed a sign saying the room had been reserved. This was somewhat odd for, at this time on a normal summer afternoon, it would have been a lively place, with groups of four people playing bridge at any number of tables scattered around it, or various people sitting in the large green couch beside the now darkened fireplace.

For a moment though, as she walked into it, she felt it was deserted.

It came to her that she had been invited by a ghost to a haunted hall.

Then she saw him.

Seated over there, on the far side on a large green easy chair, a window behind him, a table in front.

"Nina! Over here!"

Pastor Rockman.

For some reason—an irrational one she told herself—she would have preferred the ghost.

She crossed the large room and took a seat in a chair almost identical to the one in which he was seated, except brown.

"We've missed you," she lied.

He smiled—and for some reason she thought Pastor Rockman's smiles were lies, too—and said:

"I've been in Jackson for a couple of days, meeting with the District Superintendent and the Bishop."

Well, she told herself, at least that was probably true.

He sat looking across the hall, hands folded upon his lap. He wore no jacket but only a starched white shirt open at the collar. His shoes glistened beneath the table, shining so brightly she feared they might catch fire.

The town banker, she found herself thinking.

"I want to thank you for coming."

"Sure, no problem."

And for the first time, she realized there was a problem.

But what was it?

What was going on here?

"There is about to be a difficult meeting. It could become unpleasant. But I don't want to have it alone."

"All right."

"Of all the people in the church," he continued, "I suppose there is no one whose judgment I respect more than yours. Actually, of all the people in Bay St. Lucy."

"Thank you. That's a lovely compliment."

"It's no more than what a great many others feel. You're the town's *de facto* mayor."

"I don't know about that."

"It's true. And by the same token, you're the church's *de facto* lay leader. So when something like this comes up, something truly extraordinary…"

There was a rattling sound on the other side of the room. She turned her head in time to see the ponderous iron-grill and glass door swing open, and Brother Tamp enter.

He stood there for a time, framed in bright morning sunlight.

She could not help but be constantly aware of the contrast between the two men. The one black white polished and shining, the other brown, free-bearded and haggard.

There was silence for a time while they studied one another.

She knew nothing to say.

Which was probably because, she realized, there was nothing to say.

She was here as a witness, not a participant.

Finally, Rockman stood and gestured at the empty chair beside him, saying:

"Tamp. Thank you for coming."

So Tamp, she realized, had been summoned here too, just as she had been.

Tamp usually had little time for pleasantries, and today was no exception.

"What did you learn," he asked, "in Jackson? Did you meet the big dogs?"

"If that's what you want to call them."

"That's what they are."

"Then yes, I met them. Come and sit down."

Tamp crossed the room, making his was gingerly between card tables and straight chairs with magazines on them, looking up from time to time at the long canoes that hung above.

She could never watch him, never see his blue eyes that flashed as brilliantly, even if in a different color, as Rockman's shoes, without expecting him to stop whatever he was doing, rear back his head, and shout:

'And now for some dern good dancin'!

He did not do that, of course.

He merely sat, folding his long frame into the padded chair as though he were a pilot settling into a cockpit.

"Nina," he said, nodding to her.

She nodded back.

The room sat waiting.

She wished it could have said something, but that was too much to ask, even of a room that probably had many tales to tell.

Finally Rockman:

"I should tell both of you that my meetings went well."

Neither of them said anything.

"There are financial concerns. It's as I told both of you last week: the long and short of it is that some people at the District level don't feel that the Bay St. Lucy congregation is paying its fair share toward national projects, our mission outreach being paramount among these."

Again, more silence.

"But I was able to buy us more time. I also was able to impress upon them the importance of this Summer Retreat to the people involved in it. They have agreed that it should continue."

"That's excellent news," said Nina.

Tamp nodded.

And now it would be so nice, Nina found herself thinking, *if we could all get up and go our separate ways.*

Just go out and fish a little.

But, of course, that was not going to happen.

It was time for the real meeting to begin.

And Brother Tamp began it by saying not, 'It's time for some real fine dancin,' but:

"Pastor Rockman, I have to ask you why Ms. Bannister is here."

"She's here, Brother Tamp, because I asked her to be here."

"Why? Do you feel you need a witness?"

"In short, Tamp, yes I do."

"Don't you think this is putting her in a very difficult position?"

"I think *you* have put her in a difficult position. You have put us all in a difficult position."

"I don't think…"

"That's the problem, Tamp; you don't think. You're a kind man. But you don't think."

"Brother Rockman…" Nina interjected, sensing the direction of the conversation.

But Rockman cut her off.

He was clearly not speaking to her now.

"My question to you then, Tamp, is simply this: what in God's name do you think you're doing?"

To which Tamp answered quickly:

"You've put it wrong."

"Then how should I have put it?"

"What I am doing is in God's name."

"Oh really! How wonderful! Because it's certainly not in the church's name!"

"Can't the two be one, Rockman?"

"Oh yes! Indeed they should be one! Except you have to pay a little attention to the church to make that happen!"

"All right. I know I haven't…"

"Tamp, I began the drive here from Jackson at nine this morning. I began to get texts from parishioners. 'Do you know what is happening here?' most of them began. I had to get off the road and go into a coffee shop just to answer my smart phone. Except I didn't know how to answer it. I didn't know how to answer the message that said, 'Do you know that Tamp is planning a gay wedding on Saturday? Or the one that began, 'Has the Methodist Church changed its position on gay marriage?' Or rather, I should have known how to answer that one. The answer to that one is simply, 'No, it hasn't.'

"Rockman, you know yourself that across the country…"

"Oh is that what I should have said? Across the country people are breaking church law, church doctrine? So that of course is what we need to do in Bay St. Lucy. We are the home of that newly inspired prophet Pastor Tamp, who is now in a position to tell the Bishop himself what the will of God is!"

"Listen. Jennifer and Meg first approached me about this thing more than a year ago. Since that time no day has passed that I haven't prayed about it."

"Tamp in the Garden of Gethsemane, is that it?"

"That's not fair and you know it."

"I don't know it. That's the first remotely accurate thing I've heard you say. For months, actually. I don't know it. Why don't I know it? Well maybe I don't know it because my Assistant Pastor doesn't choose to tell it to me. Or especially, to ask my advice about the matter."

"I didn't ask you because I knew what you would say."

"And that was not something you could be bothered with."

"We have different views on the matter. These two women are sincere Christians and they are good members of this congregation. Why shouldn't they receive, in full view of this congregation, the blessed sacrament of marriage?"

"Oh I don't know—how about, 'Because it's a sin!"

"The Bible prohibits any number of things we have since come to accept."

"We, we! Don't you see how important that word is? But it isn't really that important to the Great Prophet Tamp, is it? The Tamp who speaks directly to Jehovah! And now that I think about it, Tamp, why don't we create in the old antiquated Bible a new thing: The Book of Tamp! We shall hex the Pentateuch, and slip you in neatly between Numbers and Deuteronomy!"

With that, Tamp, glaring, got to his feet.

So did Rockman.

They were glaring at each other now.

Nina had never felt so small, so helpless.

Why had she allowed herself to be drawn into this?

Did she not know what was bound to happen?

What is wrong with you, Nina?

Rockman leaned forward, almost hissing now:

"Of course, the marriage in front of our entire congregation isn't really that important now, is it? Because when Friday comes, there may not be a congregation."

"If you're talking about the alt-right rally..."

"Why would I be talking about that? What does that have to do with me? Or the Bishop! Or any other Methodist in the State of Mississippi?"

"Listen! We learned about the rally a few hours ago."

"Yes, and so did the rest of the country."

"What was I supposed to do, Rockman? There are only two choices open to us: we stay here and face these people or we run and go home. Brother Abe and I elected to have a meeting, let the people speak, and decide the thing. We did, and they decided to stay."

"It wasn't their choice."

"Then whose choice was it?"

"It was the church's choice, dammit!"

"But they are the church!"

"No, and you never seem to be able to grasp this, Tamp. They are a part of the church, just as you are, just as I am."

"So what would you have done, ordered them to go home?"

"No. I would simply have pointed out to them, as the Bishop has been pointing out to me for the past few hours in a dozen or so calls, that without our presence in that part, there will be no Alt Right rally. We are playing right into their hands by staying here, don't you see that?"

Tamp shook his head:

"I only see that..."

"'Only' is the operative word in everything you see, or try to see. The fact is though that you've created a terrible situation here. Two terrible situations. A wedding which cannot take place and a now-nationally televised first skirmish in what may turn into racial warfare. Brother Tamp, you have left me no choice. Acting on orders from the District Superintendent and the Bishop, I am terminating your employment as Associate Pastor of the First Methodist Church of Bay St. Lucy."

Nina caught her breath.

Both men were standing now, glaring at each other over the small table.

"Sit down," she heard herself say.

Principal Nina.

Remarkably, she found herself thinking, they both did so.

She wondered if her next move should be to give a homework assignment.

Brother Tamp spoke, rather calmly, before she could do so.

"So what happens now? What do you want me to do?"

"Go home. Pack and go home to Bay St. Lucy."

"Without a chance to address the congregation? With no possibility of saying good bye?"

"That was your choice, not mine. Your actions have made any other church-related activities on your part completely impossible. Also I have to tell you that, under these conditions, your pension will be disallowed."

Tamp nodded:

"I see."

Silence for a time.

Finally Rockman nodded and said:

"All right, then that does it for now. After you've left—which I hope will happen within the next hour—I'll reassemble the two congregations and tell them..."

"No."

More silence for more time, but this time a different kind of silence. Stunned silence.

Seemingly without end.

But of course, it had to end, which it did when Rockman asked:

'What? What did you say?"

"I said no. It's a word you need to learn."

"It's a word you're in no position to say, Tamp."

"I don't know. It sounded all right to me. Let's try it again. No."

"What are you talking about? This is not a discussion we're having. This is your Senior Pastor telling you to go home now. Do you want me to get the Bishop on the phone so he can make it even clearer?"

"To hell with the Bishop. And to Hell with you."

"Tamp!" Nina could not help exclaiming.

And it was a very calm Tamp who turned to her and said:

"It's all right, Nina. I'm sorry you're having to hear all of this. But believe me, it's all right. He can't fire me. None of them can."

"That's not true," said Rockman. "And you know it's not true."

Tamp turned back toward him and said:

"So what are you going to do? Brother Abe and I, along with the Apostle Paul and Dr. King, have just inspired those people. Are you going to tell me that you—a man they've barely gotten to know—are sending me home? You're going to tell them you're sending them home, and that the race-haters win? That the people want to stay but the Bigwigs say No? And you talk about national media—yes, everything that's happened here is damned sure on national media…my announcement about the wedding as sure as the whole thing with the Alt Right. That's been reported through a thousand Twitter accounts, and it's going to be reported by WRN News out of Tupelo. They'll be here in an hour, Rockman, cameras and all. You want them to interview you? Or the Bishop? One of you is going to say, "We just fired this man?" Really? Which one? And what reason are you going to give?"

"I can't believe that you are…"

"Then you had better start to believe. Listen, Aaron, I know you want me out. Have for a long time, maybe since the day you arrived in Bay St. Lucy. And you've got your wish. I resign. That will make it easier for you and the folks in Jackson. I'll give health as a reason, and it's not too far from true. I'm tired, really tired. But all that happens after we get back home. After we face these people Wednesday afternoon the way Christians have always faced their enemies, secure that God is with them. And after I marry those two fine young women in their spiritual home in front of their spiritual community."

Nina could see for the first time a different color in Rockman's appearance.

Where there had been only starched white and glistening black, there was now sweating red.

"If you try this," he hissed, 'you will lose a lot more than your pension, Tamp. I will destroy you. And believe me, I can do it."

"Then do it."

"As you wish, Brother Kentwood. As you wish."

So saying, he rose and strode out of the room.

Nina looked at Tamp and saw the same redness began to creep across his forehead:

"What did he mean, Tamp, by calling you 'Brother Kentwood?"

But Tamp merely shook his head and said, seemingly to himself:

"The devil told him that. It had to be the devil."

There was silence for a time, as Brother Tamp seemed to be struggling with something within him."

Finally Nina:

"What did he mean, calling you that?"

Tamp looked up at her, as though forced to remember that he was not in fact alone:

"He means…well, Ms. Nina, he means something you told me a year or so ago. I've forgotten exactly what we were talking about. But it came around to sin. And you quoted from one of those books you always know so well. Whoever wrote it said: 'We are all as God made us. And some of us, much worse."

"Tamp, I was just…"

"Much worse, Nina. Much worse."

He put his palms over his face.

She could tell he had begun to cry.

CHAPTER FIFTEEN: THE TIE THAT BINDS

Nina wandered along the shore of the lake during the late afternoon and early evening, trying to make sense of the bitter argument she had had just heard. She went to bed early, and had been asleep for two hours when her smart phone rang. It was Meg.

"You need to come to our cabin, Nina."

"What is it?"

"Something on our door."

"What?"

"Just come."

She did, and found Meg and Jennifer standing ten feet from the door.

"Look."

Nina saw it.

In the middle of the door.

"It's a note of some kind," said Meg.

"What's the brown stuff behind it?"

"I don't know, it looks like jelly or something. And there are other things: torn feathers and cloth bands— and some kind of round objects, broken. Look like egg shells."

They were standing in front of the door now.

And the smell—stench actually—told them that it was.

Nina forced herself to peel the sheet of white paper off the film of excrement.

She opened the note.

The writing—seemingly in red crayon—was too large to miss.

It said simply:

"Welcome to the church. Ishtalomo."

For a time they could only stand and stare.

Finally Jennifer asked, quietly:

"What is this? What does it mean?"

But Meg's face had already begun to redden, as Nina could tell by the yellow, bug infested porch light.

"I don't think it's too hard to tell what it is. The smell should give it away, don't you think?"

"But that word, Ishta-whatever. And these shell-like things, the feathers…"

"It's filth, Jennifer. In whatever language, whatever culture—filth is filth! And I want it off there!"

She lurched toward the door and grasped the handle, but Nina stopped her:

"Wait a minute, Meg."

"Wait for what? You want to leave this—this filth—on our door all week?"

"No, but I'd like to know a little more about what we're dealing with."

"Jennifer and I know already what we're dealing with. We've been dealing with it for years. And it may come home to you in slightly different forms, sometimes on the door, sometimes in the mail, sometimes on the phone. It's always when you're least expecting it. And it's always the same thing: the worst of human excrement. And I want it off!"

She pushed at the door again, and once again Nina was able to stop her.

"Meg, wait!"

"Wait for what?"

Nina hesitated, then said what had to be said:

"Somebody might still be in there."

Meg merely breathed deeply and said:

"I hope somebody is in there. I really hope it!"

Now Jennifer:

"Nina's right, Meg."

"All right. So Nina's right. What do we do, sleep outside? Rent a tent?"

Nina:

"We get some help."

"Who, the police? I'm not sure I want a bunch of policemen looking at this. I'm not sure I want anybody looking at this."

I'm not talking about just anybody, Meg."

"Then who?"

"Somebody who might understand these words, these objects."

"I'm still not sure…"

"Then come on. I'll show you."

They turned and walked away, Nina still unable to get the smell from her nostrils.

CHAPTER SIXTEEN: WITCH STORY

Barbara Smallwood hat slept fitfully for the last few hours, moving in and out of a kind of half dream, half reality semi-slumber. The coming Wednesday kept playing itself out in her mind, big white men wearing vests, overalls, and baseball caps, and carrying assault rifles across their shoulders.

She glanced at the luminous alarm clock that sat on a reading table beside her bed: 12:10.

She went over in her mind the previous evening's drill:

'Don't speak any more than you have to; don't get drawn into shouting matches; move forward, move forward, don't allow yourself to be pushed or manipulated; above all, keep large groups from forming and continuing to grow.

Divide, divide.

Smaller groups.

And, of course, there was always the possibility to avoid this entirely.

'You were hired as a scholar of Chickasaw culture. I had foreseen that you would spend your days setting up exhibits and giving lectures, not taking part in gun battles. You can stay out of this.'

But, of course, she could not 'stay out of it.'

For a thousand reasons.

The biggest thing to remember though was...

And from this reverie she was taken by the sound of knocking on the front door of the museum down below.

She attempted to clear her mind.

Who would be knocking on the door of a Chickasaw museum a few minutes after midnight?

Best, she decided, not to speculate.

So she swung her legs out of the bed, stood, somewhat shakily, still trying to get used to the fact that the low ceiling was only a foot or so above her head, and allowed herself to look up through the two-foot square dormer window.

The full moon was right in the middle of it, luminous, perfectly dime-round, and casting enough light to flood her twelve foot square bedroom.

She dressed quickly, aware all the time that the knocking was continuous, but (and she was thankful for this much at least), somewhat even in its cadence and intensity.

Whoever was down there was calm.

At least as calm as someone might be who was knocking on a stranger's door a little after midnight.

In half a minute she had finished putting on her uniform blouse, her trousers, and her boots.

She looked over at a small chest which sat at the end of the bed.

On it lay the 45. Automatic, sleek and silver, staring back at her from the end of its belt, which, with diamond-shaped inlaid stitching, could have been the three foot long curved body of a rattlesnake.

She left both belt and gun where they were, crossed the room, and opened the door to the stairway.

It was darker here, and so she had to make her way down carefully, cursing the clumsy boots and picturing a headline in the local morning paper that might say something like 'Chickasaw Warrior Woman Badly Injured in Headlong Spill Down Museum Stairs.'

But this did not happen.

At the base of the stairway, the museum opened out to her, moonlit again through the six-foot-tall windows, so that various tribal leaders from the nineteenth and twentieth centuries could look sternly back at her as she crossed toward the door.

Upon which the knocks kept falling with the regularity of an alarm clock.

All right, she found herself whispering as she reached for the knob.

All right, let's see who you are.

And, so wondering, she turned the knob and pulled.

There upon the small slab of concrete that served as the museum's porch stood three figures.

This much she saw clearly, and immediately.

The rest, namely gender, took a second more, because each wore a flop hat, flop sweatshirt, flop trousers, flop shoes, and a generally floppy demeanor, giving the impression of first-time hikers—or canoeists, for their shoes and the bottoms of their pants were drenched—back from a long night in the wilderness.

"We're so sorry to bother you…"

This from possibly the most haggard of the three and also the shortest.

Also the only one of the three whom she knew.

"Nina! Nina Bannister!"

"Yes. We met Saturday."

"You found some young men to help me unload boxes!"

"Well, actually Lannie Baker did, but I helped out in the process."

"At any rate, thank you. They were a big help. And the museum is set up now."

"I'm glad."

"So, what can I do for you? I'm guessing you're not here for a midnight tour of Native-American artifacts."

"No."

"What's going on?"

"I want you to meet Meg Brennan and Jennifer Warren. Meg and Jennifer are..."

"Gay."

Silence for a second, Nina spoke:

"I don't know if..."

"They're labeled 'gay.' I'm labeled 'Chickasaw.' Don't worry about it, you two. It's nice to be known for something."

"I don't know, since you put it that way," said Nina, "what I'm known for."

"Common sense."

"Sounds kind of boring."

"Yeah, it is, but somebody has to have some, and it might as well be you. What's wrong?"

"Somebody has defaced Meg and Jennifer's door."

"Defaced?"

"Put shit on," said Meg.

"That would be 'defaced,' all right."

Nina stepped forward:

"There's something else."

"What else?"

"We don't know."

"Well, I guess common sense will take you only so far. So you think I'm an excrement expert?"

"There are some words, some objects..."

"All right, let's go and see for ourselves."

She took a step forward; Nina stopped her, momentarily, saying:

"Do you need a gun?"

"I deal with excrement in my bathroom two or three times every day and I've never had to shoot it yet."

"Well, I guess that's comforting."

"Best I can do. Come on."

It took them perhaps five minutes to reach Meg and Jennifer's cabin.

Barbara looked at the door for no more than a second or so and said:

"Teenagers. Small-scale vandalism. I wouldn't worry about it. If you want, and have a bucket with soapy water in it, I'll help you clean it up."

Meg shook her head:

"I think we'd rather do it ourselves. Thanks though."

"Are you certain," asked Nina, "that they're all right?"

"They'll be fine. People who do this kind of thing do it and run. They're cowards. Which you two are obviously not. No, go on in, clean your door, and try to get a good night's sleep. Nina, I'll walk you back to your room, if you don't mind. Some things about tomorrow I'd like to clear up."

"Sure."

So saying, the two of them said good night to Meg and Jennifer and began to make their way to Nina's room in the main park headquarters.

"Nice people," said Barbara Smallwood.

"Yes. Lot of guts."

They walked for a time.

Finally Nina asked:

"So why did you lie to them?"

The other woman did not change her pace or move her gaze from the straight and forested path in front of her.

"Was it that obvious?"

"Pretty obvious."

"Then again, you've got common sense."

"Damned stuff."

"Yeah. Without it you'd be ten minutes away from a good night's sleep."

"Whereas, with it…"

"With it you have to talk to me for a while. Or at least listen. Is there a good place?"

"The big meeting room with canoes hanging from the ceiling. I've been hearing horrible things in there all day."

"Well, that's church for you."

"Come on. I'll take you there. Who knows, maybe someone has left out a bit of coffee. Of course, it might keep us from sleeping."

"You're not going to need coffee," said Barbara, "to keep you from sleeping."

And on they walked toward the lodge.

Finally the narrow pathway made a turn, and the main lodge loomed up before them

"You live in there, Nina?"

"Yes. There are a number of rooms in there. They usually go to us 'older singles.' The younger couples want cabins. More privacy."

"I understand."

"Come on. We go through this main entrance and make a right."

They did so, then continued down a hallway.

Finally a second door led them to a large room with couches and easy chairs strewn around it. The first thing to catch her eye was the number of inane yet colorful magazines lying on the small end tables. This entire hall, she found herself thinking, could have been a giant hospital waiting room.

The second thing was the canoes hanging from the ceiling.

Just the sight of them stopped her in her tracks.

"Wow," she found herself whispering.

"Pretty impressive, aren't they?"

"That they are."

"Chickasaw?"

"Yes. They need to be over in the museum. Of course, if they were there, only the museum visitors would get to see them. Now everybody does. Just look at them. Twenty-five-feet long, able to carry a whole war party. God knows how heavy each of them is. Well, we can talk about the canoes later. Come on, let's sit down."

They did, on opposite sides of a table in approximately the middle of the room.

Nina was the first to speak.

"So what are we looking at?"

Barbara merely shook her head:

"I don't exactly know. except it doesn't really make sense. And it's not good."

"Are Jennifer and Meg in danger?"

"Yes."

"Shouldn't you have told them?"

"I'm not sure what good that would have done. Kept them up all night."

"Maybe they need to be up all night."

"Maybe. At any rate, I'll be up all night. I'm going to go back to my room and get a sleeping bag. I'll bed down fifty yards or so from their door. They won't know I'm there. I also need to call my boss. Maybe he can send somebody over to relieve me."

"You still haven't told me what we're fighting here."

"Witches."

"Pardon?"

"I said we're fighting witches."

"You've got to be kidding."

"Wish I were. But the truth is, that word 'Ishtalomo?'"

"Yes."

"It's the Chickasaw name for a witch. Not just any witch though. You see, the Chickasaw believed that the forests were filled with witches. Ishtalomo was a particular one, with a story all her own."

"I guess I'm going to need to hear that story."

"Yes."

"And I'm also pretty sure I'm not going to like it."

"You're right there, too."

"So go ahead."

"Okay. This is the way it was told to me, I don't know how many years ago. An old witch called Ishtaloma was dead, and her people buried her in a tree, up among the branches, in a grove that they used for a burial-place. Sometime after this, in the winter, a Chickasaw and his wife came along, looking for a good place to spend the night. They saw the grove, went in, and built their cooking fire. When their supper was over, the woman, looking up, saw long dark things hanging among the tree branches. "What are they?" she asked.

"They are only the dead of long ago," said her husband, "I want to sleep."

"I don't like it at all. I think we had better sit up all night," the wife is supposed to have answered.

The man wouldn't listen to her, but went to sleep. Soon the fire went out, and then she began to hear a gnawing sound, like an animal with a bone. She sat still, very much scared, all night long. About dawn she couldn't stand it anymore, and reaching out, tried to wake her husband, but could not. She thought he was asleep. The gnawing had stopped.

When daylight came she went to her husband and found him dead, with his left side gnawed away, and his heart gone. She turned and ran. At last she came to a lodge where there were some people. Here she told her story, but they would not believe it, thinking that she had killed the man herself. They went with her to the place, however. There they found the man, with his heart gone, lying under the burial tree, with the dead witch right overhead. They took the body down and unwrapped it. The mouth and face were covered with fresh blood.

They sat for a time.

Finally Nina asked:

"What does this mean for Meg and Jennifer? Something dead is going to eat them?"

Barbara shook her head and said:

"You have to look at the other things on the door. They were actually turtles' eggs and eagle feathers. These things were used in stomp dancing, which the Chickasaw do for every major ceremony. But on the door the turtles' eggs were broken and the eagle feathers ripped. That means the roles of male and female are mixed up; they have become unspeakable and vile. Which explains the…"

"I know, you don't have to say. So what does it all mean?"

"It means their lives are being threatened. And by someone familiar with Chickasaw culture."

"Who could that be?"

"I don't know. I've only just arrived here in Mississippi. But these are ancient Chickasaw lands. Any number of descendants could be around, and I wouldn't know it."

"Barbara, what do the Native Americans think about gay marriage?"

"It's very complicated. There are over 900 tribes in The United States. A third of them have no problems with a gay lifestyle; another third are debating the issue. And the last third are dead set against."

"The Chickasaw?"

"Last third I'm afraid. I looked it up when I learned about this whole problem. Chickasaw law says something like: "a marriage between persons of the same gender performed in any jurisdiction shall not be recognized as valid and binding in the Chickasaw Nation as of the date of the marriage"."

"Well, at least that's clear."

""Something else is becoming clear, I'm afraid. I've been afraid of this for some time, and I haven't mentioned it. But now I've got to."

"What? What else?"

"All those people coming Wednesday?"

"Yes?"

"They may be the least of your problems."

CHAPTER SEVENTEEN: AND SOME OF US MUCH WORSE

Well past midnight now. Sleep impossible, thought Nina. Witches. Not bad enough that the Alt Right was threatening them—no, now evil spirits, though long dead, had to get in on the fun too.

She thought about getting up and pouring herself a glass of red wine.

She would take it outside and sit on the porch of the lodge, listening to faint tidbits of late night conversation. Perhaps a bit of music from someone's radio.

Then perhaps even a second glass of wine.

A Merlot.

Yes.

Yes! She should do exactly that! Why not?

Oh, right.

She didn't have any wine.

It was, after all, church camp.

She could sip orange juice, she supposed.

Except that she didn't have any of that either.

Sill wriggling around on the horns of this dilemma, she had almost decided to take up painting, when there was a knock on the door.

She almost did not answer.

She could feign sleep.

But she was already feigning sleep, and it wasn't much fun.

So…

"Yes?"

"Nina? It's Tamp."

Of course.

It would have to be Tamp.

After the horrible scene with Rockman this afternoon, he would have had a great deal of thinking to do.

And he would have had to talk to someone.

So…

"Come in, come in!"

He did so, looking haggard, which he always did, and miserable, which he never did.

"Sorry to bother you so late."

"It's no bother, Tamp. You know that."

"It's just—I've been wandering around for the last few hours."

"Did you eat dinner?"

"No. Not much appetite."

"Do you want something to eat now?"

"What do you have?"

"Nothing."

"Well, that kind of solves that problem, doesn't it?"

They each laughed, softly.

"Pull up a chair, Tamp. If you don't mind, I'll just stay here where I am. I've got a little cave hollowed out in the covers. You wouldn't think I'd need covers on a summer night like this. And I don't really. Not for warmth anyway."

"Then what do you need them for?"

"Protection."

"I see. You think they'll work?"

"As well as anything else, probably."

At least against witches, she thought of saying.

But she did not.

Tamp almost certainly knew nothing of the door effacement and its attendant complications. Nor did he need to know.

He was facing his own problems.

"So. You've been thinking."

"And praying. I went up to the clearing where you and I were earlier. I thought of myself as Jesus in the Garden of Gethsemane—then I realized how hypocritical that would be. Me, trying to be like Jesus."

"It's not such a reach as all that, Tamp."

"More than you know. More than anybody knows. Well, almost anybody."

Silence for a time.

Finally Nina:

"What did Rockman mean this afternoon, Tamp? What did he mean when he called you 'Brother Kentwood'?"

"He meant the end for me, Nina. Not the end as a man of God, because I've never really been that. But the end of being someone the congregation could trust, admire, have confidence in."

"Do you want to tell me about it?"

"Yes. It's been inside for so long…"

"All right. Maybe it's time to let it out."

He took a deep breath.

Then he began to let both things out: the breath, and, with it, the story of Kentwood:

"It happened the second summer of The Retreat. I was not a young man then, but, well, a good deal younger than I am now."

"That's true of all of us."

"Yes. Well, at any rate, there was a woman. I didn't know her; she wasn't from Bay St. Lucy. She had begun to show up in the congregation, during my sermons. One evening toward the middle of the week she came up to me, and said she found great comfort in what my message had been. She asked if we could meet later on that night. We did, in the chapel. I asked for her name, as you might have expected that I would. She told me she had rather not give it. I accepted that and went on with the meeting. She said she needed counseling. There were problems with her marriage. Her husband loved her, but, for reasons she herself could not understand, she couldn't stand to be with him. So I tried to advise her as best I could. We had several meetings. They extended beyond the Retreat. I would drive up here once a week and meet her, at some place she would choose. Finally in mid-August she told me she was pregnant. The baby was her husband's—she had never been unfaithful to him—but she couldn't stand to have it. She hated the man so much that she couldn't stand the thought of having his child. She begged me to help her find a way out of the dilemma. Well, the long and short of it is that as a very young man—a rather wild young man—before I found Jesus, I was wild, as young men often are. In short, I knew of a clinic in a town in Louisiana not too far from my own home village of Bay St. Lucy, where such a situation could be dealt with."

"The town was named Kentwood?"

"Yes. She made some excuse to her husband, and we went there. The procedure was done. I paid for it and signed my name, claiming to be her husband. Some clinics would have demanded proof of marriage. This one did not. As I knew they would not."

"Then you were to take her back home, and it would be as though nothing had happened."

"Yes. Except that something did happen. She died. Bled to death."

"Oh my God."

"Those were my words. Except that He didn't answer."

"What did you do?"

"What I should have done, of course, was to set about trying to ascertain who she really was. Then I could have gone to her husband, told him that I was a Methodist pastor who had been counselling his wife, and finally explained that she hated him too much to have his child. I, acting as a good Christian, had taken her out of state, without his knowing it, so that she could have an abortion—which she did not survive."

"You didn't do any of these things."

"No. I assumed that, if he learned any of these things, he would have killed me. And I was terribly afraid. Even if he had not killed me, my reputation would have been destroyed. So I bought a small burial plot outside of Kentwood and, with a small funeral service, had her interred there. A husband had buried his wife. No one in the town saw anything particularly out of the ordinary."

"And back at her home? Her parents? Her relatives?"

"I knew certain things from the talks we had. I knew that she was, at the time of this affair, quite alone in the world. Her parents were both dead. She had no brothers or sisters. Only her husband, who, though passionately in love with her, knew quite well that she did not return those feelings. He assumed, I suppose, that she had run away."

He was silent for a time, then said:

"And, in a way, she had."

"It's a terrible story, Tamp."

"I know."

"How do you think Rockman got wind of this?"

"I doubt if he did, at least in so many words. But I was a wild kid. Everyone knew that. I'm sure word of it reached Rockman, too. But this is the computer age. I'm sure he just set about checking court records for Mississippi and Louisiana. He wanted to see whatever dirt he could come up with. He found more than he could have expected."

"Tamp, what do you do now?"

"I have to go to see Rockman. I know it's late, but…well, it's just something I have to do. I'll tell him that he's won. I'll offer to resign immediately, and not perform the gay marriage. Also, if he chooses to make Kentwood public, so be it. I will only beg of him one thing: let me be with Brother Abe on Wednesday afternoon to confront these Alt Right people. The congregation expects that of me, and so do I. Otherwise, he's won."

"How do you think he'll respond?"

"I know how he'll respond if he has any decency in him. Whether he does or not—who knows? But for now, Nina, I just need to go and get this confrontation over with. Thank you—thank you for hearing me."

"Tamp, I…"

She could think of nothing to say.

It would hardly have mattered, though, since he had left the room and closed the door behind him.

CHAPTER EIGHTEEN: THE VALUE OF CULTURAL STUDIES

On the trail back to the museum, Barbara Smallwood thought of very little. She was in the woods and it was after midnight. That was enough. She became a creature of the senses, aware that no more than twenty yards to her right was a larger animal, probably a deer, hopefully not a black bear, although that would have been a possibility. To her left was a break in the undergrowth, through which she could see flashes of lighting. That meant rain, not tonight, but probably tomorrow afternoon.

And as she watched for a time, she became certain.

Mississippi or Oklahoma.

It would be more than just rain.

After an indeterminate amount of time and an equally indeterminate amount of distance— indeterminate because time and distance were things of numbers not of instinct—she reached the museum.

She went upstairs to her bedroom and gathered several things: her sleeping bag, which she had stored in the room's only closet, a flashlight, a two way radio—she would have to call her boss and tell him about this, no choice there—a hunting knife, and, yes, the 45.

She took the things downstairs and prepared to walk toward Jennifer and Meg's cabin. She was almost certain that no one would return to bother them this night, but she felt the need to sleep lightly, somewhere within fifty yards or so of the door, just in case.

Before doing these things though, she did something else, something dictated by no more than a hunch.

By the doorway of the museum was a light switch. She reached up and to the side with her left hand and switched it on.

The great room loomed before her, just as she had arranged it during the day.

Or?

Again, it was no more than a possibility.

But the museum had been open for several hours during the afternoon.

Some of that time she had spent at the cash register, selling various trinkets and artifacts to the public.

But for some of the time she had been gone.

She crossed the room, halting before the big picture window on the south side, and looking carefully at the third shelf, which was the height of her belt.

And upon which lay a small stack of paperback books, all the same book, all entitled *Chickasaw Legends: Wood Witches and Forest Ghosts*. How many copies were there?

There should have been seven; that much she remembered from stocking the shelves this morning.

And the story of the Ishtaloma was in that book.

Anyone wishing to appear knowledgeable about Chickasaw culture, or wishing to blame something—such as a threat—on any Chickasaw descendants who might be living in the area—would have only needed to do a quarter hour's reading to have found a 'villain.'

She began to count the books.

She had just ascertained that there were six—and only six—when the window exploded around her.

It was as though she had walked into a rainstorm of glass pellets, or rather the storm had come raging into the room to engulf her. The thunderclap that came with the shattering panel still reverberated in her ears as, voluntarily or not, she sank to her knees. There were an infinite number of stinging sensations on her forehead, her neck, her wrist and hands, and the floor, for a large surprisingly symmetrical circle around her, glittered, as though someone had made her the centerpiece of a display of diamonds.

For an instant or so she was capable only of perceiving, not of actually moving or acting. She felt a fresh breeze on her face and saw the lightning, not so distant now, flash in conjunction with a low rumble of thunder. This mild bass sound counterpointed strangely with the still incessant tingling of pellets falling from the tables and shelves they had covered for an instant following the blast.

This muscle atrophy that came from a bizarre feeling of aesthetic appreciation—as though she had found herself in a movie and was applauding the director— lasted for only an instant or so.

Then she was on her feet.

Act quickly, she told herself, *but don't panic.*

And so thinking, the first thing she did was to take off her boots.

Clumsy things that they were.

She even let her glance fall on one of the shelved black and white photographs on the wall beside her as she prepared herself:

James Adair, long time trader among the Chickasaws. He described their strength and endurance, and the fact that they were exceedingly swift of foot. "In a long chase they will stretch away, through the rough woods by the bare track, for two or three hundred miles, in pursuit of a flying enemy, with the continued speed and eagerness of a staunch pack of bloodhounds, until they shed blood."

Almost ready now, she looked one more time around the room.

Ten feet away from her lay a large stone.

A note, she could see, had been taped around the middle of it.

Let that go: she could read it later.

Secure in that knowledge, she picked up the hunting knife and stuck it between her belt and her pants.

The gun she left lying on the floor.

Twelve forty a.m.

Nina Bannister lay in her room, looking up at the ceiling.

She had no illusions about going to sleep.

Ever again.

She was not disturbed, then, when Frank entered and sat down on a chair beside the bed.

'What in God's name is going on?' she asked.

'Nothing.'

'Nothing is going on?'

He shook his head and answered:

'A lot is going on. Just not in God's name.'

'Thank you, Frank, for clarifying that.'

'Well, you're the English teacher. Be precise in your language, Frank, be precise in your language. If I've heard that once…'

'All right, all right, let it go.' Suffice to say, too much is happening."

'Not yet.'

'What?'

'You haven't even opened the door yet.'

'What?'

But he had disappeared.

And someone was, in fact, knocking on the door.

"Come in," she said.

But to the just-departed Frank she said:

'Wherever you just went, I wish I was there and you were here.'

He did not answer, though, and the door, as though to spite her, opened.

Kayla Morgen and Darius Johnson.

What were they doing here? she wondered.

"What are you two doing here?" she asked.

Neither answered.

So she sat up in bed and said, "Come in and sit down," although she knew she should have said, "Go back to the girls' area and the boys' area and get to sleep."

The two teenagers entered the room, Kayla walking in front and sitting in a chair beside the bed, Darius lagging back and sitting in the corner.

"We're sorry to bother you, Ms. Bannister," said Kayla, looking down at the floor as though she were a fourth grader admitting to breaking a vase.

"Yes, ma'am, we really are," echoed Darius, staring in front of him at the jagged shards of that same imaginary vase.

Kayla:

"We know it's late."

"What are you talking about?" asked Nina. "It's only a little after midnight. Here in First Methodist Las Vegas that's nothing at all."

As soon as she said that she felt guilty, even though both of them seemed to smile ever so slightly as soon as they heard it.

Ever so slightly; then the broken vases reappeared.

Kayla, even blonder than she had been at the campfire last night, and, impossibly, bluer-eyed:

"We didn't know who else to tell."

"All right. I'm here. But I suppose the first question I have to ask is, why aren't the two of you in bed?"

Kayla looked back at Darius, who looked back at Kayla, and Nina knew why they weren't in bed. Or at least in bed where they should have been.

"Oh damn," she could not stop herself from saying.

The two continued to exchange glances at one another. Kayla had begun to blush; Nina had read that it was quite possible for African Americans to blush, but to her the question remained open. Suffice to say that, if Darius had been capable of blushing, his deep black almost purple skin would have done so.

"You're in love with each other."

They both nodded, sheepishly, or at least in the manner that two sheep in love would have nodded.

"How long has this been going on?"

Kayla:

"A couple of months."

"Well. I'm happy for the two of you. Congratulations."

Both simultaneously:

"Thank you."

"How many people know about this?"

Darius:

"Only a few. Some close friends. It was just a short time ago that we—well, that we realized how we felt for one another. Normally we would have announced it on Facebook, that kind of thing. But now—well, it's kind of difficult. Kayla's going back this fall to a college on the East coast, I'm heading back to USC. We're not sure how we can make it work."

"I understand."

"And there's the other thing."

There was silence in the room for a time while 'the other thing' came in and sat down.

"You mean," said Nina, "the thing that one of you is white and one of you is black and fifty or so armed alt-right supremacists are coming in here to tell us we're all going to Hell after they shoot us all with automatic assault rifles, which they're allowed to have because we're all Americans?"

No response to that.

So Nina continued:

"Well, I'll say again, it's wonderful that the two of you have these feelings for each other. On the other hand, you haven't picked the most auspicious time to make a 'We'd like to teach the world to sing' Coca Cola commercial."

"No," said Kayla, "we realize that. But...well, actually that's not what we're here about."

"There's something worse?"

"Yes."

"Don't tell me."

"What?"

"I'm just kidding. Of course you've got to tell me. What is it?"

"Well, we had left one of the trails and gone into the forest with a blanket."

"You're right; that's worse."

"No, that's not it."

"All right, go on."

"We were just about to..."

"I don't want to know."

"All right. The main thing is, we heard something coming through the undergrowth. We were scared; we thought it might be a bear. They say there are bears in these woods."

"You don't usually have to worry about them if you're in the teenagers' bunkhouse."

"I know; we're sorry."

"That's all right. The course of true love never did run true."

"What?"

"It's Shakes—no, on second thought don't worry about it. What was it? What was coming through the undergrowth?"

"An Indian."

"Native American."

"Sorry. A Native American."

"Okay, but I'm still certain I didn't understand you."

"There, looking at us, from maybe ten feet away. There was this Ind...Native..."

Nina sat forward on the bed:

"Kayla, now that I think about it, I'm not sure that being politically correct is the most important thing we have to worry about right now. Let's just go ahead and be insensitive. No one will know. You saw an Indian?"

"He just stood there looking at us."

"What did he look like?"

Darius:

"He was a big Dude."

"That's good. We'll call him a 'Dude." That way we won't offend anybody except all the other Dudes in the country. How big was the Dude?"

"Well over six feet. And muscled? Man, that guy was ripped."

"Tell me more."

"We could see him pretty well in the moonlight. He had shaved his skull, and the top half of his head was painted red. The lower half was painted jet black. There was one long feather stuck behind his ear. He had a necklace of some kind...white...and his chest and shoulders were covered with black markings, like tattoos. But they made all sorts of patterns."

"And what did he do?"

"He just looked at us for a while, and then he shook his head. Real slow."

"Did he say anything?"

"No."

"Did either of you say anything?"

"Are you kidding?"

"No, and I guess that was a silly question. So what happened?"

"He just stood there shaking his head for maybe half a minute. Then he disappeared. It was like the forest just swallowed him up."

"Maybe it did. Maybe it did."

"Ma'am?"

"I'm just babbling. Don't worry about it."

"So, what should we do about this? Should we tell somebody else?"

"No, anybody else will just think you're crazy."

"Do you think we're crazy?"

"I think I'm crazy."

"Really?"

"Given all that's happened in the last few hours, the last few days, I don't know. Just, go on back to where you're supposed to be sleeping. I don't think there's anything we can do about this tonight without causing more trouble than it's worth. And, besides, if you think about it, what is there to it anyway? The ghost of a fierce Chickasaw warrior likes to watch an underage interracial couple have illicit sex: nothing very interesting there."

"Well, if that's what you think..."

"It is what I think. The only other thing is, maybe you should try not to advertise your feelings for one another too much in the next day or so."

"We understand."

"All right, then, good night."

"Good night, Ms. Bannister."

And, so saying, they left.

Except that, after a second or so, Kayla returned, stuck her head in the door and asked:

"Ms. Bannister?"

"Yes?"

"I have to ask you this."

"Ask."

"Would you have loved your husband Frank if he was black?"

"I love him right now and he's dead."

"And that's worse, isn't it?"

"Didn't used to be."

"All right, and just one more thing."

"Sure."

"It may be hard for Darius and me to hide completely how we feel for one another."

"Why?"

"On Friday night we're cast in *Jesus Christ: Superstar*. I play Mary Magdalene."

"Who does Darius play?"

"Jesus. Good night, Ms. Bannister."

She closed the door, leaving Nina to think:

"Well, somebody has to do it."

And, within a matter of minutes, she was asleep.

At slightly before one a.m., Barbara Smallwood returned to the museum, cursing herself.

She had failed completely.

For some minutes she had been supremely confident of her ability to catch the man—because the sounds she heard coming from the forested trail leading away from the building were that of a man, and a big man—who had thrown a stone through the exhibit hall window.

She was in the woods with bare feet and a hunting knife, all she needed.

If this was a deer running from her she could have caught it.

Not quickly perhaps, but she would have worn it down.

This was no deer.

But—and this bothered her more and more as the trail became more densely forested and the moon became less visible behind the low hanging vines—it seemed less and less to be a man.

A man would have grown clumsier, would have tired out, would have made mistakes.

There would have been more broken branches, and these branches would have been lower as the prey stopped and bent to catch his breath, then scrambled on, bent slightly with effort and exhaustion.

No such thing happened.

And it was she who began to tire.

What was she chasing?

Whoever or whatever it was took her more than a mile into the deepest part of Tombigbee Forest. She now found herself surrounded by yellow pines, and—barely able to see the ground before her—she realized that there were no more tracks.

Worse, stopping, standing completely still, she found herself able to hear only a low rustling wind, the moaning of an owl, and the very faint sound of music coming from one of the cabins back in the park.

Whatever she had been chasing had completely outrun and outdistanced her.

Unless…

Unless it was waiting for her.

Watching her now, as she stood wondering what to do.

That meant, of course, that there was nothing left to do, nothing except go back.

And so she did, re-tracing her steps while every now and then looking over her shoulder, ashamed that she had been beaten.

These feelings, mixtures of fear and shame, accompanied her as she re-entered the museum.

The first thing she noticed was a glaring hole on one of the shelves.

How had she missed that?

And what had been stolen?

She had walked half the distance to the shelf before she realized: a hatchet.

A war tomahawk almost two feet long.

Then she spied the stone that had shattered the window. It still lay in the middle of the floor. She picked it up and unwrapped the yellow paper that had been taped to its handle.

And she read, scrawled in large clumsy letters in red ink:

"THEY HAVE DEFILED THE LAND AND THEY WILL DIE STARTING TOMORROW"

THE END OF PART TWO

CHAPTER NINETEEN: THE POWER OF THE PRESS

Somehow Nina had gotten a few hours of sleep, she was not sure how.

A part of her brain had told her—at 2, 3, 4, and 5 a.m. respectively—to get out of bed and go report what had happened last night.

But another part of her brain had told her not to.

Brain part #1—the parietal?—had told her that the sign on Meg and Jennifer's door was a warning and that people running around in the woods dressed like Chickasaw warriors needed to be found and told to stop.

Brain part #2 though—the medulla oblongata?

Good old seventh grade science.

—this part, whatever its name, had told her that Barbara Smallwood already knew about the warning on the door and was taking all necessary precautions, and that, as for the second problem, there was no way she could report it without telling where its source had come from, namely two teenagers who had sneaked out of their rooms in the middle of the night to go and have sex.

Interracial sex at that.

And, racial or interracial, it was not the sort of thing they would like advertised.

And so, when she woke once again at seven o'clock, she told her brain not to think of these matters.

Make a cup of coffee.

Do not turn on the television.

So, she made the cup of coffee and it was half drunk when there was a knock on the door.

She thought of shouting out, "Nina Bannister is not here; she has been taken to the emergency room!" when she remembered what it actually had been like to be taken to the emergency room (something that had happened to her only six months ago), and shouted out instead:

"Come in!"

The door opened.

Revealing Meg and Jennifer.

She was attempting to say, 'Good morning!' and had gotten as far as 'Good mor—' when the two of them strode into the room, Jennifer obviously near tears, Meg obviously near hitting someone.

They would, she found herself musing, really make a good couple.

Meg spoke:

"Have you had your television on?"

"No. I never watch television anymore. Well, except for this one monster movie that I've got recorded. These scientists go to a place called 'The Black Lagoon,' and they find…"

"Turn it on."

"Do I have to?"

"Yes."

"Is it more stuff about the alt right coming?"

"No."

"Then how bad could it be?"

"I'll show you; they're re-running the tape every ten minutes. We should be getting in on the first of it right now."

This was not precisely right. When Jennifer picked up the remote from Nina's bedside table and pressed the small red 'on' button, the screen was showing a woman obviously in hideous shape, skeletal, and trying to smile, but unable to speak. A script running beneath the picture said, 'Marjorie died last year from smoking. Never smoke.'

"Is this," said Nina, suddenly feeling hoarse, "what you wanted me to see?"

"No. Just wait."

Another commercial, with another horribly deformed man/woman (hard to tell which), accompanied by the words "Just ask your Gastroenterologist."

"I hope the two of you realize I haven't had breakfast. Now I'm not even sure I can get this coffee down."

"This is not funny, Nina."

"No. It's depressing."

"It gets worse."

"How can it get worse than death?"

"Watch."

Given that she was lying trapped in bed, there was little else for her to do.

Blessedly the commercials were at an end.

In their stead, a screen with a lightning bolt, and below that the words, 'Breaking News!' written in a font which might just as well have said: 'Superman!'

Meg:

"Now watch—if you really want to get sick."

Flashing lights on the screen.

Camera pulling back, revealing—oh damn, a van parked in front of the main building of Tombigbee State Park.

It must have been—at least a short time ago—right outside her own room.

And now a newsman, microphone in hand, speaking earnestly, as though there were actual human beings standing just in front of him and not merely a row of cameras:

"The news this morning comes from Tombigbee State Park, only a few miles north and west of Tupelo, Mississippi, where it has been known for some time now that tomorrow, Wednesday afternoon at eleven o'clock, a group identifying themselves as the 'alt-right' will gather to protest the combining of black and white churches."

"All right," Nina found herself saying, "but that's what they've been reporting for a solid day and a half now. What's different about this broadcast?"

Meg and Jennifer merely stared at her, as though whatever was wrong was her fault, as the announcer's voice intoned:

"This morning though, CMRS News has learned that yet another group has added its voice in heated and dramatic protest: The Chickasaw Nation."

"Oh," she said, quietly.

Then:

"Damn."

It was the worst word in her vocabulary.

Barbara Smallwood had no television in her attic room, but she was able to watch the broadcast—it was not the first time she had seen it this morning—from the smart phone she normally carried in the glove compartment of her jeep.

She had no idea why she kept watching the tape again and again.

Perhaps she expected it to get better with each subsequent playing.

It did not.

It did not get worse, either.

It remained exactly the same.

"Our news department has learned several disquieting things. First, late last night or early this morning, the room of a gay couple planning to be married in a church service—the service to be performed in front of the Bay St. Lucy Methodist Church and the Bay St. Lucy Bethel AME Church, which is Black—this coming Saturday night, was viciously vandalized. Vandalism is bad enough of course, but this particular incident was worse. The couple's door apparently was smeared with human excrement, and in the center of the door was hung a Witch's symbol cursing the unnatural union of same sex couples."

She thought about turning the thing off but knew she should not and could not.

So the report continued:

"In yet more frightening new, an interracial couple apparently having sex in the woods near Tombigbee Park Headquarters—CMRS News is currently attempting to verify the couple's names, and obtain direct statements from them—was attacked by a man dressed in the full battle regalia worn by Chickasaw warriors. There is no news available at the present time concerning the extent of the couple's injuries."

"But that's not even..." she found herself whispering.

The thing should end.

Let it end!

But that did not happen.

What did happen was a continuation of the same Chickasaw report, which had begun as 'somewhat true but confidential,' moved to 'a grain of truth but mostly falsehood,' and now ended with:

"Most frightening of all, The Chickasaw Museum near the park's headquarters—was broken into only hours following the attack on the young couple. Several weapons of war were taken, including tomahawks and spears. Approximately one hour ago, the museum's curator, newly-hired Ms. Barbara Smallwood, herself a full-blooded Chickasaw, made a phone call to CMRS Headquarters. In this call she confirmed the station's version of events and stated, quote: 'The spirit of the Chickasaw Nation fills this park, and is obviously outraged at the perversion of nature that is going on within it. Whether something supernatural is going on or not, gay marriage and the mixture of races are *un*natural, and they will not be tolerated."

Barbara switched off her smart phone.

For a time, she merely stared at it, knowing that it would buzz at any moment, and practicing what she would say when it did:

'I never made such a call. I don't know how they got their information. I never made such a call.'

She said these things over and over for a little over two minutes.

The phone buzzed. She opened it and heard:

"This is Starnes! Dammit Barbara, what's going on"

And, attempting to answer, she found that she had no voice.

CHAPTER TWENTY: CONVERSATIONS

Nina's open window gave out onto the vast Park Lawn, where yesterday Tamp's and Goforth's twin sermons had galvanized two congregations, but where two things were happening, and had been happening since sunrise. First, breakfast was being set out, gleaming platters of eggs, sausage, bacon, and whatever else could be imagined, on long tables, these punctuated at either end by canisters of coffee.

Second, the fishing tournament was beginning in earnest.

Yesterday practice.

Today, the real thing.

And, not to forget, The Youth, under the direction of Cindy Baker, were giving a 'dramatic presentation' (title strictly kept secret) in the 'huge canoe room' (no other name for it seemed to fit) at ten o'clock this morning.

It would, she was certain, be a re-enactment of The Good Samaritan, or another parable.

Something like that.

"Hey, can I sit with you?"

"Cindy, of course. Sit right here—put your plate down. What have you got for breakfast there?"

"Oh just a piece of toast. This darn diet…"

Cindy. A diet. Cindy, who, standing a good five feet four, must have weighed all of sixty three pounds.

It wasn't fair.

"Okay, Cindy, you've been very good and haven't mentioned this morning's radio broadcast, or the possibility that the camp is being haunted by the ghosts of the Chickasaw nation."

"No, I don't engage in small talk. Either you don't know anything about this crazy gossip—in which case you can't talk about—or you do know, in which case you almost certainly don't want to spoil a beautiful morning dealing with it."

"You're very perceptive. So—I would much rather ask about the play your youth are doing this morning."

"Good for you and thanks for asking. You'll be there, won't you?"

"Just try and stop me. But you've got to let me in on a little bit of the secret."

"Then it wouldn't be a secret."

"Okay, but let me be certain I've got this right. All the middle school youth will be involved."

"Right. The high schoolers are in the big musical that Jack Fox is doing Friday night."

"I understand. And you've had how long to rehearse? Just yesterday, right?"

"Two hours Sunday evening after everybody arrived, and two hours yesterday."

"So, let me guess what play you're doing."

"All right, go for it."

"You're going to dramatize 'The Good Samaritan.'"

"Nope."

"Okay, it's not 'The Good Samaritan.' But it's one of the parables, right?"

"Not even close."

"Then, with a few kids, many of them really young, it must be something that you can do…"

"Nina, it's *Everyman*."

Silence for a second or so.

Or at least as much silence as there could be with a fifty or so people chowing down and gossiping.

"What?"

"It's *Everyman.*"

More not too near silence.

Finally, Nina, trying to mask astonishment, could ask:

"Are you talking about the Medieval Morality Play?"

"Sure am."

"Cindy, *Everyman* is one of the masterpieces of English literature!"

"I know. It's very good."

"It's also an entire play—anonymous masque composed sometime in the fifteenth century."

" According to my sources, the year was 1453."

"According to…Cindy you might as well be doing *Hamlet*!"

"No. Too depressing. And not very religious."

"You are working with how many children?"

"Fourteen."

"And you had how much time to work? Four hours?"

"Three and a half actually. We had snacks."

"You know this is called a Miracle Play."

"Fitting, huh. Hey! I've got to go. Don't tell anybody what play we're doing though."

Cindy rose, and Nina said:

"I won't."

But what she thought was, *They won't believe me, anyway.*

By eight o'clock, breakfast was over and the fishing tournament could begin in earnest. The youngest participants clambered around the short piers, getting advice from dads and moms and older siblings. Middle schoolers fished from boats that sat languidly in the water some fifty yards from shore. Nina had found a lawn chair from which she could watch everything, delighted at the little screams from little people who, fishing mostly with cane poles, drew gold and red and ice-blue sunfish out of the lake. These fish were weighed, of course (forty five ounces, fifty three ounces), and named (Angel, Golden Boy, Starburst) before being dropped carefully out into the water. Occasionally one of the older children in a boat would catch a catfish. This was a dangerous situation, of course, because the catfish sported spear-fins that could inflict painful injuries, and the fish were thus dutifully removed from the hooks by fathers or uncles, and, upon some rare occasions, even kept for the evening fish fry.

It was the contest, just as it always was.

Except no Pastor Tamp.

Tamp who, several hours earlier, sometime around 1 a.m., had confronted Rockman and admitted defeat.

How had that gone?

And where were the two men now?

By eight thirty she had digested breakfast.

By eight forty five, she had gotten over her guilt feelings concerning the sausage gravy, jam rolls, eggs, etc., and the completely clean plate that had been left before her.

By eight fifty, she had begun to think about lunch.

She was thus glad to be rescued from these fantasies by a voice behind her—in physical as well as temporal space, as it turned out—saying, somewhat plaintively:

"Ms. Bannister?"

She corkscrewed around in the plastic folding chair and looked up.

It was a familiar face, certainly, but an out of place one.

She panicked for a second or so.

This was someone she should have known, did know, but could not immediately call to mind.

Thirty years in the classroom would do that.

"Ms. Bannister, they told me I could find you out here."

Who was it who was it who was it…

"It's May Ellen. May Ellen Gentry."

Of course.

She beamed, partially because she was always—well, almost always—glad to see former students, partially because the guilt of having forgotten this young woman's name could now be replaced by the slightly less agonizing guilt of being hungry again.

"May Ellen Davis!"

"Yes ma'am. That was my name when I had you as a sophomore. Would have taken you junior and senior years too but you went on and got to be principal. You were a great principal, everybody thought so—but I'm still sorry I didn't get to take you for more English classes. You was the only one made it fun."

And how well I taught you grammar, she found herself thinking.

"May Ellen! It's so good to see you! You were such a hard working student!"

"Well, like I say. You made it fun."

"And you're married now?"

"Randy Gentry. Boy from up north."

"Up north?"

What did she mean by that?

Michigan?

New Hampshire?

"Yes, ma'am. Tupelo."

Oh.

That kind of up north.

"We met at an FFA convention in Jackson. Only a few months after I graduated. He was a little older, but we just hit it off, you know how it is."

"Sure. And what does Randy do now?"

"We have a farm. Not too far from here. Used to raise cotton, but you can't do nothing with cotton now. Price too low, the Chinese, market just went to...well, it doesn't matter."

"So what do you raise?"

"Corn mostly. Big demand for that. Ethanol."

"I see."

"Got us three kids, oldest in fifth grade. Wish they all could have a teacher like you. I still remember some of that stuff."

"Really?"

"Oh yes, ma'am. Even Shakespeare. 'There is a destiny that shapes our ends rough.'"

Good job, May Ellen. The line is, 'There is a destiny that shapes our ends, rough-hewn though they may be.'

But good job anyway.

Between the corn market going and the ethanol market coming and three kids in Tupelo...good job anyway!

"Well congratulations, girl! You seem to be prospering."

"We're doing all right. We can't complain."

"I would think not, a successful farm and three kids. It really is nice to see you. But...was there something in particular you wanted to see me about?"

"Yes, Ms. Bannister, they was."

"Tell me then. Whatever I can do."

The woman turned and peered around.

"It's kind of...I don't know. I wonder if we could go somewhere and talk where it was a little more..."

"Private?"

"Yes, ma'am. I guess that's what I'm tryin' to say."

"That sounds good."

"All right. Let's go."

And, so saying, Nina got to her feet.

Soon they were in Nina's room.

They sat down, and Nina asked again:

"So how can I help you?"

May Ellen took a deep breath.

"Ms. Bannister, I had to come and tell you this myself. When I found out what was happening, and that you were over here, I had to come tell you myself. So that's what I'm going to do. Ms. Bannister, that group of men that's coming over here tomorrow at eleven o'clock: Randy's going to be one of them. And, before all of this goes down, I just had to talk to you, to tell you why that group—why we all, really—feel like we do."

"All right. Tell me."

"All right. Well then, Nina…I guess the major thing is, why are so many people trying to promote race-mixing and this 'race equality' thing? Why? I'll tell you: because, it's Satan's goal to have us violate our Heavenly Father's law on mixing our seed with the other people of the world. What used to be wrong is now right. What used to be bad is now good. Our world has been turned upside down and we have only ourselves to blame for letting it happen."

"The government is destroying our race with all these 'programs' that they got going. They make you hire 'cause of race and not real qualifications, they call this 'affirmative action.' The government stands up for all this not-white integration. When all the third worlders coming into the country can't work, they go on welfare. The welfare program makes white people pay for the not-whites to eat and live, and that just means we don't have enough money to feed our own kids. Our race, just because of what the government's doing, has the lowest birth rate in the country, did you know that, Nina? Our own white race, that founded this country!"

There was something that should be said to this, Nina knew. She felt guilty for not saying anything.

But she felt at the same time that any human response would have been inappropriate, because she was not talking to a real person. She was listening to a recording. May Ellen Davis high school student who had become May Ellen Gentry young farm wife and mother had ceased to be either and had been transformed—through whatever agencies had been at work on her—into a phonograph.

And Nina had as good a chance to alter it as she had to change the newest recording of 'White Christmas.'

So it went on.

"We're scared. They call us hateful people. They write terrible things about us and say we're killers and monster-people. But we're the ones that are threatened, we're the ones that won't keep on existing if things keep on going this way. And it's more than that. Nina, I pray for you. We all pray for you, and that's why the men are coming over here tomorrow afternoon. To tell you. Because you are a church, and you're going against what God has ordered for you."

Some automatic response mechanism inside her prompted Nina to ask:

"How do you mean that, May Ellen?"

"You can read it in the Bible. It's so clear there."

"Where?"

Exodus 33:16 "So shall we be separated: I and thy people, from all the people that are upon the face of the earth." Leviticus 20:24 "I am the Lord thy God which have separated you from other people." Joshua 23:12-13: "If you do in any way go back and cleave unto the remnants of these Nations, even these that remain among you, and shall make marriages with them, and go in unto them and they unto you: Know for a certainty that there shall be snares and traps unto you, and scourges in your side and thorns in your eyes, until ye perish off from this good land which the Lord your God has given you."

She paused for a second to catch her breath.

She was reciting *Hamlet* in ninth grade English.

And she had done her memorizations very well.

"Listen, Nina, listen to me: I don't want you to be lost. Listen to Deuteronomy 7; 3: 'Neither shalt thou make marriages with them; thy daughter shalt thou not give unto his son, nor his daughter shalt thou take unto thy son, for they will turn away thy son from following me, that they may serve other gods.' And listen to Colossians 4:1: 'Masters, treat your slaves justly and fairly, knowing that you also have a master in heaven.' And better than that, Nina, is Ephesians 6:5: 'Slaves, obey your earthly masters with fear and trembling, with a sincere heart, as you would Christ."

Silence for a time.

May Ellen sat across the table, staring at her, waiting for a reply.

As for Nina, she simply wished that someone would come into this vast room, which had been built to house and support small conversations, bridge games, etc.

Why were there no bridge games going on now?

Why were there no distractions?

Why did no raucous teenagers stumble in, laughing and horse playing and punching one another and giggling and guffawing and preventing May Ellen from saying:

"The bottom line, Nina, is that we, the chosen people of God, the true tribes of Israel, are commanded not to race mix. Not in the bedroom; not in the church. And that slavery is not a sin; it is a commandment."

"Are you saying, May Ellen, that Jackson Bennet and his family, and Alanna Delafosse, and Jack Fontenot, and Brother Abe—should be our slaves?"

"No, Nina."

"Good. Because I honestly…"

"I'm not saying it. The Bible is."

Upon stating this, May Ellen extended her hand across the table and asked:

"Will you take my hand, Nina, and pray with me?"

But Nina merely shook her head and said:

"I don't think I can ask God, May Ellen, to make slaves out of my best friends."

"All right. All right. But I will continue to pray for you. I want you to know that."

"I need all the people praying for me that I can get," Nina said, quietly.

"And I want to tell you one last thing, maybe the most important of all."

"Tell me."

"The way it's been in the past, the liberal media lumps us all together. We're the radical conservatives, the poor uneducated right wingers. But this demonstration will be different. I promise you, it will be different. We won't be alone—we'll be joined, and by people even the liberals have to listen to."

There was nothing left to be said to that.

So after a few seconds May Ellen stood up:

"Thank you for seeing me, Nina. And for hearing me out."

"You're welcome, May Ellen. Many blessings on you and on your family."

"Thank you. Good bye for now then."

She turned and had taken several steps toward the door when Nina stopped her by asking:

"May Ellen?"

She turned back:

"Yes?"

"I have to ask you something."

"Please. Go ahead. Anything at all."

"These people who are coming tomorrow…will they have guns?"

A short pause and then:

"That is their right. As Americans."

"Do you think Jesus would have had a gun?"

But May Ellen merely shook her head and said:

"I don't think Jesus would have been forced into this situation."

And so saying, she left.

And so she simply sat for a time, thinking about these things, wondering.

Thinking of Alanna, Jackson, the Bethel Church, all of its members.

And of the horrible things they had been forced to endure for centuries.

But their sufferings had, at least, done one thing for them.

The sufferings had given them tolerance.

They were not like May Ellen.

They would never cast aside an individual or a race simply because of…

But these musings were interrupted by the glass door, which, so long closed and silent, finally opened.

It was Alanna.

Nina brightened and almost shouted:

"Alanna, it's so good to see you! How have you been?"

But Alanna, clearly upset, took two paces into the room and said:

"Our Bishop has learned about the gay marriage. We're leaving."

Around nine o'clock Tuesday morning

My Room

So what has happened since I last wrote something here?

Let's see if I can get you up to date.

Somehow the media learned about the defacement of Jennifer and Meg's room. They also got wind of Kayla and Darius and the warrior they saw—except they made it a little more dramatic and said there was an actual attack—which is nonsense. Then they said there was an attack on the museum and gave a 'quote' from Barbara, which I'm sure she never gave them.

Poor Barbara. I'm sure her boss is outraged. And she didn't do anything wrong.

Well, we'll just see what happens with all that.

Over breakfast I met with Cindy and tried to guess what short parable the youth were going to dramatize for their little play and she told me they were going to present a fifteenth century morality play that would take any good Shakespearian company a few months to produce and nobody would understand it anyway because it's in Latin.

But it's all right because the average age of the actors is around twelve and they've had a good three and a half hours to work on it (They had to have refreshments.)

Then one of my old students sought me out and said she wanted to talk to me. I said ok why not and we went into my room. She told me her husband was one of the fifty or so Alt Right men coming over tomorrow to demonstrate and she told me why (Because we're all going to Hell if we keep mixing with the Bethel read Black Church). She had it all thought out and had memorized a lot of Bible verses to support her opinions. I would have been very impressed except that somehow in the last few years as well as becoming a loving housewife and (I'm sure) a loving mother she has also turned into a MAJOR LOON.

Then, after I gave up trying to figure out what had gone wrong with her mind and how I could tell her that the people of Mississippi were not the children of Israel (at least not the people of southern Mississippi I'm not sure about how they do things here in the north), and she left—Alanna came in and told me that her church, which was composed of liberal long suffering broad minded people who knew better than anybody else what it was like to be discriminated against had decided to pack up and go home because Tamp was going to perform a gay wedding and the Black Church doesn't tolerate gays.

Are you getting all this?

Good, because it only gets better.

We all wound up at another meeting, this one in the building we use as a church. Once again, everybody couldn't get in, and that's probably all right because if they had if would have been even more chaotic. But it sounds like what happened is this: sometime yesterday evening Rockman had called the Jackson headquarters not of our church but the Bethel African American Church. He had told me yesterday after dinner that he was going to contact them, but I thought he was going to tell them about Tamp and this Kentwood thing, whatever it is. But it was the gay marriage. When he told their Bishop we were having joint services and that a joint service on Saturday was to feature a gay wedding, their front office went crazy. It seems the Bethel national and international church is not debating the subject of gay weddings in church like we are, or even having gays as members. To them it's just wrong, no ifs ands or buts.

So, of course, that set fire to everything. Some members of Bethel said yes, they should all go home *rather than go against the Word of God but some other members of Bethel said if they all went home it would look like they were running away from the alt-right group that was coming on Wednesday and that would be cowardice and no way ever would they run away from those racists and they would rather burn in Hell first and somebody from our church (Inez I think) said "How can you say that have you ever really burned in Hell even for a minute (and, of course, nobody had so there was quiet for a time but not long) then somebody asked Jennifer and Meg if they would consider just postponing their wedding just for a few weeks until we could get all of this worked out and Jennifer looked for a minute or so like she might be getting ready to say 'okay,' but Meg got up and said, 'We might have said okay even as late as yesterday but not today because somebody smeared our door last night with...well, you know...and left us a hateful note and to that we say...well, she said the same word that somebody had smeared their door with and that I can't write here, and so that stopped being an option and so there we were.*

At least for a few seconds or so.

Until somebody asked Brother Abe for his thoughts. He said he was without any power in the matter. His supervisors had made it clear to him. The Bethel Church could in no way support gays in church or especially gays getting married in church. If the Bay St. Lucy First Methodist Church kept on with this plan and he stayed along with his congregation then he would be removed from his Pastoral position. And then somebody (I've forgotten Black or White it didn't really seem to matter too much at this point) asked if it wasn't a little bit hypocritical for African Americans, who had been discriminated against for four hundred years or so, to be the ones doing the discriminating now. Somebody else, after hearing that said:

"NO."

...and that led us back into the 'going to hell' part again

But then, before it could get wild again—and it was starting to get very wild indeed, believe me—Lannie did something crazy.

He said:

"I think we should be advised by someone who hasn't spoken up yet."

Silence to that.

"Who is he talking about?" everybody seemed to be thinking.

And I was wondering if he meant Jesus or God but since I knew that those two were saying entirely different things to entirely different people it didn't seem to help very much, so I kept racking my brains about who we should be getting advice from when he said:

"I think we should hear what Nina Bannister has to say."

What?

Can you believe that?

And, even crazier, there was this kind of murmur, and everybody started nodding and looking at me.

Me!

What was I supposed to know about things like this?

But they were all looking at me.

Silently, at least, they all seemed to be asking me:

'What do we do, Nina? How do we know what's right and wrong? What's the moral thing to do?'

So I stood up.

And somehow it just came to me.

I looked around and saw Cindy standing in the back of the room.

"Cindy, is your play beginning at ten? That is, in twenty minutes?"

"Yes."

"Over in the big room with the canoes?"

"Yes."

"All right. Then here is my advice for everyone. If you aren't sure what's moral, then go to see a morality play; and if the adults seem to be making a mess of everything, then let's listen to Cindy's kids."

And since that was all I had to say, I left.

I had to. In fifteen minutes Everyman *is set to begin.*

Solo Deo Gloria

CHAPTER TWENTY-ONE: EVERYMAN, I WILL
GO WITH YOU...

Nine fifty-five Tuesday morning.

As soon as she entered the 'big canoe' room and saw
Cindy's actors, Nina knew how it was going to be done.

Each of the players carried a carefully typed out (by
Cindy, of course) script, which they were simply going
to read. All of the action would take place in one small
area not far from the window looking out over the lake.
No blocking to worry about.

They could do it.

Middle schoolers though they were, they could do it.

Was it a play meant for people that young?

No, but...

Who else was making any sense these days?

At any rate, the room was packed when Cindy stood
up and spoke:

"This is a play about how God sends Death to
summon every human being in the world to come and
give account of what they have done with their lives,
lives which are gifts from God almighty."

Then she disappeared into the crowd.

For a second the small area where the action was to
take place was empty, and Nina found herself with
nothing to look at but the massive canoe hanging
directly over it.

Then the intercom was turned on, and a voice,
speaker unseen, filled the hall:

"Where art though, Death, my faithful and almighty
messenger? Your God calls thee forth!"

(Enter Death, played by Tommy Simmons. Skinny, bespectacled, Tommy, who would almost certainly grow up to be an accountant)

He stammered a bit as he read, but he seemed to gain confidence as he went along:

D: Almighty God, I am here at your will, your every commandment to fulfill.

G: Go thou to Everyman and tell him in my name of a journey he must take, that he can in no way escape. Tell him I want a reckoning, and I want it now.

D: My Lord, I shall do as you command. Lo, there, I see Everyman walking. He's not thinking about me. His mind is on his pleasures and his treasures.

(Everyman enters, played by Marcellus Washington)

D: Everyman, stand still! Where are you going? What are you thinking about? Have you forgotten your God?

E: Who are you? And what do you want from me?

D: I come from God. From your God, the God who made you. And even though you may have forgotten Him, He has not forgotten you!

E: What does he want from me?

D: He wants a reckoning.

E: A reckoning of what?

D: Everything you have done in your life.

E: But when does he want it?

D: Now.

E: But that's impossible! That will take...

D: Now.

E: Who are you?

D: I am Death, that spares no one.

E Death? But this is a mistake! You can't be death! Death is supposed to wear a big black cape and have a scary mask! You just look, well, common.

D. There is nothing in the world more common than death.

E: All right but still, you can't come for me now! I'm young! I'm in the Youth class! You must want someone from the Adult class, or the White-haired Senior Class!

D: No. You.

E: But..

D: You. Did you think you were exempt? Why, because you play football? Because you're planning to go to college?

E: But this just can't be! I'm healthy! I've been accepted to one of the best colleges in the world: Mississippi State! And I...that is my parents...have money! I'll pay you whatever you want. Just pretend you couldn't find me!

D: You think that's going to work? Read the Medieval Morality Play called "Everyman," written by an anonymous author in the fifteenth century.

E: What is a Medieval Morality Play?

G: Yes, you are a Mississippi State student. Nevertheless, here's what it says: "Everyman, it may not be by no way, I set not by gold, silver, nor riches, nor by Pope, Emperor, King, Duke, nor Princess, for, and I would receive gifts great, all the world I might get: but my custom is clean contrary, I give thee no respite, Come hence, and not tarry." So there it is, Everyman. You think I couldn't have all the money in the world if I wanted? Now stop insulting me and get ready. It's time!

E: But if I take this journey, can't I come back?

D: You can never come back.

E: But but but but...

D: Did you actually think that your riches, your health, your friends—that these things belonged to you? No. They were leant to you. And no payback has come.

E: But this journey—it's so scary to think about it. I can do it, but not alone. May I take someone with me?

D: Just try to find someone who'll go with you. This journey, the journey with me? Try. I dare you. I'll even give you an hour. But that's all. Remember: an hour. Then we go.

(Death Exits)

E: What must I do? My friends! I'll tell my friends what's happening. They'll see that I don't have to endure this alone. We've been so close for so many years. We've been through everything together. Now that I desperately need them, they won't let me down! There they are, waiting for me as always, as though nothing had happened. Hail! Hail my dearest friends!

(Enter Friends)

F: Hey, E.M. Buddy, where've you been man? Let's get moving, the big game starts in little more than an hour—and we've got great seats!

E: You don't understand, I don't think I can...

F: Then we'll go by Ernie's for drinks! Florence will be there! Remember Florence, E.M.?

E: No, but...

F: I'll let you in on a little secret.

E: Now that you mention it, I've got a little secret too.

F: Bet it's not as big a secret as I have for you!

E: You'd be surprised.

F: No, it's Florence! She called me this morning, really, she did.

E: I got a call this morning too.

F: She said, I hope old E.M. is going to be there this morning. We only got to talk an hour or so the other day—but I feel so close to him! You can SCORE with her, Buddy! Maybe tonight!

E There's something else I have to do tonight. And I need you to come with me!

F: Of course, we'll come with you! We're Buddies, always have been! One for all and all for one! Wherever you go, we go!

E: Oh that's so good to hear!

F: No problem, Pal! So what do you have to do, deal with those gambling debts? We can handle those guys! If we stand together, we can pay them off!

E: No. It's not that I have to pay off the gamblers.

F: The drug dealers? You still have to deal with them?

E: No. That's not what I have to do.

F: So tell us what you have to do? What is this big bad thing you have to do? Tell us now so we can make plans. What do you have to do?

E: Die.

F: What? You have to do what?

E: Die. I have to die. And I want you to go with me. I want...

Friends disappear.

Everyman is left alone

E: Where are they? Friends! MY GOOD FRIENDS! They're gone. Now what? The time is growing shorter. Who can I turn to?

(Enter Goods)

E: My belongings! I had almost forgotten you! I worked my whole life to get you! My house, my dwelling, the place where I'm safe! My clothing, the hats and shirts and ties that define me. My wonderful goods, I need you to...

G: We've heard. Good bye.

(Goods disappear)

E: What? Gone, like that? But what do I have left? Ah, my relatives! My dear brothers and sisters, my...

Enter Relatives: (The Guidry triplets)

E: Dear brothers, dear sisters, dear aunts, uncles, dear..."

R: Don't even think about it.

Relatives disappear.

E: What is left? Only my parents. My father and my wonderful mother, my mother who bore me. Heart of my heart, flesh of my flesh.

Enter Parents:

E: My father who taught me everything. My mother, who bore me!

M: Heart of my heart you are, Dear Son Everyman, and flesh of my flesh!

E: You bore me out of nothing. Now I need you to go with me to...

M: So look! I've packed you a nice suitcase!

E: You've what?

M: Seven suits of underwear. You can go a week. Then, surely, there will be a place to do washing there. Otherwise, you shouldn't stay.

E: But mother I...

Parents disappear.

E: Now it is over! I have no more hope! I am alone, in the face of death. No one, nothing can help me!"

(Everyman screams)

E: Will no one help me?

A spotlight shines on one chair, in which a young girl sits, chains around her)

E: Who are you?

GD: I am your good deeds. And I would help you. But your sins have chained me here.

E: How can these chains be removed?

GD: You know that. You have always known that.

E: (Falls to floor, prays) Oh God my Creator! Oh Christ, may salvation! I am the most miserable of sinners! Please, oh please, forgive me! For without thy grace, I am certainly lost!

GD: (Chains fall from her. She rises, walks to Everyman, places a hand on his shoulder, and says:) "Now, I am freed to speak for thee.

Death Appears, stands in front of Everyman and says:

D. It is time. Follow.

E. (Rises. Good deeds takes his hand, leads him to follow Death)

GD: Everyman, I will go with thee, and be thy guide. When all else fails, to be by thy side.

E: What must we do now?

GD: Let us leave this place, and never return again.

(They exit together. The lights go out, and the church is left in darkness)

For an instant after the play ended, Nina wanted to cry.

How could anyone in the audience not want to cry?

But, in the room, which was still completely dark because of the thick curtains, a voice cried out:

"Actors!"

Then another, then another:

"Actors! Actors!"

Applause was breaking out.

A spotlight came on, illuminating the small space where the play had taken place.

It was empty.

Of course, Nina thought.

The actors had scattered throughout the audience, an audience which was in fact Everyman.

In it was in the audience where the spotlight was to come on.

When?

And where, she could remember thinking sometime later, was Death?

And it was at that moment when the canoe fell.

It splintered on the floor, exploding like so many wooden bombshells,

Its middle, though, stayed relatively intact.

So that everyone in the room could see, lying face upward, attired in black robes of the ministry, the body of Pastor Aaron Rockman.

He seemed, Nina later remembered, perfectly at ease, almost as though sleeping.

She might even have thought to walk over and wake him, except for the tomahawk half-buried in his chest.

CHAPTER TWENTY TWO: WHAT WENT WRONG
IN CHARLOTTESVILLE?

They met in a Fieldhouse.

Just outside, beginning to bake in the summer heat, lay the football field of the Plantersville Harvesters.

On the field had been placed rows of traffic cones, bright yellow and red.

By ten-thirty a.m. the Fieldhouse was full of law enforcement personnel.

Park rangers from three state parks in northern Mississippi.

State troopers and town police from small towns like Sherman, New Albany, Nettleton, Pott's Camp, Blue Albany—even a few from Tupelo.

Sitting in one of the back rows of metal folding chairs that had been packed into the already nearly airless building. More patrol cars were still arriving.

A few mounted State Troopers, sun-glassed and blue-helmeted, sat stiffly on their mounts, the horses well-trained and looking straight ahead at nothing at all, as though wishing they too could be wearing sunglasses.

Barbara Smallwood tried to pretend she was invisible as Captain Frank Davis Starnes walked to the podium.

"I won't waste your time with introductions," he said. "Some of you know each other, some probably don't. Hopefully you'll get acquainted in the next hours, or in the next day or so. Also hopefully we'll take care of what's in front of us, and we won't have to come together like this anymore."

A few assenting nods at this, some murmurs.

"This thing is getting worse. It was bad enough that fifty or so alt-right people were coming over here tomorrow to protest the mixing of a black church and a white church. If I had had my way, both groups would have just gone back to Bay St, Lucy, the right wingers would have called off their protests, and this all could have been avoided. But the churches didn't want it that way. They felt like it would have been cowardly, and if they ran away this time, when would they stop running away? And I've gotta say, I have respect for that way of looking at things, too. The bottom line though, is that things have escalated. As soon as the Alt Right people called the TV and the radio and the newspapers and the Twitter feeds and all the rest of the digital media and whatever else is out there, it began to get worse. We've gotten word that counter protesters are coming. Among them, the group known as Antifa."

Collective 'moan' from the audience.

"There may be some colleges or universities involved, there may be some others. We got word that in a day or so that there's going to be a gay wedding planned by the churches, and that brings in a couple of other bunches, LGBTQ, anti-LGBTQ—you get the picture. In addition to all that, I'm sure you've all heard the radio reports this morning. According to the media, the woods are now haunted with Chickasaw ghosts, who feel the same way the Alt Right does. The bottom line is, we will not let this thing get out of hand. We will not become Charlottesville. To avoid doing that, I want you to remember one thing: the police had sufficient manpower there. But they forgot one major rule. This is word for word what it says in the book: In protests [or] counter-protest situations, the police separate the groups with barriers and by enough distance so they can see and hear each other but not engage in violence."

He looked around the room, then went on: "Now, tomorrow afternoon our groups are going to be confronting one another on the large green lawn sloping down from the main park building to the lake. We're going to be out there later this afternoon putting up metal barrier fences, in just the design of these traffic cones you see out on the football field here. We're going to go out in a second, we're going to arm ourselves with shields, just the way we'll be armed tomorrow, and we're going to assign teams to each sector. We must channel these people the way we would if we were driving cattle. It can't be brutal. We're not Nazis. It has to seem the most natural thing in the world. 'You go here, just right through here, and you go over there."

He paused.

"You understand?"

General nods.

"All right, let's go outside. We're going to form our teams."

He left the podium.

The room emptied, except for Barbara, who made her way to the podium and waited to be addressed by her superior.

Finally:

"All right. Just let me get all of this straight again."

"Yes, sir."

"You were never called by this radio station?"

"That's right."

"Now as I understand it, a Ms. Bannister and the gay couple to be married came to you in your room about midnight. They took you and showed you the defaced door. You sent the couple inside, then went to the park headquarters with Ms. Bannister and told her the symbolism of what had been left on the door."

"Yes, sir."

"When you got back to the museum, a rock was thrown through one of the windows. It had a threatening note on it. You gave chase, but could not catch the person or persons who threw the rock.

"That's right."

"Only this morning, when you heard the broadcast, did you learn about the couple in the woods, and about this alleged 'warrior' that they say, and that the radio says attacked them."

"Again, sir, that's right."

"And nobody else knows about these things, or could know."

"No."

"Then my question is, who the hell called the radio station?"

No answer possible.

Starnes, with what seemed genuine reluctance:

"Barbara, I'm only going to ask you this once. I've know you only a matter of days. You seem thoroughly professional. Your references are first rate. But I also know that the Chickasaw culture, the Chickasaw values, are deeply important to you."

"Yes, Ranger Starnes, they are."

"And the Chickasaw do not believe in Gay Marriage."

"No."

"You also realize that the more publicity you can gain for your culture, the more people are likely to come here and want to learn about it. A few ghosts running around the woods—it would draw a lot of tourists."

"Sir, are you asking me if I made all these things up and then called the station myself just to get attention?"

"I'm assuming you did not. Anyone could have left this. I was on the road, getting patrolmen together for what we have to do tomorrow. As I understand it, Ms. Bannister and the gay couple were kayaking on the river. Anyone could have left this 'witch warning' on their door. Except not many people—no one but you as far as I know—know that such a thing exists. As for the stone and the warning, that's only your story. The window is broken…"

"…but I could have broken it. And I, an accomplished tracker, could find no one, even though I pursued immediately. Also, I know how warriors paint themselves. I could have played the 'warrior ghost' that the kids saw in the woods."

'All I'm saying, Barbara, is that as far as publicity goes—this could get to be the 'big foot' of Tombigbee."

A buzzing sound came from the walkie-talkie attached to the Captain's belt.

He put the instrument to his lips; his low voice rumbled into it:

"Starnes."

Pause while he listened.

Then:

"Yeah. I got it. We'll be right there."

He closed the walkie-talkie, then looked at Barbara Smallwood and asked:

"Then tell me once, and that will be it."

"Sir, I have no idea who did these things."

He nodded.

"All right, I believe you, Patrolman. And now, that war tomahawk that was stolen from the museum?"

"Yes, sir?"

"I think we've found it. Come on."

She rode with him as he told her about the murder of Aaron Rockman. She kept her eyes on the road, which was filling up with emergency vehicles, most of them passing fast, red lights flashing, sirens screaming.

They were entering the park now, approaching the main building. The entire area resembled a war zone, with red lights everywhere, and troops, having been drawn from the drill at Plantersville—a drill that had been immediately cancelled, of course—doing precisely here what they were training to do tomorrow, which was to put as much of a damper as was possible on extremely strong emotions, and divide people into smaller groups.

"What is the plan?" she asked quietly, somewhat ashamed that all other police officers and park rangers seemed automatically to know it, while she did not.

Not to mention her shame at being accused of fabricating a huge system of lies.

"We've got to get people calmed down," Starnes answered. "Then we have to get them into their cabins."

"Are they all going to want to go into their cabins?"

He shook his head while parking the patrol car.

"No. Some of them are—understandably—going to want to leave. Just get in their cars, or on the church bus, whatever—and drive straight back to Bay St. Lucy. It was one thing to stay up here and face the alt-righters. But when people start getting murdered…"

"I understand."

"We have to keep them here, though. This is now a murder scene. These people have to be questioned."

"All right, I understand. So what do you want me to do? Come with you to the main building?"

He opened the patrol car door, got out, and looked around.

"No," he said. "Look, down there by the lake. There are a lot of people milling around. They seem to have been fishing. Some are still out in boats. It looks like there's been an event of some kind. I want you to get them off the lake and away from the piers."

"Do you think they're in danger?"

He shook his head:

'I don't know who's in danger. All I know is that somebody murdered Aaron Rockman. It had to have been done late last night or early this morning. Whoever did it is still out there somewhere. I want people inside."

"What do I tell them?"

"Tell them to go inside."

"Do I tell them what's happened?"

"They may already know. Or they may just think they know. The main thing is, get them off that lake."

"Yes, sir."

So saying, she got out of the patrol car and strode off down toward the water.

CHAPTER TWENTY-THREE: NOTHING BEATS A GOOD CUP OF COFFEE

Nina had brought coffee back to her room.

"Ms. Bannister?"

"Yes?"

"I'm Ranger Davis Starnes. May I come in?"

"Of course."

He did so.

"I'm sorry to bother you."

Someone else seemed to be speaking for her; she listened to the lines:

"You should be sorry. I was having a great time. Now you've spoiled it all."

Was that a smile?

How could anyone be smiling now? Or ever again?

"May I sit down?"

"Of course."

He did so, taking the chair by the television set that she had hoped to see Frank sitting in.

"Would you like some coffee?" she asked, thinking the question idiotic as soon as she had asked it.

Why not simply offer him lobster and champagne?

"No, ma'am. Thank you anyway though."

Good. Enough of that nonsense.

He was silent for a time, looking down at his interlacing fingers. She liked him, liked his being here with her. In some ways he reminded her of Pastor Tamp. They were approximately the same age. Each had a calming quality about him. This man was a bit more blue-blonde morning-shaven whereas Tamp was brown-brown never-shaven. And this man was a bit more powerful looking, muscles under uniform as opposed to Tamp's bones under clerical garb.

But still she felt comfortable around him.

He was carrying a gray, official-looking briefcase. When he opened it, she saw that it contained a small, rather old-fashioned even for her way of thinking, tape recorder.

He smiled and shook his head:

"There are better ways to record conversations, I guess, but I'm a traditionalist. Hope you don't mind."

"Not at all."

He pressed a button; the two plastic recording discs began to spin slowly.

"My office," he said, "is always littered with these things. People say I'm nuts, but, like I say, I'm a traditionalist."

She did not answer.

"I hope," he said, "you're not too upset to answer a few questions."

"No, I'm all right. First though, I have a question for you."

"Ask it."

"How are the middle schoolers, the ones in the play?"

"We're lucky there."

"How could we be lucky?"

"Most of them—all of them, really—were in the back of the room. The director of the play wanted them to scatter through the audience. They elected to sit in the rear rows. As soon as the canoe fell, there were quick thinking adults who got them out of the room. None of them saw anything."

"That's good."

"It is. But as for you—well, I've been able to talk with quite a few folks from both congregations. Your name keeps coming up. People trust you."

"I guess that's good."

"Of course, it's good."

"Well. Ask away then."

"I don't have many specific questions. As I'm sure you realize, something terrible has happened. Pastor Rockman is dead. The body is being Medivacked out now by helicopter. A couple of first responders have had a chance to look him over—their initial response is that he seems to have died very early this morning, sometime after midnight."

"I see."

"Now, my job is this: I have to ask the same question of everyone in this camp. I'm certain you don't know anything that you feel relates directly to the crime. But think. Rack your brain, Ms. Bannister. Is there anything, even the smallest detail that might relate to the murder? Take your time. And once again, there is nothing too small. Now, is there anything, anything at all that might help to give us a lead?"

Nina remained silent for a second or so.

The tape recorder made a faint whirring sound.

Then she said:

"A couple of things."

"Good! Remember, let me know about them, no matter how insignificant they seem."

"Okay, well, then: yesterday morning at about ten o'clock Aaron Rockman threatened to destroy Brother Tamp. He said he had information about Tamp's past that would ruin him. Last night, just after midnight, Tamp came to my room and said he was going to Rockman's room."

Starnes sat watching her, seemingly too stunned to speak.

"Shortly after he left my room, a young couple who had been making out in the woods after curfew told me they had been threatened by what seemed to be a Chickasaw warrior carrying a tomahawk which must have been very similar to the one buried in Rockman's chest."

She got to her feet, and, looking down at him, asked:

"Are you sure you don't want a cup of coffee?"

CHAPTER TWENTY-FOUR: TO DRAW OUT LEVIATHAN

Canst thou draw out Leviathan with an hook? or his tongue with a cord which thou lettest down?

Psalm 41:1

When Barbara Smallwood got to the shore, she found a confused welter of rumor and confusion, mixed with the clatter of people dropping things into the water and running into each other.

All of this being compounded, of course, by the presence of digital media. Twitter, Facebook, Instagram, etc.

So that all of the people standing and milling around the lake shore were looking alternately at the water, at each other, at their parents, at their children—and at the palms of their hands, which, glowing a constant pale pink or blue, had become their primary, even though often completely false, source of information.

'Can you tell us what happened up there?'

'We heard something blew up in the main lodge!'

'Is anybody hurt up there?'

'I just got a text that said a boat fell on somebody!'

'Is there a shooter? My son just texted me that there's a shooter loose in the camp!'

She tried to calm these people as well as she could, happy to see that a narrow trail of more officers and park rangers were arriving to help her.

Also arriving up at the camp was a Medevac helicopter, which, though possibly useful, did not help to lower the emotional intensity of the people watching it land.

She tried to ignore the helicopter, and she answered most of the questions by saying things like, 'We do have a situation,' and 'Everything is going to be all right' (Which was not true, of course, especially if you had been Aaron Rockman)—and, most consistently, 'We need for you to return to your cabins.'

So that within twenty or so minutes most of the one-time fishing contest participants, coaches, and spectators, were filing calmly up the hill toward their cabins.

There was only one group of three teenage boys who, concerned looking, approached her, saying;

"Officer?"

"Yes?"

"Over in the far southwest corner of the lake, there beyond the last pier, where those reeds and cattails are?"

"Yes?"

"Well, we were standing on the pier when we heard all the sirens begin to go off."

"Yes?"

"There's something in the water. There are still a bunch of kids there now, trying to see what it is and maybe get it out."

"What is it?"

"We don't know. We couldn't really see it. But— well, it sounds like an animal of some kind. And it's crying. Or screaming."

"All right, thanks for telling me. You boys go on back; I'll check it out."

So saying, she walked off in the direction of the pier which they had indicated.

As she passed the pier she could hear the sound.

She had an idea of what it was.

Immediately she shouted at the kids:

"Get away from there! Now!"

"But we just want to..."

"Now!"

Reluctantly they left.

But she could not leave.

If she did, other kids might hear the same high pitched sound and return to see what it was.

The water was brackish; she could see nothing.

She stepped from the shore into cold, foot-deep marsh.

She saw only driftwood, logs, moss-pads, and clumps of grey-black bramble overhanging the eddying swamp currents.

Inert objects, hardly moving, only slightly darker than the backwater itself.

And there, nailed to one of the trees, was the kind of warning object that she had seen last night on Meg and Jennifer's door. Eagle feathers and shells.

For some moments she stood motionless, having no idea what she was looking at or what might happen.

The thin cries continued, as though oozing out of the lake itself, not far from where she was standing.

Then she could see movement of a log just beyond the pier.

The log itself seemed to be crying.

It flopped gently, weakly in the water, a living black log with ridges on its back.

She realized then that it was what she had feared, an alligator. A film of water glistened on its ridged back and tail; it could not have been more than a foot and a half long.

It had been tied by a twenty foot rope to the pier post.

She also realized the danger.

Someone had done this on purpose.

Someone thinking children would be here.

She could now see that the rope circled the gator's body in the middle of its abdomen, precisely between head and tail. Submerging in the brackish water, lifting itself out, thrashing, whining, the animal could not bend its head in such a way as to get its teeth upon that rope.

"Cut it loose."

The command came from Lannie Baker, who was standing perhaps sixty feet away, having helped to clear children from the docks.

"Cut it loose now!

"I know!" she shouted back.

Because she did know.

She knew only too well.

She pulled out her hunting knife and walked quickly to that part of the vibrating rope that ran closest to the ground, aware now that glistening logs, some of them huge as fallen trees, were rising and falling in small lake currents just beside her.

She slashed once, twice...

One more and the animal would be free.

"Do it quick!" cried the man behind her. "If you don't let him get out of here..."

She could not allow herself to panic.

Just cut the rope, cut the rope...

But it was too late.

Suddenly the swamp exploded over her, roaring and drenching her as she fell back into it. Then she was under water, choking, her mouth and nose pressed against a noxious smelling tree-like form that crushed her windpipe and chest.

She could neither breathe nor cry out.

She knew that she had dropped her knife; but she was paralyzed, unable to breath or move.

Then she felt herself lifted; her head burst from the water. She gasped, swallowing water; but now she could see the eyes of the alligator, gold-green marbles boring into her, jaws gaping and ready to snap.

"Aaahh…"

It was as close to a scream as she could manage.

And at that moment, she saw it.

It was as clear in her mind as the most vivid dream she could remember.

The sky, dark.

Black as the blackest night.

And below that sky…

…a vast field, once green.

Now completely white.

And covered with coffins.

It lasted no time at all; and it lasted forever, would never go away.

And then somehow it ended.

She felt herself being thrown clear as, she realized, Lannie had dived upon the alligator.

She was now half out of the water, lying in what seemed to be reeds or cattails, her upper right pant leg torn and drenched red…while two feet from her she saw the two trees, the two body-thick limbs, one white shirted, the other horrible-scaled and glistening.

From neither creature—Lannie, nor the alligator—as there a roar or a shout.

They were locked together, the man, his own knife in hand, riding the gator's crusted back, his arm encircling the mouth while the knife plunged into the neck…and the alligator, convulsive, scythe-tail mowing and spraying water, bellowing as it bled, and roaring while it threshed its trapped head wildly.

With a huge surge it rolled on top; Lannie, buried beneath and choking in reeds and moss, still locking the jaws shut, still thrusting the butcher knife hilt deep into white flesh, sucking it out, thrusting again…

…and she herself, sickened, terrified, lying half on land and half in water, forcing herself to feel her own leg.

The uniform pants leg had been ripped open and was soaked in blood; but the wound itself, she could see now, was not deep.

She could move her legs.

The entire struggle in front of her began to slide out into the swamp.

The alligator, much stronger, was pulling Lannie deeper under water.

She got to her feet somehow, slipping as she did so, hands wrapping themselves around a broken tree trunk that seemed to have jutted up immediately beside her; she looked desperately to her left, and saw her knife, lying just beneath the water.

In two steps she had it, and with one motion arched another swing at the rope, which still lay embedded in the mud.

Cut through, it recoiled in opposite directions. She lunged to her right and riveted her grasp around the now-freed segment, tugging back at the baby gator that was jerking itself away from her and heading desperately into deeper water.

She could not allow it to do so.

Pulling with all her strength, trying desperately to remain upright with nothing solid under her, she reeled the thing toward her, while, ten feet away and out into the lake, the water churned and bloodied itself, cries and roars mixing as though a huge engine were bellowing and fuming beneath the surface, two growths battling to subsume each other.

She had the baby alligator out of the water now, hanging a foot above the surface, snapping and twisting as it fought to find and bite the rope.

Holding it at arm's length, aware of the blood gushing now from the freshened wound on her upper leg, the ripped trousers patch trailing behind her in muck and ooze...she lurched toward what now seemed a kind of formless whirlpool of spray, blood, teeth, scales, flesh, and glinting knife blade.

"Here! Here you...! HERE!"

She held the thing hanging from the rope, dangling it out until she could see the two marble eyes looking straight at it...held it until it began to whine again, began its tinny scream...held it until it was inches away from the gaze of its mother, her own mouth still held rigid and harmless by the rope-cord muscles of Lannie, who, choking, silent, face buried still beneath the water...would not let go.

"HERE! GO GET HIM!"

Whirling with all her strength, she flung the rope and the baby gator as far as she could into the lake.

The alligator looked straight at her with black-eyed dispassion, opened its monstrous red mouth a full two feet wide...

...and slid back into the water, corkscrewing away with slow, sidling motions of its stony-ribbed tail.

In two seconds it had disappeared...and the cries of the baby gator died away.

CHAPTER TWENTY-FIVE: FIRST INTERROGATION

They had taken Nina Bannister to the Park Patrol Office, which was a nondescript building on the far western edge of Tombigbee State Park. She was not in chains, nor was she treated like a prisoner. But, comfortable as they had made her, she felt ashamed as she looked out the windshields, both front and side, of the patrol car.

Everywhere chaos.

Or, if not chaos, near chaos.

More rangers and officers—she was aware of uniforms, sky-blue uniforms, brown uniforms, black uniforms, but, of course, she had no idea which garb went with which branch of law enforcement—but more of them seemed to be arriving with every moment.

On the other hand, fewer and fewer church members could be seen consoling each other, crying in each other's arms, or kneeling together in prayer.

This was because the church members had been, as gently as possible so as not to feel like prisoners of war, led to their individual cabins, to be questioned.

They had stopped now; the driver, young, blonde, hardly more than a teenager, turned and smiled at her while he said:

"Here we are, Ms. Bannister. You can get out now. Just walk on up the stone path there and go into the headquarters building. Ranger Starnes has just called me. He'll be with you in a few minutes."

"All right."

She did as she was told.

The door opened for her just before she reached it. A trim and official-looking woman stood just inside, smiling, her graying and short-cut hair, her gold-rimmed glasses, her perfectly fitting navy blazer with its Mississippi Forest Patrol patch sewn evenly across the jacket pocket—all giving the impression that here inside this door was a realm where order reigned.

The woman could have been a librarian.

And indeed, as she took the first steps into the first hallway, which was to lead to a second hallway, which was to lead to the main office, where she was offered a chair, she felt the urge to check out books.

Starnes's office contrasted completely with the woman who led him into it.

It was, in short, a mess.

A pile of plastic circles that she recognized as tape recordings lay beside a desk.

On the desk lay what must have been last week's mail, large yellow manila envelopes, smaller official looking government documents.

After a time, he entered, followed by another woman, a younger one, who was pushing before her a clattering metal table upon which lay the same tape recorder that Starnes had used in her room.

"Sorry to keep you waiting, Ms. Bannister," he said quietly, seating himself behind the desk and motioning the woman accompanying him to position stenographic material in its appropriate location.

"This is Ms. Grimes. She's going to take down what you say. We'll also be making a recording, of course. You don't want anything to drink?"

"No, thank you."

"Well, then, Ms. Bannister. Or...may I call you 'Nina?'"

"Of course."

"Well then, Nina. The first thing is, we don't want you to feel ill at ease."

I have, she could not help thinking, just watched a canoe fall and splinter itself a few feet in front of me. My pastor was in it, murdered, with a massive hatchet embedded in his chest. This was just the type of hatchet, when one thinks about it, that had been seen a few hours earlier—by two of the town's leading young adults, who had been out in the woods having illicit sex—in the hands of what could only be described as the ghost of a Chickasaw warrior, who had it seems only a short time before defaced with a death threat the doorway of the gay couple whose upcoming marriage was splitting the church and would have been splitting the state had not the issue of racial hatred pretty much already succeeded in doing that.

Why would she feel ill at ease?

"No, I'm fine."

"Good. Now, you have to imagine my surprise—shock, really—when you said the things you did back in your cabin."

"Yes. I can imagine."

"In the first place, this couple that were having sex. They came to you last night—well, very early in the morning as I understand it now—and told you they had seen a warrior with face painted for battle?"

"Yes."

"And what did this warrior do?"

"He pulled a tomahawk out of his belt and shook his head, as though telling them to stop."

"Just as was reported on the radio this morning?"

"Yes."

"But you weren't the one who called in the story?"

"No, I was not."

"And why didn't you report the incident to the police?"

"I don't know. I guess I thought any policeman or a member of the Park Patrol would have just laughed at it. And, to himself if not out loud, he would have imagined that the two young people were high on drugs."

"Do you think they were high on drugs?"

"No. They aren't the kind to do that."

"But they are the kind to sneak out after curfew and have sex?"

"No."

"But that's what they were doing."

"Yes."

"Why?"

"Love."

"Well, that's inspiring. But it's possible that the tomahawk they saw could have been the one embedded in Aaron Rockman's chest."

"I know that now. But then—well, to tell you the truth, I didn't mention the incident for two reasons: first I thought it was so crazy that no one would believe it. Second, I just—I just—"

"You didn't want to sully the reputations of the two young people involved."

Nina nodded:

Starnes did too, and, in response, spoke in comforting tones:

"All right. I understand your position. And I'm not going to make you give me their names. I've just done this: I've sent a couple of park rangers over to the area where the youth were sleeping last night, and where almost all of them are gathered now. These rangers have been instructed to be as diplomatic as possible. They've asked simply that the couple who were out late and after midnight curfew report here to the Ranger Office. They have reassured everyone that the couple did nothing wrong, nor will they be reported or in any way punished. It's just possible though that they may have seen something else connected to the murder, and we need to know precisely what it is that they actually did see.

He paused for a moment, then continued:

"This way, we'll still get their story, but they will realize you haven't 'told on them.'"

"Thank you. Thank you very much."

"Of course, if they don't come forward…"

"They will. I know the two of them. They will."

"Good. Now, as for the other matter, let's talk about Rockman and Pastor Tamp."

"All right. Well, I suppose it's a long story. I'm one of the lay leaders of the church, so I know it as well as anyone. Tamp has been with our church for years. Most of that time he's served as an assistant pastor without pay. He's very loved. Pastor Rockman on the other hand was only appointed by the Bishop last year. Clearly there were issues from the start. They began with economic problems, this camp being one of them. It costs a lot to come up here. Rockman felt—and, I suppose so did the District Supervisor and the Bishop that those funds, which have always come from individual offerings—should go into the central fund to be used for things such as Missions or Habitat for Humanity. Tamp disagreed."

'I see."

"In the last few days though the issues became more sharply defined. The idea to pair with Bethel came from their pastor, Goforth, and Tamp. They've been friends for years. Rockman, I suppose, felt left out of the circle. There wasn't much he could do about it though without appearing to be racist. So he let it simmer. But the straw that broke the camel's back was the wedding. Tamp announced some days ago that he would perform the wedding of a gay couple. This matter of gay weddings in the Methodist Church has been extremely controversial for years now. It's threatening to split the entire church wide open. Rockman hated to see us involved in that."

"I see. Go on."

"I'm not sure anybody knows a lot more than that. Or what will happen in the end. What did happen yesterday is this: at about 4:30 Rockman asked me to sit in on a meeting he was having with Brother Tamp."

"Why did he want you there?"

"I believe he wanted a witness."

"And you went to the meeting?"

"Yes. I wish I hadn't."

"So what happened?"

"Rockman ordered Tamp not to perform the marriage. Tamp said he was going to do it. Rockman fired him. Tamp in effect said he refused to be fired."

"What were the two men like at that point?"

"Standing. Glaring at each other. I had to tell them to sit down, to get control of themselves."

"Did they?"

"Not really. Rockman said he would destroy Tamp."

"Are those the words he used?"

"Close enough. Finally Rockman charged out of the room."

Silence for a time.

"Didn't you think you should tell someone about this?"

"Who? When I have questions about what to do in a situation, I usually ask my Pastor."

"Pardon?"

"Nothing. The bottom line is though, I didn't know anyone to tell. And, in looking back at the whole thing, I'm still not sure it's that important."

"Not that important? Nina, Aaron Rockman was murdered only a few hours ago!"

At this moment the receptionist stuck her head in the door and said:

"Chief?

"Yeah?"

"You know we asked for those kids who were out in the woods having sex after curfew to come by?"

"Yes?"

"They're out front."

"Tell them to wait a minute; I'll be right there."

"All right."

She disappeared.

Starnes looked at Nina again and said:

"Now tell me again why you didn't think it was important to tell me that Pastor Rockman threatened to 'destroy' Pastor Tamp only a few hours before he himself was murdered?"

"Because Pastor Tamp could never, would never, hurt a fly. Talk to him; I'm sure he can tell you exactly where he was last night. And also, whoever killed Rockman did so with a tomahawk and then someone put his body in a canoe twenty five feet in the air. Even if Brother Tamp had wanted Rockman dead, he could never have done those things!"

Silence for a moment.

Then Starnes shook his head and said, quietly:

"There are just a couple of problems with all of that, Nina."

"What? What problems?"

"We can't talk to Tamp, because he's disappeared. He's not anywhere, as far as we can tell. And we've just gotten the preliminary medic's report on Rockman. He wasn't killed with that tomahawk; he was stabbed to death with a hunting knife. We've been able to learn that it was the same kind of knife Tamp bought from the Outdoors Shop when he was up here last week. Now, if you will excuse me, I've got to go and interview the young people who were out in the woods having sex."

Stunned, Nina sat for a time while he left the room.

Then she followed him out.

Then she looked in the parking lot.

She saw at least twenty teenagers standing there.

CHAPTER TWENTY-SIX: AND THE WINNER IS…

They had taken Barbara Smallwood to a small infirmary not far from the park's main building. Two people worked on her, a young man and a young woman. These people were, she imagined, used to working on mosquito bites and sunburns.

Alligator attacks not so often.

The young man was leaning over her now, the woman just behind her.

Both were looking at the bandage that had been placed carefully over the wound on her upper left leg.

"Hurt much?"

She shook her head.

The truth was, it did not hurt at all, and she told them as much.

Both smiled, both seemed to say at once, as though enjoying the process:

"That's probably the anesthetic. When it wears off, you'll be sore for a while."

"I understand."

"You were pretty lucky."

"Right. Lucky me."

"Neither one of us has ever treated an alligator bite before."

"So it's been a pretty big day for all of us."

The young man:

"We've given you two shots of antibiotics. Shouldn't be a danger of infection."

"That's good."

The young woman:

"It wasn't that big a wound. A little more than two inches long."

"I guess I didn't taste too good."

Smiles throughout the infirmary at this.

She hated infirmaries.

On each of the four antiseptic green walls were small magazines with titles like "Diabetes and You," and "Want to Avoid Unwanted Pregnancies? Then don't have sex!"

"Ranger Smallwood?"

Which one of them had asked this?

She was getting them mixed up.

Oh well, there was really only one answer anyway:

"Yes?"

"There are a couple of people waiting to see you. One of them is the guy who went through the attack with you."

"Lannie Baker."

"Yes."

"Is he all right?"

"He is. Didn't get bitten. His wife is with him, too. And there's a little crowd of people outside, too."

"Send the Bakers in first."

"Okay."

Lannie and Cindy entered.

Group hugs followed, or at least the closest things to hugs that she could manage, sitting on the observation table like she was.

It was a bit difficult to speak for a time, first because the Bakers needed to disentangle themselves and sit on plastic chairs beneath the huge gold and black poster with a concerned looking young man and the words "You and Liver Cancer!"—and second, because there was not much to say, or at least nothing that came immediately to mind.

Finally she broke the silence:

"Hey. I guess I need to say 'thank you,' for saving my life."

He merely shook his head and replied, somewhat sheepishly:

"All in a day's work."

"You should think about getting a different job."

Before he could think of a reply to this, his wife leaned forward and said:

'You're Chickasaw, aren't you?"

"Yes, full blooded."

"Okay then: I have a question."

"Ask it."

"Well, do the Chickasaw have some kind of a tradition, when one warrior saves another's life? Like, there's an offering-present or something?"

"Yes."

"What is it? Your first born son or something?"

"Usually it's a bottle of scotch."

"Oh. I hadn't read about that."

"We try to keep it quiet."

"I can understand."

Lannie:

"Other than that, there's something you probably need to know. I mean, if you're in shape to hear it."

She took a deep breath and said:

"If it's about the missing pastor—Pastor Tamp I think—and the medic's report, I know about all that. I've had my two-way on."

"It's something else."

"Lannie…" Cindy attempted to interrupt.

Barbara stopped her:

"No, whatever it is, tell me."

"You're sure?"

"Yes."

"All right. It's why all those people are outside."

"So why are all those people outside?"

He smiled:

"You won the fishing contest."

Half an hour later she was ready to be discharged.

Starnes was waiting for her in his patrol car.

"I thought," he said, holding the door open for her, "that I might at least offer a ride to our resident hero."

"I'm not," she said, wincing a bit as she adjusted her leg to get it into the vehicle—and, oh yes, the anesthetic was wearing off—"much of a hero."

"You'll do. There were kids playing around the pier post where the baby gator had been tied up. If they had gotten close enough…"

"Yeah. Well, good that they didn't."

"And as I understand it, the signs hanging on the pier were the same Chickasaw markings that you saw on the gay couple's door last night."

"Yes, as far as I could tell. It got kind of busy there for a while."

Starnes smiled grimly as he started the engine.

"I sent a man down to retrieve them. They're back at headquarters. You might take a look at them as soon as you're able."

"Of course."

"And Barbara…"

"Yes?"

"That crap I was dishing out to you this morning about being responsible for the things that went on last night, and for breaking the story—it was no more than that, just crap. Please forgive me for having said it."

"Nothing to forgive."

"Of course, there is. You're a first rate ranger. I'm just—well, I'm not sure right now whether I'm coming or going. Dealing with the rally is hard enough. Now people pretending to be Chickasaw, and the murder itself…"

"I understand. There's one thing I need to tell you, though. I didn't think of it because—well, you may understand after I try to make this clear."

They were moving slowly over one of the park roads now, a breeze coming through the open window of the patrol car.

"Go on, Barbara."

"It's just that, last night, after I got back to the museum and before the rock came through the big window on the south wall."

"Yes?"

"I was looking on the shelf. There had been seven books about Chickasaw lift, culture, legends, etc. I counted them. There were six."

"Meaning someone…"

"Someone, during the afternoon while I was out of the museum doing errands or whatever, took that book. I haven't thought much about it, because the rock came through, then I was chasing whoever threw it…"

"I understand."

"But the point is, anyone could have learned how to make the sign on the door. There was also a picture in the book depicting how a warrior might have painted himself."

"So we're not necessarily dealing with an expert in Chickasaw culture."

"No, we're just dealing with a book thief. And, earlier this morning, I would have accused kids. Childish vandalism, that sort of thing. But now of course…"

Starnes downshifted to avoid a chug hole and grunted as he said:

"Now is different. Now there is murder."

"And you have a suspect."

"Yes. The assistant Pastor, a man named Tamp."

"I met the man. He was up here last week, making last minute preparations, or so he said."

"Did you form an opinion of him?"

"Nice guy as far as I could tell. Why do you believe he might have done this?"

"You know Ms. Bannister?"

"Nina? Yes."

"She witnessed a vicious argument between the two men late yesterday afternoon. Rockman threatened to destroy Tamp."

"How?"

"I don't know. Ms. Bannister didn't say. But they were ready to come to blows. Also, Tamp came to Ms. Bannister's room late last night or early this morning and told her he was ready to go see Rockman. During that visit, it seems possible to me, the two men may well have fought. Also, we know that Rockman was killed with the kind of scaling knife that Tamp had recently bought. To top all of that off, Tamp has as you probably have heard, disappeared."

"Yes, I know that."

"At any rate, he's our leading suspect."

"How could he have moved the body into that canoe, and how could he have raised the canoe twenty five feet off the floor? Also, what motive would he have had for using the tomahawk in an effort to involve the Chickasaw culture?"

"I don't know. Maybe he can tell us. At any rate, this leads me to the assignment I want to give you."

"Give."

"You think you know this Ms. Bannister pretty well?"

"Yes. I met her on the Saturday before their camp began, and we had to work pretty closely together last night. Nina chose to come to me for advice about the room desecration. I appreciated that. Still do."

"Do you think she trusts you?"

"As much as anybody can trust an Indian. Sorry, Native American."

"I'm glad you're still able to see some humor in this."

"That was the last of it. Go on."

"I was able to interview Ms. Bannister an hour or so after the body was discovered. I think she knows more than she's telling me. I also think she may know where Tamp is hiding. I'd like you to spend some time with her this evening. Then, after you've said good bye for the night..."

"You want me to spy on her."

"Well, if you want to put it that way..."

"How would you put it?"

"I want you to spy on her."

"All right."

"If she goes to Tamp, arrest him. Explain to both of them that he's the number one suspect in a murder case. We're looking for him now, and my patrolmen have orders to shoot on sight."

"Would you shoot on sight?"

He shook his head, while downshifting and slowing as the vehicle approached the museum.

"I don't know. I don't want to be put in that position. That's why I very much hope you're successful tonight. You understand your assignment?"

She unbent her stiff leg, corkscrewed out of the car, gave thanks for the slight East breeze that had sprung up, and leaned back through the window, saying:

"There's one more thing I need to tell you. It's a warning, actually."

"All right."

"At one point this afternoon I saw a vision. That's all it could be called: a vision. You see, sir, the Chickasaw believe..."

He merely laughed as he put the patrol car in reverse, and he said:

"Barbara, I don't have time for ghost stories right now. Let's deal with real problems; then you can tell me some fairy tales."

She straightened, nodded, and said:

"Yes, sir."

"And good luck tonight!"

"Yes, sir."

"Good bye for now!"

"Yes, sir."

And, softly, as his car disappeared around the first wooded curve, she whispered to herself:

"Ghost stories and fairy tales."

Then, visualizing and still hearing his laugh, she said a word that she felt described him.

It was a Chickasaw word that had no equivalent, as far as she knew, in the English language.

Or any other.

CHAPTER TWENTY-SEVEN: THE WHITENESS
OF THE WHALE

Not far from Nina's room—she had only to walk
down one hallway whose walls were decorated with
tree memorabilia—was a small porch, which
overlooked the lake. The chairs were pale blue and
wooden, and there were also deck lounges, which one
might have found on an ocean liner.

At six o'clock in the evening she found herself there,
looking out over the water and the empty piers,
remembering how the children had looked playing there
a few hours before.

She heard a noise behind her, thought about turning
to see who it was, and decided time would tell if she
simply waited.

She did; time did.

"You mind if I bother you?"

Barbara Smallwood.

Strange, one of the few people she would have
chosen to talk to.

She was beginning to like this woman.

"Of course, I don't mind. Sit down."

"Thanks. Little sunny out here."

"It's not bad."

There was a rasping of wood on concrete as Barbara
pulled a chair from the wall and scraped it a foot or so
toward Nina.

They were silent for a time.

Finally Nina:

"Heard you got attacked by an alligator."

"Yes."

"How was that?"

A shrug.

"You get attacked by one alligator, it's pretty much the same as getting attacked by all alligators."

"That makes sense."

A bit more silence; the sound of birds flying low over the lake.

"How," asked Barbara, "have you been spending your afternoon?"

"Well, I got interrogated."

"I heard. Did you kill anybody?"

"I don't know. If I did, they weren't able to break me."

"That's the stuff; be tough. So what have you been doing the last hour or so?"

Nina shrugged:

"Funny thing. I usually bring a book or so to Retreat. I spend the late afternoons lying in bed and reading. Or sitting out here."

"What kind of books?"

"Murder mysteries mostly."

"But now?"

Nina shook her head:

"They all seem so boring. No race riots; no gay marriages; no tomahawk murders; no falling canoes; no Indian...sorry, Native American—"

"It's all right. We got over that a long time ago."

"Anyway, no ghost warriors running around the woods after midnight; no door excrement; no alligator attacks..."

"I know what you mean. Just 'same ole, same ole.'"

"Exactly. Of course, that's probably all going to change tomorrow afternoon. How many policemen are now going to be protecting us?"

'Fifty or so, I guess. Starnes keeps getting volunteers as more protesters and counter protesters say they're coming."

"You like Starnes?"

She could tell that this was not an easy question for Barbara to answer.

"We live in different worlds. But he does the best he can."

"What's his story?"

"I'm not sure about all the details. He lost his wife some years ago."

"How?"

"'Drug overdose. Anyway, since then I'm told he pretty much lives for his work."

"So what do you think about tomorrow? Are we crazy to stay here? It would have been a lot easier just to do what they told us, to go. Avoid violence."

Barbara nodded:

"Yeah. That's what they told The Chickasaw, too. Don't stay where you are. Just move along. That way no one will get hurt. There's a famous letter. It's written by the Bureau of Indian Affairs to the Chiefs of the Tribe. I read it so many times that I've got it memorized now. It goes something like this: 'Your father, the President, proposes to give his Chickasaw children a fine tract of country on the other side of the Mississippi River, of equal extent, in exchange for your present lands. We know that you are attached to the country of your birth, and the lands in which the bones of your fathers are buried; but if the United States offer you one of equal advantages, and are willing to pay you liberally for your improvements, would not the nation best consult its real interest by making the exchange?"

Nina could think of nothing to say to this.

Barbara finally spoke:

"Sometimes you have to stand your ground, Nina."

"I know. But I'll admit it. I'm afraid. All those people. All that hatred. I'm afraid."

"You should be afraid. Nina, I know you were a teacher. I hear people talking about how much you've read, and how you were able to make the books real to them. So I have a question for you."

"All right. Ask it."

"In all the books you've read, is there a character who can see the future, and who tells people what will happen, but no one believes it?"

"Yes. Her name was Cassandra. She insulted the God Apollo. So he spat into her mouth. And whatever came out—even true prophecies, because she could see the truth—people thought were lies."

"The ancient Chickasaw had prophets, too. They were called Hopais. They told the people what would happen in the future. Big difference between your people and mine: mine always believed the prophets, always followed them. Yours never do. Especially when it's critical."

"Are there still Hopais around, Barbara?"

"Yes. They speak through a few chosen people, at a few critical times: usually when the Hopais is about to die and can see death in the face."

Nina was silent for a time. Then she said, quietly:

"Are you one of those people?"

"Yes. I didn't know before. But now I do. It happened a few hours ago, when the alligator—well, it happened."

"You saw the future?"

"I did."

"And you can't tell anyone about it?"

"I tried to tell Starnes, but he wouldn't listen to me."

"Who else?"

"No one. I could have told my father. He was the one who taught me all the Chickasaw legends. I loved him a great deal. He passed away last year."

"I'm sorry."

"I am, too. On one of our last nights together, out in a canoe, I asked him what my life would be like, and if I would ever marry and have children. I expected him to be encouraging, nod his head and say, 'Of course you will!' or something like that."

"Sure."

"But he didn't. He said some Chickasaw women were different."

"Different how?"

"Various ways. But there was The Panther Woman. She was a great warrior and strategist. She planned the battle against de Soto's men in the 1500's. Other women, though, serve as prophets. He told me he thought I might be one of those. He didn't know why he felt that way; but it's what he had come to believe."

"That you might be an Hopais?"

"Yes. And when I came near to dying this morning, I knew he was right. I saw so clearly…well, I just knew he was right."

"What did you see?"

First, it was what I knew. You need to understand, Nina. We believe that there is a Supreme Being."

"Like ours."

"In many ways, yes."

"What do you call this Being?"

"Ababinilli. There are four parts to this being: They're called The Four Beloved Things Above. Those things are the Sun, Clouds, Clear Sky, and He that Lives in the Clear Sky."

"There's great beauty in that."

"There won't be tomorrow."

"Why not?"

"Because He that Lives in the Clear Sky is offended by hatred, and will punish people who allow themselves to be ruled by hatred. That's going to happen tomorrow, Nina. I saw it. Saw it so clearly."

"What did you see?"

"First, the sky was black. Not just dark, but black, like the sun had disappeared. Then that whole vast green lawn leading down to the lake. It was white. All white. And covered with coffins."

Nina sat for a time, then whispered:

"The whiteness of the whale."

"What?"

"Nothing, Barbara. It's that maybe I'm a prophet too. There's a book by a man named Melville. The book's name is *Moby Dick*. He talks about the color white and how, although people think of it as pure and beautiful, it can really mean horror. No color at all. No life. Absolute atheism. Nothingness. In a way, an angry He that lives in the Clear Sky would be better than..."

"Than what, Nina?"

"Than nothing at all."

Silence for a time.

Then Barbara:

"All of our prophets, all of our gods, all of our beliefs, all of our faith changes—they boil down to one thing, Nina, one thing that I have to tell you."

"And what is that?"

"Don't go out there tomorrow."

But, of course, there could be only one response to that.

"I have to go. It's my church, my people."

Barbara nodded and said:

"I understand. Of course, I understand. Nina, Starnes has asked me to sit with you tonight."

"Why?"

"He just thinks you might be upset. Maybe it's best that you not have to be alone."

"Nice of him."

"Well, like I say: I'll never understand him. But he's my boss, so…"

"Yes," said Nina. "So, you want to stop lying now and tell me the truth?"

"All right. We're not good at lying to each other, are we?"

"No. Probably we never will be."

"All right. The truth is, Starnes knows that you and Tamp are close friends and have been for years. He thinks you might know where Tamp is, and that you might go to him some time tonight, just to listen to his side of the story, take him a little food, etc. I'm supposed to follow you and arrest him."

Silence for a time. Then Barbara:

"So do you know where he is?"

"Yes. I think so."

"And are you going to see him tonight?"

"Yes."

"And you know, I guess, that I won't be following you."

"Yes, Barbara. I know that."

Barbara got to her feet and said:

"Go with God, Nina."

"And you go with The Spirit of the Clear Sky."

Barbara Smallwood nodded, squeezed Nina on the shoulder, and walked away.

Eight o'clock, Tuesday Evening
My Room
    No idea where to begin.
    Pastor Rockman, I suppose.
    No, I didn't like him. In fact there were a lot of people who didn't like him. But he was just trying to

lead the church in a way he thought it needed to go. At any rate, he didn't deserve what happened to him.

They're transported the body back to Bay St. Lucy. I'm not sure when the funeral services will be, but sometime after we all get back from Retreat. Of course, the question is, when will that be? The truth is, we're all, at least in a way, being held prisoner here. It is, according to Ranger Starnes, a crime scene. There are people still to be interviewed.

Not that we would want to leave anyway.

Whatever is going to happen tomorrow, we have to face it.

Barbara Smallwood made that clear to me a couple of hours ago. You can't run, and you can't allow people to push you around.

I know Jesus said, 'Turn the other cheek,' but he didn't say run away.

And they're different things.

Barbara is right about that.

As for Barbara, I'm beginning to like her. We see things the same way, have the same quirky sense of humor that nobody else understands.

She said some frightening things about a vision she had.

I might write to you about them a little later; I don't think I'm able to right now.

I've got to turn them over in my mind.

But, as for other things...

I know where Tamp is hiding, or at least I think I do.

There's only one place he would go.

And I'm going there later on tonight. I can't believe he would ever hurt a fly. Whoever did kill Rockman, it wasn't Tamp.

I know they had that terrible argument, but that's not the same as actually killing someone.

But why did Tamp run away? And what about the knives, the fingerprints?

He'll explain everything to me tonight, I'm sure. And then I'll tell you.

More about tonight: there's a big meeting. It was called by Brother Abe, who is our leader, now that Tamp is missing and Rockman is, well, you know.

It's to be held at the amphitheater, where we had the sing-along a couple of nights ago. Sunday night was it? Gee, that seems ages ago.

The high school students, under direction of the Rapp star Jack Fontenot—I can't believe I'm even writing that—have begun working in the amphitheater on Jesus Christ, Superstar. *They had to stop, of course, because of all that's happened.*

I don't see how they could have done a full length Broadway musical anyway—but I didn't see how Cindy's middle schoolers could do Everyman. *We live and we learn.*

Anyway, it's about time to go.

The next time I write, I'll hopefully be able to tell you about two meetings.

The first with the two congregations.

The second with Tamp.

Until then...

                              Solo Deo Gloria

CHAPTER TWENTY-EIGHT: TRY NOT TO GET WORRIED...

By nine thirty the sky had darkened completely. Stars would have glittered like polished jewels above Tombigbee Forest's mid-summer Mississippi sky except for two things: first, the lights of the amphitheater glared blue-white, much as the sun would have done at mid-day, except that the sun would not have drawn instincts to circle around itself, and the sun would not have given off a strange buzzing noise, being too busy burning itself up to worry about such things.

And there was the moon.

Not quite perfectly full now, the way it had been when they all met here two nights ago to be joyous and sing, it still did its best.

Of course, the same could be said for all of them.

She sat exactly where she had that Sunday evening. This time she was holding Alanna's hand. All of them in the row—Jackson Bennet, his wife, his daughter, Allison Baker beyond them, then Lannie and Cindy, and so on, all along the row—all of them were holding hands.

Looking down at the circular stage below them, the larger than life screens, blank now, but making Nina think that they were in some university lecture hall, where power point presentations on chemistry or physics or elementary Spanish or economics or some other completely trivial in the face of murder and racial hatred subjects were about to be taught and tested and forgotten.

So those were differences between this Tuesday night and the clean pure blessed Sunday night they had spent before.

Those and the fact that, on that Sunday, only a few more than two thirds of the audience had been riveted to palms glowing pink and blue with various digital messages or songs or films or gossip: half of the adults, that is, and all of the congregation twenty-five years old or younger.

Now that fraction had jumped to ninety-nine percent, or rather, everyone in the crowd except Nina.

What were they looking at? she wondered.

Well, it had, she told herself, changed.

In previous hours, days, weeks, months, years, and perhaps decades—had she been old and out of digital touch for that long?—at any rate, in these time periods, they had been looking at images of friends and loved ones with cats.

Now things had changed and they were looking at news broadcasts.

More and more of them, all talking about this little group of disciples gathered on the shores of Lake Galilee-Tombigbee, ready to take on The Roman Empire.

The original group of Alt Righters had not been bad enough.

Now there were counter protesters.

Not only from Mississippi, but from California as well.

Did people not have enough problems in California with forest fires?

Why did they need to come here?

At any rate, it all made her wish she had a smart phone, so she could snap it shut and throw it away.

She was just in the middle of these thoughts when Brother Abe walked onto the stage, stopping just in front of the middle of three screens.

The audience was silent.

Well, that was not true, of course, but the audience was as quiet as it could be given half of the smart phones were still turned on.

Goforth took a deep breath, as though about to speak. He did not speak, however,

He simply pointed to his right.

Jack Fontenot appeared.

He was a true rap star now, long waistcoat, dreadlocks, and dark glasses.

Two teenagers rolled a small piano console close to him, and he sat down.

Once settled, he said to the audience sitting above and around him:

"You may know that I and a dozen high school students have been working on a production of the rock opera *Jesus Christ Superstar*. We were going to do it Friday night. And I want to say this right now: despite all that's happened, we're still going to do it on Friday!"

Cheers at this.

"Brother Abe and I have talked about what could be said to you tonight, when things seem so difficult. We've decided on what follows. We hope you take some comfort in it."

He made a gesture with his right arm. The glaring blue white lights went out, and the screens seemed magically to illuminate themselves. For an instant Nina saw only blurred shapes, but then she realized she was looking at a biblical scene. Or rather the film version of such a scene.

Then she realized the magic of the thing: as recorded rock music began to blare, the figures began to move. But only some of the figures were filmed images; others were the teen-agers in the production, dressed and illuminated exactly like actors who were only celluloid images.

The audience, realizing this at the same instant Nina did, gasped.

As did Ranger Starnes, who was part of the crowd.

Music grew louder: Judas was chastising Jesus; other disciples joined in the argument.

More scenes: entry into Jerusalem, betrayal, Judas hanging himself.

The teenagers merely moved in time with the beat, and moved their lips as though singing.

Somehow they had become swallowed into the production.

But then things changed.

All motion stopped as did the music.

And one young woman stepped forward, as though exiting the film itself.

It was Kayla.

And Nina remembered: she was to play Mary Magdalene.

She was now facing the audience.

Jack Fontenot began to chord lightly on the electronic keyboard in front of him.

Da Da—Da Da Da Da…

And again.

Ever so lightly.

Until Kayla began to sing.

Not to the characters in the opera, but to the congregation seated above and around her:

"Try not to get worried, try not to turn on to
Problems that upset you, oh…"

And the audience sighed as one.

Kayla, smiling ever so reassuringly, kept on:

"Don't you know

Everything's alright, yes, everything's fine.
And we want you to sleep well tonight.
Let the world turn without you tonight.
If we try, we'll get by, so forget all about us tonight
Everything's alright, yes, everything's alright,
Having sung that much, she stopped.
On one of the three boards the film images disappeared.
And the text came on.
The audience stood.
And smiled, and hugged each other, and laughed.
It all began again:
"Try not to get worried, try not to turn on to
Problems that upset you so…"
Don't you know
Everything's alright, yes, everything's fine.
And we want you to sleep well tonight.

Possibly no one in the audience knew how many times this refrain was repeated.

Nina was still singing it when she met Barbara Smallwood outside the amphitheater.

"Walk me to where I tell you," she said. "Then let's assume I gave you the slip."

Barbara smiled.

"Well. You're obviously pretty crafty."

"Damned straight."

"I have just one bit of advice for you, Nina."

"And that is?"

"Try not to get worried, try not to hang onto, problems that upset you so."

"I'll try to remember that."

And, so saying, she strode off to meet Brother Tamp.

CHAPTER TWENTY-NINE: ARDEN FOREST

Finally there was a noise in the undergrowth and her Oberon for the evening, Tamp, emerged from the woods.

He stood looking at her, his tall and even more meatless and muscle-less frame half illuminated by the waning moon, half darkened by the thick yellow pines, which, whatever non-color they seemed to be now, were certainly not yellow.

"Did you think," she asked, "that I would bring someone to arrest you? Did you think I was that disloyal, Tamp?"

He shook his head while taking one long stride into the clearing.

"I thought they might have followed you without your knowing it."

"So you just thought I was stupid."

Another step, then another.

Then, bending himself like an accordion, he was sitting beside her.

"Did you bring food?"

She nodded and said:

"I knew you would be hungry, so I brought you dinner."

"What?"

"I thought for a while about veal scaloppini with a nice hollandaise sauce. But then I decided that wouldn't be appropriate to the season, so I brought you something different."

"What?"

"Weenie. Here."

She took the thing from her pants pocket and handed it to him.

He inhaled it and said, "Thanks."

"My pleasure."

"So, who won the fishing contest?"

"Tommy Springer," she answered, "finished second. Two and a half pounds. Catfish."

"Who finished first?"

"Barbara Smallwood. Little over two thousand pounds. Alligator. Lannie Baker helped her. They threw it back though."

He smiled.

"Your sense of humor…"

"Actually it's not really…well, don't worry about it. So what's happening, Tamp?"

He took a deep breath, and then began:

"All right. There's a lot to tell, so I guess I should get started. I did just what I said I would do when I came to see you last night. I went by Rockman's room. He hadn't gone to bed, and, as he let me in, I thought things might be all right. He seemed almost friendly. Offered me a cup of coffee. While I drank it, I told him that he had won. I would be glad to go back to my own cabin, pack and take one of the church vehicles back to Bay St. Lucy. Once there, I would clean out whatever belongings I had at the church, and write my letter of resignation to the District Supervisor. All I asked was that he let me stay long enough to stand with the church against the Alt Right."

"That should have satisfied him."

"It didn't, though. He went from smiling to laughing. I realized he wasn't trying to patch things up with me, Nina. He was mocking me. He said that he had sent all relevant information about Kentwood, including pictures and official documents, to the proper

legal authorities—I'm still not certain who those were–
–hours earlier. Even before the meeting that you
witnessed, Nina! He said these authorities would be
contacting me at any time, and that I would face
charges of kidnapping and even double murder. While I
was still trying to get my mind about that, the phone
rang. It was the Bishop of the Bethel Church.
Apparently Rockman had put a call in to him late that
afternoon or early in the evening. The Bishop said…"

"I know what the Bishop said. We all do. He said the
Bethel Church had to leave, or Goforth would be fired."

"Yes. Well, at any rate, all of it coming together, I
just lost it. We both did. We fought. Both of us yelled at
each other and rolled around like kids on the
schoolyard. We also both got scratched up a little, him
under his chin, me on the cheek. But after a little while
of it we were both exhausted. So we glared at each
other for a few minutes. Then I left. I just went back to
my cabin and washed up, trying to think. I went to
sleep, exhausted I guess. Anyway I didn't wake up until
around ten o'clock this morning when the sirens started
going off. I wandered outside. That's when I found out
that he had been murdered. But I didn't do it, Nina!"

"I know that, Tamp."

"I heard his body was found in one of those canoes,
and he had been murdered with an ax. I have no ax, and
I certainly couldn't have gotten the body into a canoe!"

Nina leaned forward:

"Nobody knows how the body got into the canoe,
Tamp. But Ranger Starnes came to see me, and he
questioned me. I had to tell him about the argument
between you and Rockman."

"Of course you did, Nina. I don't blame you for
that."

"It gets worse, Tamp. Rockman wasn't killed with an ax. He was stabbed to death with a hunting knife, like the knife you bought up here last week."

Tamp seemed to catch his breath, and he whispered:

"That would explain it."

"Explain what, Tamp?"

"Last night when I went to see Rockman, I left the knife on my bed. I locked my door, like I always to. But when I got back, after the fight, the knife was not there."

"Someone had broken in and taken it?"

"Not 'broken in.' The door and lock had not been damaged. No, whoever came into my room and took that knife—had a key."

"But that doesn't make sense."

Tamp, obviously stunned by these revelations, could only stare straight ahead and shake his head. Finally he could only whisper:

"It's all impossible."

"They're searching everywhere for you. They're certain you did the murder. If they see you and think you're trying to escape into the woods, or that you're trying to steal a car—they might shoot to kill."

No response from Tamp.

Nina:

"Why don't you come down the mountain with me, Tamp? I can at least help insure that no one will shoot you while you're trying to surrender."

But he merely shook his head and said:

"I'll come down. But I know when. And I know where. Thank you, Nina. You're the best."

And, so saying, he disappeared into the forest.

When Barbara Smallwood located Starnes, he had just returned to Patrol Headquarters.

She looked at her watch: ten thirty.

For some reason, that seemed very important.

He was just about to enter the building, but, seeing her get out of her jeep, he turned.

"Did you follow Ms. Bannister?"

"No."

"I don't understand."

"I resign."

"You…but you…"

But she, driving away, did not hear the rest.

CHAPTER THIRTY: NABBED

When Nina got back to her room, at just after midnight, Starnes was waiting for her, the ever-present tape recorder running.

"Sit down," he said, curtly.

She did so.

"You've been with Tamp, haven't you?"

"Yes, I've been with him."

"You know the man is the primary suspect in a brutal murder?"

"I don't believe he did it."

"You don't believe—well, let me ask you if you believe this, Ms. Bannister: do you believe you could be, and I think should be, charged with aiding and abetting a criminal?"

"You do what you have to do."

"I was told you were one of Bay St. Lucy's leading citizens. Someone I could trust."

"Apparently you were misinformed."

"Are you trying to be funny?"

"No."

"A hundred white supremacists are going to show up here tomorrow. I'm doing everything I can to organize police protection for all of you. And for them, in reality."

"I realize that."

"You don't act as though you realize it. Every man and woman in law enforcement needs right now to be focusing on tomorrow morning. We have no idea how many people are going to try to pour in here, either to protest the churches meeting together, or to support their right to meet together. But instead of concentrating on that issue, we've got to have people combing the woods looking for Tamp. Who, despite your quaint beliefs, is to my mind as clear a murder suspect as anybody could want. Let me just go over this one more time: Rockman and Tamp disliked each other from the first. That dislike grew, over months. It came to a head yesterday morning in a near-violent argument, which you yourself witnessed. Rockman threatened to destroy Tamp. Rockman was, to put it bluntly, blackmailing Tamp because of a failed abortion that had cost the life of a young woman in the Louisiana town of Kentwood. And I need to add, Ms. Bannister, that what Pastor Tamp did with this young woman constitutes a crime in itself. Two crimes: kidnapping and homicide. And we add to this the fact that Pastor Tamp signed a document falsely stating that he was the woman's husband? All of this information Rockman had, and it was clearly enough to ruin Tamp, if not have him imprisoned. Tamp may only have disliked Rockman before; but now he had cause to both hate and fear him. At any rate, at ten o'clock this morning Rockman's body was found with a tomahawk embedded in his chest. A brief autopsy showed, however, that the actual murder weapon was Tamp's knife. Is all of this clear to you, Ms. Bannister?"

"Yes."

"And in addition, we are now dealing with the fact that you know where Tamp is hiding right now."

"Yes."

"I assigned Ranger Smallwood to follow you and locate Tamp if she could."

"I know. She told me."

"You should also know, she just resigned."

"That's too bad. She's a good officer."

"And how would you know that?"

"I'm sorry; I wouldn't. The best I can tell you is, she's a good human being."

"We'll leave that for now. The bottom line though is still, you refuse to take us to him?"

"That's right."

"Why in heaven's name not?"

"Because I gave him my word."

Starnes took several deep breaths, then continued:

"I'm begging you, Ms. Bannister. I'm literally begging you. As long as this man remains at large, his life is in danger. My officers have no choice. If they see Tamp in the woods and he runs away, they are to shoot. And I mean shoot to kill. Is that clear to you?"

"Yes."

"And still you won't tell me where he is hiding?"

"No. I have no choice in the matter. I can't tell you."

A pause, then:

"All right. I have no choice in the matter either."

He stood up and said:

"Ms. Nina Bannister: you're under arrest."

CHAPTER THIRTY-ONE: RACE CHANGE

She sat for a moment, stunned.

Her first thought was, she had never been arrested before.

Then, upon further reflection, she realized that, yes, she had been arrested before. She had been arrested two and a half years ago and charged with International Art Smuggling. And then, yes, she had been arrested one and a half years ago at Huntington University and charged with—what had she been charged with? Oh yes, murder.

The fact is, when one really thought about it, she was always getting arrested these days.

She might as well have been the heroine of a murder mystery series.

So…what was she supposed to do now?

"You're really arresting me?"

Starnes nodded.

She was still seated; he was standing over her now.

She had never realized how big he was.

"This is for your own good. And Tamp's."

"Thank you."

"You don't have to be sarcastic."

"Sorry. So where are you going to take me?"

"Security Headquarters on the other side of the park. I don't have time to take you into town."

"Can I take a suitcase or something? Some toiletries?"

"Yes, but hurry."

"I will."

Her small travelling suitcase lay in the floor of the closet.

She picked it up and was trying to remember her, 'being arrested' routine, when one of the most important parts of the procedure came to her.

She would need—ah, there it was, small, plastic, and blue, sitting where she had left it, on the desk.

Her smart phone.

"I believe," she said, sounding much calmer than she really was, "I have a right to make a phone call."

"Yes."

She picked up the phone, punched the button on the bottom of the phone, looked at the screen, and touched the icon labeled, 'Contacts.'

There it was, fourth on the list:

Jackson Bennet.

Given her proclivity for getting arrested more and more as she got older, she realized she needed to move that name higher on the list.

That, or simply memorize it.

She touched the green phone icon, then held the phone to her ear.

One ring, two rings, three rings…

Except they weren't really 'rings,' anymore, were they? What would one call these digital disturbances?

Funny, she mused, the things that ran through one's mind while under arrest.

Finally the recording:

"This is Jackson Bennet, Attorney at Law. I can't come to the phone right now…"

Maybe because it's just after midnight, she found herself thinking.

"… but if you'll leave a message, I'll get back to you."

Another beep told her it was time to record, and she said:

"Hello, Jackson, this is Nina. Sorry to be calling so late. First, say 'hi' to your wonderful wife, and hug your daughter Latoya for me. I saw you at the *Jesus Christ Superstar* mini-concert tonight, but I didn't get a chance to come over and say 'hello.' I do hope you all are having a wonderful Retreat. I'm being arrested now and taken to Security Headquarters. Please come by if you get a chance. Yours as always, Nina."

So saying, she ended the call.

The ride from her room to Security Headquarters to her room took no more than five minutes, but Jackson had already arrived when she got there.

Any number of other officers wearing all kinds of uniforms were also there, making plans for what would be happening later on in the day.

Trucks were being unloaded, and what seemed to be portable fencing was being hauled away, she assumed, to serve as crowd barriers.

"Come with me, Ms. Bannister."

Starnes had parked the patrol car and was now standing beside the open back door.

She had just gotten out when Jackson strode up, placing her in the middle between him and Starnes.

She could never remember feeling so small.

"I'm Jackson Bennet. I'm an attorney from Bay St. Lucy."

"I know who you are. I heard your talk about how everybody's got the right to carry a gun."

"Nice to know you. Now what the hell are you doing?"

"I'm arresting Nina Bannister."

"I can see that; now what the hell are you doing?"

"I'm getting ready to charge her with aiding and abetting a fugitive."

"That's ridiculous. And by the way, do you even know what the word 'abetting' means?"

"It means that if she doesn't tell us—and I mean RIGHT NOW—where Pastor Tamp is—she's going to be taken to jail."

"And what possible proof can you have that Ms. Bannister knows this man's whereabouts?"

"She admitted it."

This seemed pretty damning to Nina, but Jackson shook it off as though it had no meaning at all.

"That's doubly ridiculous!"

"All right. You can hear it for yourself. Ms. Bannister, do you know where Tamp Neufeld is right now?"

She was about to answer, 'Yes, I do,' when Jackson shook his head, took her firmly be the arm, and said, "I advise you, Ms. Bannister, to make no statement in regard to this matter until you've had a chance to confer with your attorney."

God, she found herself thinking, *I love the law.*

"Mr. Bennet," stammered Starnes, "you don't seem to understand. There is an accused murderer who is even now as we speak..."

"Ranger Starnes, I'm to understand that you have spoken with Ms. Bannister about this matter?"

"Yes, that's what I'm trying to tell you! I asked her..."

"And when you did speak to her, did you advise her of her rights to have an attorney present?"

"Well, no, but..."

"Your answer is 'no?'"

"There just didn't seem to be any..."

"Your answer is 'no?'"

Finally Starnes could only nod.

Jackson Bennet:

"I can call any of four federal judges right now, at this moment."

Starnes clearly had no idea what to do.

More cars were arriving.

Cars carrying people Nina knew.

Alanna Delafosse, for one, who embraced her and said, weeping:

"Oh my dear Nina! What are they trying to do to you?"

And then Brother Abe:

And then Jack Fontenot.

And then Darius, and some of Darius' teen-aged friends…

and more of Darius' teenaged friends.

And finally what seemed the entire Bethel Church, forming a tight circle around Nina and Jackson, who now said, ominously:

"You need to let her go into the custody of the Bay St. Lucy Bethel AME Church. If you don't we're going to charge you with police brutality directed against a Black Woman."

"But she's not Black!" countered Starnes, desperately.

To which the entire congregation gathered ever more tightly around Nina and shouted as one:

"YES SHE IS!"

Nina could only whisper, tears forming in her eyes:

"That's the nicest thing anyone's ever said about me."

Jack Fontenot put his arm around her and said:

"Come on. We'll take you with us. We're going somewhere you've always wanted to go, or so I hear. Once we get there, you can get some sleep and forget about all this."

"Where are we going?"

He merely smiled and said:

"Beyonce."

And with that, they were off.

CHAPTER THIRTY-TWO: I WILL ARISE AND GO
NOW, AND GO TO BEYONCE

Within half an hour—what time was it? One
o'clock? Two o'clock? Did it make a difference?—at
any rate, within what seemed a short amount of time,
she had become ensconced in her new home. Twenty
cabins had been reserved for the members of The
Bethel Church, and one of those happened to be vacant.

A few of the younger children were sleeping. But
most of the congregation had built campfires and were
sitting around them. Somehow the scene reminded Nina
of what many Civil War evenings must have been like,
on the eve of great battles.

And, when she thought about it, the idea of this
being a 'great battle' was not too far-fetched at that.

The Civil War continued, the campfires still burned,
and, any minute now, instead of the soft laughter and
subdued chat that was actually taking place, she might
have expected to hear the first verse of "We're Tenting
Tonight on the Old Campground."

No one had to tell her what the campfires were for.

Nor did anyone have to explain the presence, beyond
the fires, of armed police officers and park rangers
stationed every fifty yards or so, two-way radios
rattling in their belts the way Nina had remembered
squirrels chattering in the dry leaves a day or so earlier.

A day or so earlier—that is, back in time, when the
world was itself again.

The alt-right would be here at eleven o'clock this
morning.

Both congregations had been instructed as to where they were to stand, where the demonstrators would be standing, what they could be expected to hear—and see and read, for yes, of course, there would be signs—and in general how they were to behave themselves.

As though, she thought looking from campfire to campfire and the faces, the taut mouths, the eyes sparkling in firelight—as though these people, whose parents and grandparents and great grandparents and on back and on back and had been through Selma and uncounted Selma's before it—as though they needed instructions on 'how they were to behave.'

But those things would all happen in some hours, of course.

Who could say that things might not happen well before then?

This park was not fenced. Anyone, or any group might sneak in and stage any kind of 'demonstration'—or in other words 'lynching'—in the darkest hours of the morning.

And the group did not have to share officially the frequent broadcasts being forwarded to the officers—an armed group arriving in pickup trucks on Highway 72 south of Belleville, another group leaving Tupelo, a counter protest group having just passed through Newton, approximately forty miles to the East—to know what was coming, and to realize simultaneously that no timetable could be counted on as reliable.

Nina was sitting by one of the campfires, talking with Jackson Bennet about Pastor Tamp.

"Do you think he did this thing, Nina? Could he have really killed Rockman?"

"No."

"All right."

"I just can't…"

"You don't have to say any more."

"Jackson, will you defend him?"

"I may not have time; I'll be too busy defending you."

It took her a moment or so to realize that this was a joke.

Or was it?

No matter.

He was continuing though, joke or not, without waiting for a response.

"We know that he fought with Rockman—physically fought—at around one o'clock yesterday morning. Then he left. Sometime in the next hour or so someone armed with a knife stolen from Tamp's room arrived. We assume Rockman let this person in, not perceiving a threat. That was a mistake. Whoever came in at that time stabbed Rockman to death, then changed his clothes, carried him into the main room of the Park Headquarters, and somehow got him into one of the overhanging canoes."

"But why would anyone do that, Jackson? Who else hated Rockman that much?"

He shrugged:

"I don't know. I'm also worried about what might be a larger problem, if I've understood you correctly."

"Yes?"

"This entire 'Kentwood' situation that you just told me about," said Jackson. "Tamp took a woman whose identity he did not know across a state line to some sort of an establishment—we assume was an abortion clinic—where both she and her unborn child died."

"Yes," Nina replied, "and, according to what Starnes said just before he arrested me, all that could add up to kidnapping and homicide. Since Rockman had somehow learned about it, Tamp would have reason—and these were Starnes's words, 'to both hate and fear him.'"

They sat for a time.

Finally she got to her feet, saying:

"Well, there's nothing more we can do now. And thank you especially for getting me un-arrested."

"It's nothing, Nina, you know that."

"It's everything. And Tamp will see that too, in the next days."

"I just hope we can help him," said Jackson. "When he finally decides to show himself, that is."

"I think I know when that will be. And I think you do, too."

"Eleven o'clock tomorrow morning?"

"Yes. He wants to join with Brother Abe in leading the two congregations when they face the Alt Right."

"You have to admire him for that, Nina."

"I have to admire him for a lot of things. And as for the Kentwood situation, he's been living with that 'sin' for years. It's his dark secret. But the truth is, he did nothing wrong. He didn't impregnate the woman, whoever she was. He was just trying to help her."

"He should have at least found out who she was."

"But she refused to tell him! Jackson, I'm not a priest. But if someone comes to confession, admits to a crime, and asks for help, isn't the pastor, priest, father confessor, or whatever, required by the church to offer help, even if the individual insists on remaining anonymous?"

He shook his head:

"I'm no expert on these things, either. But I know according to the law, Starnes is in the right. We've all got to deal with the demonstration tomorrow morning. But after that, Tamp has to give himself up, probably be arrested, and almost certainly face trial. The evidence is too overwhelming."

"All right. I'm going to wander around a little now from campfire to campfire."

And she did.

Until finally she came to Alanna's fire, five or six people listening, Alanna sitting with a small stack of books at her feet, the brown rims of her glasses matching the color of her skin, her bright eyes reflecting the fire or the moon, or part of each.

She nodded to Nina, but did not interrupt her reading of Langston Hughes, and could not interrupt it, of course, because she was reading, "The Negro Speaks of Rivers," her voice dark and sonorous as the night as she recited:

I've known rivers:
I've known rivers ancient as the world and older than the flow of human blood in human veins.
My soul has grown deep like the rivers.
I bathed in the Euphrates when dawns were young.
I built my hut near the Congo and it lulled me to sleep.
I looked upon the Nile and raised the pyramids above it.
I heard the singing of the Mississippi when Abe Lincoln
    went down to New Orleans, and I've seen its muddy
        bosom turn all golden in the sunset.
I've known rivers:
Ancient, dusky rivers.
My soul has grown deep like the rivers.

There was nothing to be said to that, of course, so for a time the five or six of them simply sat, the others looking at the fire in front of them, Nina looking at the sky. Finally she asked Alanna:

"Do you have Zora there in that stack of books?"

"You know I do."

"And you know the lines you need to read now."

"Do you think we're going to have a hurricane here at Tombigbee Park, the way Janie and Teacake had to go through?"

Nina, though, could not stop looking at the sky.

"Look at Scorpius, the giant stinging scorpion right there in the middle of the heavens. No, I think we've offended The One Who Lives in the Clear Sky. And we'll be punished. Soon."

"And who told you that, Nina?"

The answer came automatically:

"My sister."

Alanna simply nodded and picked up one of the books, saying as she opened it:

"Well, *you* are my sister, Nina. So here it is:"

And she read:

"The wind came back with triple fury, and put out the light for the last time. They sat in company with the others in other shanties, their eyes straining against crude walls, and their souls asking if He meant to measure their puny might against His. They seemed to be staring at the dark, but their eyes were watching God."

Three a.m.

Barbara Smallwood knew that she could not be in any kind of enclosure.

So she had gone to the lake.

There were several canoes tied to each small pier.

One would do as well as another.

She was very careful to put the paddle in the water. It was not just a need to be quiet—she felt such a need although she did not know why, because the tents were a quarter mile distant and the main building even farther than that—but there was a kind of spell that had been placed on the lake and the trees and the sky. She had always been aware of this spell, even from her earliest memories as a little girl. She did not know, and never had, which Chickasaw spirit had cast it; but the spell made everything under it magic and even sacred, so that one had to move oh so quietly lest being guilty of disrespect to major forces.

Thus she slipped the paddle into the dark waters of the lake as though they were parts of some living animal that might feel pain if intruded upon too harshly.

And now, that first immersion done, she could rock back slightly in the boat and paddle.

She always began on the left side, she did not know why.

There came then the slightest rippling sound as the bow of the canoe slipped out into ink-black water. She changed hands and paddled now on the right side. That was all that was necessary to send her out toward the center of the lake, on the surface of which she saw the million gold and silver stars reflected.

All of those stars.

And, of course, she, as she rocked her head back oh so slightly, travelled back in time, being back in Oklahoma, on a lake, with her father.

Asking the thousand questions she had grown used to asking him. As soon as she knew that she was somehow different.

"Will I be a wife? Will I have children?"

And her father, merely shaking his head:

"It is for the great forces to say. But remember The Panther Woman. She planned the great victory over the Spaniard Desoto. There was no need for her to bring children into the clan. She had the heart, and the mind, of a warrior. And there were the women prophets."

Was she such a person?

She had just resigned from her job.

Why had she done that?

She had never done such a thing before.

She let her eye become fixed on a pattern of stars directly overhead.

There was the great "s," whom the people of this culture called The Scorpion.

Strange, the stories they had.

But as she watched it, another strange thing took place.

It was as though the stars in the pattern brightened.

Ever so slightly.

But they brightened.

It was as though people very close to her were watching the same stars.

And at that moment, even though she did not know what The Spirit of the Clear Sky had in store for her tomorrow—or for any of them, any day.

Even though she did not know any of these things— she knew she had sisters.

END OF PART THREE

CHAPTER THIRTY-THREE: A MIND LIVELY AND AT EASE

When she awoke, the sun had already risen.

She had no memory of actually going to bed. She must have done so in the very early morning hours. She propped herself up on an elbow and peered through the window on the opposite side of the room. A shaft of white dust hung motionless and imprisoned in the sun's ray. Otherwise the world on her side of the wall was motionless.

It was almost motionless on the other side of the wall.

But not quite.

A ring of twenty or so people encircled one of the park rangers, a young blonde boy who should have been talking to them about nature trails or flower identification or soil conservation or bird watching walks—but was not.

His voice filtered through the open window, riding along that ray that still kept fifty thousand or so minute dust particles paralyzed and hanging, prevented, at least for several more morning hours, from doing what dust was otherwise ordered by God to be spending its time doing.

"We've managed to close," he was saying, "a number of county roads leading through Parkersburg, Belleville, Hays Center, and other small towns."

There was Brother Abe, standing just to the young man's right, stepping forward into the middle of the circle and asking:

"What reason did you give for closing them?"

"Road construction. From seven a.m. until noon today."

"Is there any road construction?"

The young trooper nodded:

"Yes. There's about a ten foot stretch in each one of them that has to be resurfaced."

"Why?"

"The Mississippi Department of Public Safety tore the asphalt out of them about four o'clock this morning."

Some laughter at this.

The boy continued:

"A lot of people are mad about this. People coming in to see the demonstration. Or take part in it."

Jackson Bennet:

"Those folks are free to do their demonstrations in whatever towns they happen to be stranded."

"Yes, sir. That's what the state troopers are telling them."

"How many are going to be here then?"

"About fifty. In fifteen to twenty vehicles."

"Where are these people now?"

"Just outside of Cannonville. They're putting together a kind of procession. Signs on their trucks, that sort of thing."

"And they're still planning to show up about eleven?"

"Yes, sir. As far as we know."

"Mason Baily is leading them?"

"Yes, Mr. Bennet, he is. He promises there won't be any violence. Not unless the church groups start it."

Laughter again.

But a different kind of laughter.

A laughter born in that gap between reality and fantasy that also spawned so much hope, and so much misery.

It was now Alanna Delafosse's turn to be heard.

Nina bent forward a bit on the bed. She was not exactly certain what Alanna was wearing, but whatever it was, it was longer than full-length, and it made her resemble a chrysanthemum .

"And these people are armed, I presume."

"Lots of them are."

"With?'

"We don't really have the right to search them. We could see their weapon licenses, but it wouldn't do much good."

"How do you know that they in fact are armed?"

"All the trucks have what look like hunting rifles mounted across the back windshields. And then a lot of the men—there are mostly men in the group but a few women—have gun belts on."

No laughter at this.

No speech at all in fact.

Nina, upon visualizing the scene that was to come, realized that she should have been filled with dread. Strangely, she was not. Grown men wearing gun belts, as though re-enacting the Westerns they had all seen in their youth. There in the safety of their living rooms.

She felt an urge to laugh.

And it was only after realizing that laughing now would have been insane that she knew she must get out of bed and out of this room.

Because, looking out of the window, she was in fact watching a television show.

Channel four, the CBS eye.

No—no more television for you, Nina.

Or at least, if it is to be merely a television show, then she needed to be a part of it.

And, so thinking, she got out of bed, put on her sneakers, walked to the door, and, ignoring the crowd, took a short walk through the marvelous forest.

When she got back to her room, she saw that she had company.

Sitting in a chair in the corner of the room was her old student, May Ellen Gentry.

For a time she could only stare at the woman.

Finally she was able to ask:

"How did you get into the park, May Ellen? I know you didn't come through the front gate; they're not letting anyone in. And there are troopers stationed around the perimeter."

May Ellen did not move, but simply shook her head, saying:

"My husband grew up playing in these woods, inside the park, outside the park. He took me to a good place and dropped me off there a little before sunrise. There's a trail, kind of hidden. I can get back without anyone seeing me. What are you doing staying in this room, Ms. Bannister? This isn't the room where I talked to you before. This is the Negro part of the camp."

"I had to come here."

"Why? You're not black."

"There's some debate about that."

"What are you talking about? I don't understand."

"No, May Ellen, you don't."

But May Ellen could only shake her head, looking through the window, seeing the black faces that seemed, Nina knew, must have seemed to her completely hostile, totally alien.

And a part of Nina wanted to step back onto the porch, throw open the door, and shout to the Bethel Church now gathered in the front yard:

'Come in, all of you, and meet my best student of years past! Meet May Ellen Gentry, who has much to teach you about the current problems with our society! About how 'it's Satan's goal to have us violate our Heavenly Father's law on mixing our seed with the other people of the world.' And about how 'What used to be wrong is now right,' and 'what used to be bad is now good.' Listen to May Ellen recite scripture: Exodus 33:16 "So shall we be separated: I and thy people, from all the people that are upon the face of the earth.' And Leviticus! And Joshua! And you, May Ellen, tell the good people of the Bay St. Lucy Bethel Episcopal Church how the good Lord Almighty has ordained for them to be our slaves, slaves of the Chosen White Race!'

But Nina did none of these things.

She merely asked:

"What are you doing here?"

To which came the answer:

"I have to tell you. I have to tell you all, but especially you."

"Tell me what?"

"You remember, Ms. Nina, when we talked in your room?"

My real room, thought Nina. *My white room.*

But she only said:

"Yes, I remember."

"Then you also remember me telling you that the Alt Right was always being blamed for being ultra conservative, ultra right wing, and things like that?"

"Yes. And you also said that was going to change."

May Ellen nodded, then took a smart phone from her purse beside her, held it up, popped it open, and pressed a button.

The glowing screen was ten feet from Nina, but she could still see the face of Mason Baily, see his slicked back white hair, see his slicked back white smile, and feel the slicked back white confidence that exuded from him as he answered a reporter's questions:

"So where is your group at this moment, Mr. Bailey?"

The face moved some inches toward the camera, or the camera moved some inches toward the face. It hardly mattered which.

"We're gathering in a field, on a farm approximately five miles east of Plantersville. The farm belongs to one of our members."

"And how many of you are there?"

"Almost a hundred at this moment, both men and women."

"And again, what is it exactly that you are protesting?"

"Things unnatural and anti-scriptural. The mixing of races, which the Bible clearly tells us is wrong, and the joining of same sex couples, which the Bible also tells us is wrong. And, having said that, I wish to go even farther. Our group has been criticized as representing the so-called Christian Right. But we represent many more people than that. I'm sure your audience is now aware of what happened in the park last night. There were organized protests by groups of Native Americans, who also abominate these violations of natural laws. The truth is, people of all color and political leaning are coming together to finally say 'No," to perversions of the natural world. Today is only a beginning."

May Ellen turned off the smart phone.

"You see, Nina? This is what I told you about yesterday."

Nina thought back.

And finally she did see.

"May Ellen, you knew that these Chickasaw 'protests,' the defacing of the door, the rock through the window, the warrior appearing to the two young people, the baby alligator—you knew these things were going to happen."

"Yes, I knew."

"How? Did you plan them?"

"Oh no, ma'am. I'm not smart enough for that. But Mr. Baily is. He has a vision: he doesn't want people thinking of us in the old ways."

"I see. So Mr. Baily's vision…"

"Was to get a few people together and come into the park last night."

"And pretend to be Chickasaw."

"Yes. Randy, my husband, was one of them. He was the one painted himself up and warned the two young people out in the woods with a blanket."

"And you?"

"I helped. We needed to know everything we could know about these Indians. So during the afternoon I went to that museum. No one was there."

"So you took the book on Chickasaw legends."

"Yes. I would have stayed to buy it…"

"But you didn't want anybody knowing that the Alt Right was interested in Chickasaw culture."

"No, Ms. Bannister. You're right as usual."

"Meg and Jennifer's door?"

"That was another member of the group that's coming today. One of our neighbors. He had the idea after we read about the feathers and things in the book. He owns a cattle farm, so…"

"So it wasn't hard to come up with the…"

"Yes, ma'am. You can always find that where you find cattle."

"And your people were responsible for catching and tying up the baby alligator?"

"That's right."

"So the Chickasaw haven't been involved in these incidents at all. It was members of your group pretending to be Chickasaw, so that the nation would think you were joined by all aspects of the American culture."

May Ellen nodded:

"It's like I told you in your room, Ms. Bannister: we had to get smarter. And Mr. Bailey made sure that we did."

Nina nodded, then said:

"May Ellen, I have to ask you one thing."

"Yes, Ms. Bannister?"

"The man who was killed last night. The Pastor. Rockman. Was it your people who did that?"

"No it wasn't. But that's the most important thing I have to tell you. Randy and two of his friends had got orders from Mr. Bailey to do one more thing before they left the park."

"And what was that?"

"Go and threaten one of the pastors. Just knock on his door, wait until he opened it, wave a tomahawk in his face, and then disappear into the forest. So they were able to find out where this Rockman's room was. And they found the door unlocked. They opened it."

"And found him dead."

"Yes, and that's the truth."

"But they carried him," said Nina, "into the canoe room, and put a tomahawk in his chest just to tell everyone that the Chickasaw had cursed the coming together of both churches and the gay marriage. Rockman was actually opposed to both of these things. But, of course, they had no way of knowing that. And as for the canoe falling…"

"They tried to cut the ropes holding it up just enough so that it would fall around the middle of the morning."

"And they succeeded."

"Randy never would have killed that man, Ms. Bannister!"

"I believe you. The question is still, who did kill him?"

"I don't know. I just know I have to go now."

And she did.

Leaving Nina to wander a bit.

She walked to the lake shore.

She checked her watch. Seven-thirty.

Somehow she felt guilty.

There was nothing she could do about the events that would happen at eleven o'clock today.

But the killing of Rockman?

It did not make sense.

But all that meant was, she had to make sense of it.

There was something she was not seeing.

What? What was it? What was she missing?

Frank appeared. They walked for a time, as they had done in so many past retreats.

Then he smiled at her and said:

"Good bye, Nina."

"You came all this way to tell me that?"

"It's not as far as you think. Actually it's not far at all."

"I don't know why, but somehow that doesn't comfort me right now, Frank."

"What would comfort you?"

"Knowing who killed Rockman."

"See? Then I'm not the one you should be talking to. That's why I said ,'good-bye.'"

"Who should I be talking to?"

"You know."

And he disappeared.

She did know, of course.

But not 'talking to.'

No. 'Listening to.'

And as soon as she prepared her mind to receive them, Jane Austen's words reverberated in her brain:

"A mind lively and at ease can do with seeing nothing, and can see nothing that does not answer."

You've been seeing nothing for too long, Nina.

Stop letting your mind be at ease.

What? What is there that you've missed?

What doesn't fit? What doesn't..."

And then it began to come to her.

Just beginning, just beginning...

...and now, yes, yes...

...replay those conversations, brain.

You can do it.

Replay them!

There had been three separate interrogations by Starnes. The first occurred in her cabin, only a few minutes after Rockman's body had been discovered. The second took place in Starnes's office, Park Patrol Headquarters. The final one—when he attempted to arrest her—happened in her own room, just after midnight.

She had to re-create those conversations in her mind.

Try, Nina, try.

"You can do this!

And try she did.

The first conversation was quite brief. Starnes asked if she knew anything at all which might bear on the crime. She told him about Tamp's argument with Rockman. She said very little, except that Rockman had stormed out of the room. She had also told him—again, briefly—about the warrior who had appeared to Kayla and Darius.

And that was all she had said.

The second conversation had been somewhat lengthier.

In his office, the stenographer taking it all down.

How did it go?

How—

—and there it was, clear as day, in her mind, which was not now "active and at ease," but which was actually working. She could hear herself speaking, hear Starnes replying.

She had said:

"Rockman ordered Tamp not to perform the marriage. Tamp said he was going to do it. Rockman fired him. Tamp in effect said he refused to be fired."

"What were the two men like at that point?"

"Standing. Glaring at each other. I had to tell them to sit down, to get control of themselves."

"Did they?"

"Not really. Rockman said he would destroy Tamp."

"Are those the words he used?"

"Close enough. Finally Rockman charged out of the room."

And that was all.

That was all, she could swear it!

And there followed, of course, the midnight conversation in her room. She did not have to re-create it in its entirety. She only had to remember that Starnes had said:

'Rockman was, to put it bluntly, blackmailing Tamp about a disastrous abortion Tamp had arranged years earlier for his mistress in a Louisiana town called Kentwood.'

That was it.

But that was enough.

"Thank you, Jane," she whispered. "And thank you, Frank."

Jane did not show up.

Frank did. Smiling.

"So do you understand now, Nina?"

"I think I do, Frank."

"So tell me. What's the question you have to answer?"

Now it was her turn to smile.

"The question is, since I was the only one who knew about Kentwood—Tamp told me all about it in my room shortly before he visited Rockman—and since I never told a soul about it—"

"Yes?"

"Then how in hell did Starnes know about it when he came to my room and tried to arrest me? How the hell did he know about any of that, Frank?"

He nodded, and would have put a hand on her shoulder if he had been alive. He shook his head and said:

"We don't like to use that word, you know."

"What word? Kentwood?"

"No, the other word. As for "Kentwood" and how Starnes could have known about it—well, that's the key to the whole thing, isn't it?"

And so saying, he lifted from her shoulder the hand that never could have been there—and disappeared.

CHAPTER THIRTY-FOUR: THE OLD MARRIED COUPLE

Barbara Smallwood had pulled a chair outside, and she now sat some ten feet from the museum entrance, a yellow legal pad in her lap, a ball point pen lying on the grass.

She had come outside to compose her letter of resignation.

Instead of writing, though, she found herself glancing now at her watch, now at the sky.

Sky: Colorless. Not exactly white. She knew that would come later.

No. More like the inside of an oyster shell.

The writing pad remained blank.

How could she write a letter of resignation? Did this mean she was a quitter? She had never quit anything before.

And what would she do now?

Be a waitress?

Go back to school?

And study what? The only thing in life that truly interested her was being a Chickasaw. But schools did not offer degrees in "Being a Chickasaw."

There was only one job she knew that even paid one to do that: and she was resigning from that job now. And why?

Because she had been ordered to betray a friend. And that she could never do, Chickasaw or not.

There was more to it than that, of course. There was Starnes's refusal not merely to listen to her, but to take her seriously.

The ground white. And covered with coffins.

If this had been her imagination…

But it was not. It was something much more vivid, something that was bound to happen, something…

These musings were interrupted by the ponderous growl of truck gears, as a large yellow "Park Service" vehicle crawled to a halt some twenty feet from where she was sitting.

She noticed simultaneously that a load of something or another had been covered by a tarpaulin that lay over the bed of the truck, and that a young blonde man whose name she now knew—she was proud of that fact—was getting out of the truck.

"Hello, Bob Lee!"

He smiled a young blonde smile as he jumped from the cab in the way that only the truly young can jump, and only the beginning-to-be not quite young any more can truly miss.

"Hello, Chief Eagle Claw!"

And she smiled at this.

Good for her.

Perhaps there was in fact some youth left in her, after all.

She watched him as he walked toward her. Perhaps, she found herself thinking, she should simply stand up out of this useless chair and bound toward him like a rutting deer. Perhaps she should embrace him as powerfully as possible, lift him off the ground as she did so—for she was exceptionally strong and he was quite slender—and hiss snakelike into his lovely blooming ears the words:

"Let me show you how a true Chickasaw woman makes love. And then marry me. Let me have your children!"

That would answer the question concerning her future.

But she neither rose from the chair nor embraced him.

She stayed precisely where she was and asked:

"What's in the truck?"

He was standing beside her now, as he answered:

"Security equipment."

"You think you're going to need that much?"

He shook his head:

"It's for the other groups."

"Other groups?"

"Yes. Because of the road closures."

"Oh yes. I heard on the radio. There will be several demonstrations outside of various towns."

"That's right. We've had to divert patrols to furnish security at a number of small meetings, not just this one. And those patrolmen need protection."

He was silent for a time.

So was the forest surrounding them.

It was a near complete silence, an unnatural absence not of life itself, but of the willingness of life to give itself away.

The woods were in hiding.

But hiding from what?

It had to do with that colorless sky.

And they would all learn it.

"Ranger Starnes," young Lee was saying, "told me you would probably be here at the museum. He asked me to stop by."

"I'm glad you did," she said, truly meaning it.

Maybe he would not be her future husband.

But she was glad he was here, anyway.

"He said you had resigned."

She nodded.

"I did."

"I'm sorry to hear that. We all are. I hope it's not something any of the other rangers did."

"No. I was looking forward to working with you. With all of you."

"Well, it's kind of difficult. But there's something he wanted me to tell you."

"If it's a resignation letter that he needs, I'm working on it now."

"No. It's something else."

"What?"

"He wants you to stay in the museum here for the rest of the morning. Just to be sure there's no more vandalism."

She could not hide a slight smile.

"That's another way of saying he doesn't want me at the demonstration. He doesn't trust me. Well. Tell him I'll stay here. Tell him I won't get in anybody's way."

He was blushing seriously now.

"All right. I'll tell him. I guess I'd better go now. I have to take these shields to the patrolmen outside of Belleville."

"All right. Be safe, Bob Lee."

"And you, Chief Eagle Claw."

He turned, walked back to the truck, and glanced at the tarpaulin covering its load.

Then he asked her:

"Can you come and help me secure this thing?"

"Sure."

She rose and walked over to the truck.

Then she lifted a corner of the dark green tarpaulin, which she was preparing to pull toward her.

She looked down at the objects stacked below her.

Looked at their glass—but-not-quite-glass-surface.

Looked at their curves.

And whispered down at them, her breath clouding the one which, on top of the stack, was staring silently up at her, and, beyond her, the sunless and feelingless sky.

"Oh God."

She said God, but she might well have been addressing the One Who Lives in the Clear Sky.

How could she have been so stupid?

It did not matter.

She knew now.

And there still was time.

"Bob," she whispered.

"Yes?"

"Bob, I'm going to need you to trust me."

He stared at her for a moment from the other side of the truck bed.

"What do you mean?"

"Come here."

He walked around the back of the truck, and in a moment he was standing beside her.

She took hold of both his hands. He blushed.

"Bob, I'm going to ask you to do something that may cost you your job. Probably will."

"If I do it, will it be like we're dating?"

"We won't have sex, but you'll have to do what I tell you."

"So it's more like marriage."

"Bob, I know something that's going to happen. I can't tell you how I know it, but I do. I told Starnes about it, and he just laughed at me."

"Well, Starnes can be a jerk somehow. I told you about him when you and I first met. And about how he lost his wife."

"The drug overdose."

"Yeah. That was a good many years ago, I don't know how many exactly. Anyway, I know a few Park Rangers who knew him before that happened. They say it changed him, and that he never really got over it. He still hates somebody for it. It's just that he doesn't know exactly who to hate."

"He may hate you, if you do what I tell you. And I'm not kidding, Bob. You will lose your job."

"Well. There's always the Dairy Queen. And I'll be married to a Chickasaw Warrior Woman. Even without sex, it's a turn on just to say that."

"So do you trust me?"

"I do, Eagle Claw. I really do."

"All right. We need to wait a while. But at around twenty minutes until eleven I need you to call Starnes on your two way radio. Tell him he needs to get over here to the museum, as fast as possible. You can't go into the reasons why. But he needs to come alone, and he needs to come quick. Can you do that?"

"I don't know if he'll come. That's close to zero hour. But I'm as good a liar as anybody, if it comes to it."

"Good for you."

She let go his hands and looked up.

Sky: growing darker now.

9:00
My original room
Just waiting for the phone to ring.
I think I might know who killed Rockman.
Maybe I'm crazy.
It all depends on what Jackson Bennet is able to learn.
Ring phone, ring!

If I'm right, it means we were all wrong. We were suspecting the murderer to be someone who hated Rockman. And there were, of course, a lot of people who would have fit that description. Tamp would have been the most obvious. But everyone in both congregations knew that Rockman was working to stop our summers at the Retreat, and that he opposed gay marriage. He was even opposed to the two congregations meeting here as one.

But still, murder?

And, of course, there were the Alt Right people. They infiltrated the camp last night and played a good many tricks, trying to give the world the impression that Native Americans hated the same things that White Supremacists hated.

But somehow I believe May Ellen. I think her people found the body and moved it. But I don't think they committed the killing.

Who then?

There just is no good answer.

Unless you see things from an entirely different direction.

What if Rockman was not the true intended victim? What if the true intended victim was…

…no, I can't even write it.

Not until I hear from Jackson.

Ring, phone, ring.

I need to write about other things.

The demonstration.

We've received advice about where to stand (with the lake at our backs), what to say in response to insults (nothing), and other such matters.

Some other things to review:

The children will be together in the chapel, at least those under high school age. As for them, they've been given the choice: they can stand with us if they want.

Inez and Maybelle will watch over the younger ones.

Neither lady wanted to do that, of course. They wanted to be down by the lake with us, facing whatever we were going to have to face.

But they were selected, because they were the oldest.

And since neither of them had ever said 'no' to anything the church had ever asked them to do—well, they didn't say 'no' this time, either.

Other decisions:

We've decided to dress our best. For me that meant taking off these old flop fishing clothes that I've had on for almost two days now. And what to put on? My long, flowery dress that I've had forever. It's a weddings and funerals dress.

I'm not sure which one this occasion will be.

I'm so scared. I'm not ashamed to admit it. This won't be like arguing at the City Council about what to name the new bridge that the town has built.

This will be like...

...I don't know.

None of us know.

But I can see everyone gathering outside the main building now. It's so impressive, with the men all in their navy blue and charcoal gray suits. And look! Some of the women—Alanna, of course, and Cindy, and a few others—in big hats, as though it were Easter. As though it...

Wait.

It's the phone.

I'll write again in a minute.

It's me again.

Jackson found just what I thought he would.

The records are all there, public access, clear as a bell. Years old, but clear as a bell.

All deaths recorded in this and surrounding counties, especially those deaths of a violent and unnatural cause, are matters of public record.

The name wasn't there.

Of course, it wasn't there. And it would have been. It would have to have been.

I still don't know for sure who the murderer is. But I'm getting closer.

Next step: I have to prove that, when Rockman taunted Tamp and said he had sent the Kentwood information to "the right authorities"—well, now I think I know who those authorities must have been.

But I have to prove it.

And I know just the right people for the job.

CHAPTER THIRTY-FIVE: THE RIGHT PEOPLE FOR THE JOB

In five minutes she was standing outside the cabin of Cindy and Lannie Baker.

The door opened no more than a few seconds after her first knock. There were no words. She was simply pulled inside, and a human knot comprised of herself, Cindy, Lannie, and Allison moved seemingly of its own volition around the room.

Finally she was seated on the couch, Allison beside her and holding her hand, Cindy and Lannie seated in straight chairs across the room from her.

Lannie:

"Are you ready for this, Nina?"

"No. How could anyone ever be ready for something like this?"

"I know what you mean. I know exactly what you mean. And in a lot of ways I feel responsible."

"Why, Lannie?"

"I had to open my big mouth Monday afternoon and make that speech. If it hadn't have been for that, we might be home and safe right now."

Nina simply shook her head and said:

"We might be home but we would not be safe. It's exactly as you said it: if they can terrify us here and make us run, they can do it in our own homes. Even Bay St. Lucy would not be safe. We have to confront these people."

Allison spoke up:

"Then why can't I confront them? I and my friends are just as brave as any of the adults."

It was Cindy who answered:

"There'll be plenty of time for all of you to fight. And there'll be enough enemies to go around. But, Nina, we wanted to ask you something.'

"Of course. "

"When the time comes and the Alt Right people are coming down toward us—we'd like to be standing with you."

"And I with you, Cindy. The three of you are the finest people I know. Of course, I would be honored to stand with you. But now I have a favor that I want to ask. Please, feel free to say 'no.' if you don't want to do this. It's just—well, it seems very important to me right at this time."

Cindy leaned forward on her chair and said:

"Anything, Nina. Anything at all. What is it?"

"I'd like you to break into the Park Patrol Office and steal something for me."

The three of them sat mute for a time.

Finally Allison asked:

"Can I come, too?"

Nina nodded:

"I envision you as doing the actual stealing."

Allison waved a fist in the air and yelled:

"Yes!"

It took them very little time to walk to the Park Ranger Office, which was, as Nina had hoped, almost deserted. There was the prim and perfectly organized woman Nina recognized from her earlier meeting, and whose name plate sitting on her desk read "Jeannette Richardson."

All other officers and officials were, she assumed, getting ready for the arrival of the Alt Right.

So there was no one to be surprised when she walked in and said:

"I'm Nina Bannister. I'd like a meeting with Ranger Starnes."

Jeannette Richardson simply shook her head and said calmly:

"He's out on Park business at the moment. "

"May I wait?"

"Of course. We have a waiting room right through there. Help yourself to any of the magazines.

"Thank you."

And, as demurely as possible, she sat down and began to read.

Thinking all the time:

'All right, Cindy! It's *Everyman!* If you were ever an actress, be an actress now!'

And Cindy did not disappoint.

"My car! My car's been stolen!"

She burst through the front door of the office, Allison a foot or two behind, as though she were a madwoman. Her hair was in disarray, her eyes tearstained, her hands and arms jerking uncontrollably, and her voice shrieking as though she were in the process of giving birth.

It had the beginnings, Nina found herself thinking, of an Oscar-winning performance.

It was a pity that no one was there to watch it except Jeannette Richardson.

But Cindy did not get as far as Jeannette Richardson's desk.

Instead she threw herself down in a corner of the room, beating with one fist on the baseboard while the other simply flayed the air with unbelievable violence.

"They just took it! It's a new car but we can't do without it! We'll be ruined, don't you see? I won't be able to take Lannie to the hospital. And he's sick, don't you understand? How could they just take it like that? This is a state park for heaven's sake. What happened to the law? What are we going to do?"

By this time Jeannette Richardson had reached the prostrate faux theft victim, was leaning down over her, and attempting to comfort her.

"There, there, dear! It's going to be all right!"

"No, no, it's not! We'll never get over this!"

"I'm sure it was insured!"

"No, that's just it, it wasn't insured! We couldn't afford to pay Lannie's medical bills and buy insurance too! No, it's just lost!"

"Just try to sit up, honey! I'll try to call one of the rangers!"

But the woman was not calling a ranger; she was bending over Cindy, trying to insure that she did not have a stroke and die.

Allison, meanwhile, had crossed the room and was standing in front of an open door that led, Nina knew from experience, toward a welter of offices, one of which was Starnes's.

She looked furtively at Nina, who nodded back.

Then she disappeared through the door.

Cindy's histrionics continued.

She was really a marvelous little actress, Nina observed.

Those were real tears.

One of her shoes had flown off, and just finished sliding across the center of the floor.

The performance lasted at least another three minutes, or enough time for Allison to come back into the room.

She looked carefully to be certain that she was not being observed by the administrative assistant-now-turned First Responder—then walked briskly to Nina and gave a large white envelope with the letterhead labeled 'Kentwood City Government' to Nina, who put it in her purse.

Allison walked outside.

Cindy was now sobbing inconsolably.

And she continued to do so for perhaps a minute more, after which Lannie walked into the receiving room and stated flatly:

"I found the car."

And in five minutes all of them were gone.

It took her an additional ten minutes to reach Jackson Bennet's cabin

All of the people in both congregations were milling around, embracing each other, preparing for the confrontation to come.

But she and Jackson, sitting in straight chairs on the cabin porch, were thinking of other things.

"You're certain," she asked him, "that you couldn't be mistaken?"

"No. The records are clear. No one by that name died in the way you describe."

"All right. Then I think I know, Jackson. It's the only theory that makes any sense."

"Tell me."

"It came to me when I was thinking about the three conversations I had with Starnes. In the first two I never mentioned anything about Kentwood. But in the third, the night he tried to arrest me and you stopped him, he knew everything. The botched abortion, everything."

"So how could he have known?"

"That's what I asked myself. There was only one way, since I never told anyone and Tamp certainly didn't. When Tamp went to see Rockman after midnight and the two men had their fight, Rockman taunted him and said that he had not only learned about Kentwood but had sent records concerning the whole situation to "the proper authorities." Tamp, when he and I talked, had no idea who those authorities were. But I do know."

"So who were they?"

"'They' were Starnes. He's the leading police official here. Rockman thought, since kidnapping was involved, that Starnes would act quickly. But he didn't act quickly. He just put the report from the town of Kentwood on his cluttered desk—and I know it was cluttered because I was in there—and did nothing. Or rather, he did a lot. Just not what Rockman had expected."

"Wait. Are you trying to tell me…"

"That report told Starnes something he had ached to know for years. Like, what had actually happened to his wife."

"My God, Nina, I think I'm beginning to see."

"She didn't die of a drug overdose, like Starnes had told everyone. That's why you couldn't find the name Starnes listed among the overdose victims for this or any other adjoining county. She ran away. She ran away because she hated her husband."

"She ran away with Tamp. Who took her to Kentwood."

"To have an abortion," Nina continued. "She loathed her husband so much that she couldn't stand to have his child."

"But Starnes probably never knew she was pregnant!"

"No, almost certainly she wouldn't have told him."

"So when he saw the Kentwood documents," Jackson said, nodding as things became clear to him, "that Starnes gave him, when he read about the abortion…"

"He assumed Pastor Tamp had impregnated her."

"The man he hated all these years was right here in front of him. But why didn't he just turn Tamp in, given the documents he now had?"

"Because abortion was not illegal at that time in Louisiana, Jackson. Tamp would have been disgraced when his actions came out and were revealed, but he would not have faced murder charges."

"And Starnes wanted him dead. So why didn't Starnes, if he hated Tamp so much because of this information, just go to Tamp's room and shoot him?"

Nina shook her head and said:

"That would have been too quick, too easy."

"So he set it up so that Tamp would not be the poor helpless victim of a murderer, but a murderer himself. A murderer who would be completely disgraced, would spend agonizing years on death row—and who would ultimately die in the electric chair."

"While Starnes could watch, and, as the arresting police official, attend the execution."

"It all fits," said Jackson. "Starnes killed Rockman. There's just one question left."

He was interrupted by the blare of a bullhorn, and they heard Brother Abe's voice saying:

"It is time now, brothers and sisters in Christ. Let us go among them!"

Then there was a cheer, and Nina could see, as though he had magically materialized beside Brother Abe, Brother Tamp, waving to the crowd and smiling.

"Yes," Jackson Bennet repeated. 'There are really just two questions."

"What are they?" asked Nina.

"Who do we tell? And how?"

CHAPTER THIRTY-SIX: THE GOOD BOB LEE

Just before eleven o'clock Barbara Smallwood and Bob Lee had reached the point designated by Starnes as the center for the defense posed by State and Park Police against whatever demonstrators might come. This point lay at the top edge of the grassy meadow which stretched down to Tombigbee Lake. To the left, any observer could watch the entire meadow and the calm water beyond. To the right was nearly impenetrable forest.

As she got out of the truck, she imagined herself as The Panther Woman, having outlined the Chickasaw defense against Hernando de Soto in just these woods more than five hundred years earlier.

This particular defense she had not created, but that fact did not keep her from scanning it with a degree of admiration. Starnes might well, she told herself, have been lacking in crucial insights, but he was no fool, and he had done his homework, not only with regard to Charlottesville, but also several of the demonstrations and counter demonstrations that had happened since.

Glistening silver metal fences snaked their way down the hillside, creating a kind of maze designed to filter people into definite destinations, each one separated by the others by distances as great as sixty or more feet.

Many separate groups.

Each group saying whatever it wanted, and in whatever manner it chose to.

Each group, when the time came, to be surrounded by a line—a thin line, given, but still a line—of subtly armed police.

Helmets, goggles, night sticks.

No rifles visible.

Handguns holstered, almost invisible.

And, of course, the most important thing of all.

The shields.

And Bob Lee—the good young Bob Lee who had no reason in the world to be risking his career because of the ravings of a mad prophetess—now climbing upon the back of the truck he and she had just arrived in, switching on the bullhorn and making his announcement to the twenty or so patrolmen who were now getting themselves outfitted and ready:

"Everybody listen up!"

A bit of milling around.

Mumbles, quiet jokes, nervous laughter.

The screech of electronic amplification.

"Please listen up."

Gradually diminished noise from the group.

Another face turned upward toward the truck.

Another still.

First lie:

"I've just gotten some orders from Ranger Starnes, who, as you all I'm sure know, has been called away for just a couple of minutes to attend to some matter on the other side of the park."

Now no crowd noises at all.

And for the first time this morning, the low growl of thunder.

"There are about thirty shields here in the rear of the truck."

Not a lie.

"They had been meant to be used by patrolmen at Bellevue, who, as you also know, are awaiting a demonstration much like the one that will take place here."

Also not a lie.

"We've been informed that they have sufficient defensive equipment, and do not need more shields."

Second lie.

"So Ranger Starnes has asked you to take these shields and distribute them as evenly as possible across the grass below us."

Stunned silence.

Finally a voice:

"What?"

Another:

"What are you talking about?"

Then a chorus:

"Are you crazy?"

"Is he crazy?"

"Just scatter them on the ground?"

"What the hell good is that going to do?"

"We're arming the demonstrators?"

Until finally all questions and all insults had melted into one confused jumble of confusion and disarray.

Which Bob Lee waded into again, his voice still calm, his demeanor that of a natural leader.

It was unfortunate, Barbara found herself thinking, that he would need to find a new career.

In the end, the leader succeeded in leading.

Barbara herself stayed in the truck and simply watched as the hillside became covered with neat rows of carefully laid out shields.

She only opened the door and got out when she heard the sound of an approaching vehicle which, some instinct told her, was Starnes's patrol car.

She heard his first shouts, which were, of course, directed at Lee.

'What in Christ name is going on here, Lee?' was the general tenor of his demeanor.

It was softer than it might have been, of course, because he did not want an entire crowd of law enforcement officers to realize that their leader had been made a fool of.

But upon hearing these words repeated for the third time, she glanced down the hill, saw what she was expecting to see, she stepped down upon the ground, walked around the truck, and confronted Starnes.

Red faced, he hissed at her:

"You! What are you doing here? I sent Lee over with…"

But she merely shook her head and interrupted him:

"You don't have time to question me now," she said quietly.

"What do you mean I don't have…"

"Time. You don't have time. Look down the hill. The church groups are arriving. And that man leading them is, if I'm not mistaken, Brother Tamp."

CHAPTER THIRTY-SEVEN: NO JUDAS HERE

There could be no thought now concerning Rockman's murder, Nina realized.

More important things were happening.

The two congregations were in place, standing close to one another, in as tight a circle as fifty or so bodies could form.

The lake was to their backs. Nina watched for a second a rabbit scamper across the green lawn stretching upward to the main camp building before them.

The sky continued to darken, and thunder formed a rumbling background song that they had just started singing.

"Yes we'll gather at the river,

The beautiful the beautiful river

Gather with the saints at the river

That flows past the throne of God."

She held tightly to the hands of two people, one on her left and one on her right. She was, she realized, not even aware of who the two people were.

"When we reach that shining river,

We'll lay every burden down,

Then grace our spirits will deliver,

And receive our robe and crown."

She took some pleasure in visualizing the circle they had formed as the face of a clock or watch. Jack Fox stood at 12 as he led them in the song. At eleven and one respectively were Brothers Tamp and Abe.

And now, beyond them, coming down from the top of the green hill, was a Park patrol car, the red light on its roof flashing and rotating, its wailing siren making a bizarre harmony with the rhythmic lyrics and the incessant thunder.

The circle shifted.

Like a living cell, like pictures she had seen of an amoeba, it changed its contour.

It had, in fact, left Brother Abe in his same position while engulfing Brother Tamp.

He was now simply one of the worshippers, but she could not locate him.

The patrol car came to a stop some ten feet from the outer edge of the circle they had formed. The door opened and Starnes emerged. He took three long strides toward Brother Abe.

The two men stood within six feet of each other.

Starnes stopped, looked at the two congregations massed before him, and announced sternly:

"Pastor Tamp Neufeld, I hereby arrest you for the murder of Aaron Rockman."

No movement.

The crowd was silent.

Starnes:

"You need to come out here and face this thing, Tamp. You did the crime, and you know you did. Your friends can't hide you forever. And as for the rest of you, you need to step back so that we can get this business taken care of."

Again, no movement or sound from the crowd.

Again Starnes:

"Come out here, Tamp!"

And then a voice from the interior of the crowd:

"No Judas here!"

Again:

"No Judas here!"

More people took up the chant. Then more, then more.

"NO JUDAS HERE!"

"NO JUDAS HERE!"

The crowd was getting louder.

Starnes continued to stare.

And the standoff would have continued for an indeterminate amount of time had it not been, at precisely eleven o'clock, for the arrival of the Alt Right.

CHAPTER THIRTY–EIGHT: HE THAT LIVES IN THE CLEAR SKY

It took less than two minutes for Barbara Smallwood—and all of the officers working with her—to realize that it was not going to work.

Reports that kept filtering in days later assigned the blame to various causes, the primary one being that the vehicles which should have been detained outside of the park were in fact allowed to enter it, so that instead of a line of demonstrators filtering into the upper part of the green lawn where they could be identified, sub-divided, and herded down the hillside into carefully pre-conceived trails—instead of this human line there was instead a fifty yard row of pickup trucks, vans, jeeps, old Volkswagens, and impossible-to-identify junkers, all parked as close together as possible, all disgorging people who had nothing in common but anger.

Had the mass of humanity let loose upon the otherwise tranquil setting been uniform in its belief system, some order might have been maintained. But this was not the case. Rather, any number of counter protesters had been allowed to drive their vehicles into what had begun as a file of alt-right protesters, meaning that rioting began almost immediately.

All that was needed was for bearded people to get a quick glimpse of non-bearded ones.

Even color became secondary to facial hair as an incendiary mechanism.

So that she and her fellow officers became useless spectators, just as similar officers had been all of those months earlier at Charlottesville.

They could only watch as people kept spilling on the ground, screaming obscenities, hurling themselves into whatever bodies happened to be standing closest to them, and hurling at the same time bags of urine, which exploded upon contact with the faces, arms, legs, backs, and stomachs that happened to be in their paths.

The air became instantly filled with screaming and stench.

Everyone was acting—violently—and no one knew what to do.

Barbara stood by helplessly, watching as the patrol car that had driven down to the lake began to make its way back up the hillside.

This was Starnes, she knew.

But she also knew he was much too late.

Nina could only watch in horror.

The entire mob before her kept making its way down the hill, toward the water, toward the two congregations.

All of the people who were not attacking each other were staring down at them, at what seemed an ever smaller knot of shrunken humanity, with nothing at their back to escape into except a clear wall of implacable water.

Then there was an arm around her, and a voice in her ear:

"It's all right. We're together. Hold onto us!"

Lannie and Cindy Baker.

"We're family now; just hold on, Nina."

She did so, as tightly as possible.

She felt herself beginning to cry.

The mob kept coming. Now there were not only people on the hillside but trucks too, men in bandanas with rifles, the barrels of which were sticking up into the air; the same men whose mouths were opening and shutting soundlessly, unable to be heard over the incessant roaring that was the aggregate of all the screams and obscenities.

At that moment the sky became completely black.

And it began.

CHAPTER THIRTY-NINE: THE SHIELDS OF ACHILLES

At first, Nina was to remember later on, it was mere rain, torrential and soaking but bearable. In fact the first wave of panic swept over her not because her wonderful dress, her beloved floral dress, had instantly become a cold rag-film clinging to her body—but because she could not see. Everything was grey-black and shimmering, as though, instead of water being dumped upon her from the sky, she herself had plunged into the lake. There was the mad instinct that told her she was drowning; a part of her wanted to swim upward and get to the surface.

But there was no surface to reach.

Breathe, Nina. Breathe.

She was able to do so, and she continued to do so while she crouched and put both of her hands palms down on what had seconds ago had been grass covered lawn, and was now shallow but ever-deepening water.

"Lannie!"

But he was gone.

Everyone was gone and everyone was there, hovering over her, running into her, failing completely to get around her.

While the rain intensified and the thunder drowned all of the screaming and taunting and cursing and shooting and whistling and bellowing and metal-against metal truck-collisioning that had filled the worlds of green lawn and blue lake no more than minutes earlier.

"Lannie! Cindy! Alanna!"

She was, she realized, only forming the words. No sounds were coming out of her mouth. Or if they were sounds they were stillborn, drowned instantly by a combination of exploding thunder, driving rain, and tornadic wind.

Now, though, she was on her feet again.

Making her way forward, aware vaguely that her shoes had been mud-shucked from her feet, and that she was slipping downward twice for every one stride that took her forward.

And then another pair of arms was supporting her, another face, water-blurred, only inches away from hers.

"Barbara! Barbara!"

"Nina, you have to take this!"

"What is it?"

Only then was she aware that an object of some kind had been forced into her hand.

A shield.

Dumbly, uselessly, she looked down, barely able to see it, as though it had been a curved and polished mirror.

"Take it! Take it!"

She became aware that her head was shaking.

"I can't put it on!"

Now it was Barbara who shook her head and said in a voice shrill enough to be heard the few inches distant that brought its notes to Nina's ears:

"Get under the shield! When it starts, get under it!"

"I don't understand!"

"Get your head under it! And help the others!"

"Which others! What are you talking about?"

"The heads! Everyone's heads! The rest doesn't matter! It will hurt, like you're being punched. You'll want to scream! But keep your heads, and their heads, under the shield!"

"Whose heads, Barbara?"

"It doesn't matter! Don't you see that? We're all in this! We're all the same!"

"I don't understand!"

"You will! Now go with God, Nina Bannister!"

And Barbara was gone.

It was as though she had taken with her some of the steam, smoke, water, flesh, and cloud that had been impairing Nina's vision; because, for just an instant, it was possible to see some distance up the hill.

It would have been better, Nina realized in an instant, had she been able to keep her eyes on the ground.

For she now was able to realize two things: first, the mobs of protesters were now upon them. All groups, soaked and disoriented as they might be, had begun to mix. Her two congregations had lost their identity as had the Alt Right, as had the counter protesters, as had anyone pretending to be Chickasaw, and, more frightening still, as had the Park Patrol and the State Police.

Second, worse, the vehicles lined together at the top of the hill—those at any rate which had remained where originally parked and not tried to drive down toward the lake—had formed a barrier.

No one could go back beyond the entrance of the park.

No one could cross the lake.

They were all trapped together, not as four or five groups, nor as two, but as one mass, now thrown upon each other, still willing to fight or scream or curse, but with every soaked drenched moment, less able to do so.

And then the hail began.

Nina thought of it first as a mere irritant. As she stood with the shield held uselessly in her right hand, she watched whatever patches of the hill she could see as ice-pellets began to bounce in all directions, as though the gods had dumped sack after sack of ping pong balls on the rapidly flooding half acre that sloped above and around them.

Then the pain began to intensify.

Bee stings at first on her neck and shoulders, thumps and half blows on those parts of her somewhat protected by the water-faded and skin clinging rag that had been her dress.

But worse now.

No marbles bouncing harmlessly, white and laughing on a game-board table that had once been green.

Larger objects.

She could hear now, mixed with the wind and rain and cursing and thunder, the sounds of limbs in the forest to her left being ripped from the trunks of trees.

Leaves being shredded.

Then the screams began.

She was kneeling now.

She had gone some distance up the hill.

But she was able to realize two things simultaneously:

First, it did not matter what distance she went or in what direction.

She was trapped here like all the rest of them.

Second, the pain was becoming unbearable.

The objects raining down on her were the size of baseballs.

Hurled at her back, her shoulders, her arms, her hands.

The back of her neck.

Her forehead and temples.

She was being, she forced herself to realize as she watched the blood flow first in a small stream then as a red rivulet, down upon her bare feet—beaten to death.

Then Barbara's words came back to her:

'Get your head under the shield! Get your head under the shield!"

Of course, Nina, you idiot!

You don't wear the shield—you get under it!

Farther up the hill Barbara Smallwood was stalking the battlefield—for what else could it be called now—as though she were the Panther Woman, directing not the defense of the Chickasaw against the Spanish, but humanity, imperfect and foolish and hateful though it might be but still humanity—against the forces now unleashed by Him Who Lives in the Clear Sky.

And she realized it now: she was playing the role she had been ordained to play.

Outfitted in a helmet, well-padded at the neck and shoulders, protected by the shield she had strapped around her muscular back, her eyes protected by the dark sun glasses that had been built to resist flying debris—thus protected she was able to do her job, which was to make sure that the objects lying on this field of battle were not, as she had originally interpreted in her vision, coffins, but rescue shields.

"Get your heads under! Three of you! Three per shield!"

And it did not matter which human being was being rescued at any one time.

"It hurts! It hurts so much!"

Which meant she had to kneel and whisper in the ear of whatever Methodist or White Supremacist or young or old police officer or Bob Lee or—yes, if it came to that—even Captain Davis Starnes:

"The blows to the body won't kill you! It's like you're being hit in the ribs by a baseball. You'll get over it! But your head! All three of you are going to share this shield, are going to be sure your heads are under it. Hold hands! Pray! But you three are together now. You're human beings, you're going to save each other's lives!"

And this she did, again, and again, and again…

Until the Spirit Who Lives in the Clear Sky had been satisfied.

And the horrible stones stopped falling.

And she could look out across the field once green now almost completely green now white…

Littered with not caskets but shields.

Shields that had saved the lives of human beings.

Who were now crying and praying and holding hands.

And who were all the same.

CHAPTER FORTY: WANDERING

For a time—she had no idea how long a time—Nina simply wandered.

They all did.

The scene reminded her of an old horror film. In black and white, of course, because the low scudding clouds remained black after disgorging their contents, contents which made the ground white.

There was no blue, no green. And the only red to be seen was found in the wounds that made all the wanderers look like battle victims.

Which they were, of course.

No, it was a horror film; a zombie film.

They had lost all identities, the people in front of her, around her. What had been their clothes, identifying them, giving them what they had taken to be their identity, their belief system—these were all rags now, like what had been leaves in the lush Tombigbee Forests were rags.

And they wandered, hugging each other, crying in each other's arms.

The wind was dying gradually, so that sound was decreasing. The ambulances and Medevac vehicles were approaching from every direction though, so the noise did not really lessen but merely changed in pitch.

She had trouble walking. Her shoes were long since gone, and she saw dimly when looking down that her feet seemed blistered. The bright crimson circles the size of quarters, of fifty cent pieces, were not blisters at all, she dimly realized, but wounds from the stones that had pelted her, had pelted all of them.

It was only now that she began to realize how much pain she was in.

Or perhaps she had not really been in pain before. Perhaps the shock had been too great. Lying there as in a Plexiglas womb, nose buried in the grass and mud-water, fingers interlaced with those of strangers, all of them screaming, praying for it to stop—perhaps her little insignificant brain had been too overcharged to register anything as simple as phrases such as, 'It hurts!' or 'Make it stop!'—and it was only now, walking as best she could, picking her way among these slowly melting and ever-more-slippery ice globules, that her body was able to begin the process of bruising, swelling, bleeding, and throbbing.

Vehicles had now begun to arrive, media cars and trucks as well as medical assistance units. She could see reporters holding hand-held cameras and talking into microphones, in about the same numbers as she could see first-responders wheeling stretchers out to people as yet unable to stand.

The stories would circulate for weeks. The first ones she read with some eagerness, the later ones with growing indifference, the final ones not at all.

What difference did it really mean? The stones had been the size of baseballs. No, softballs. No, grapefruits—such a comparison deemed necessary by the Mississippi media just in order to rival the great hail storm over Bangladesh in 1968 which killed more than two hundred people, their skulls crushed.

Barbara Smallwood was in charge now, and she realized it. So did everyone else. It was not only Bob Lee who continually looked to her for advice, for gestures showing him which victims needed care the most—it was all of the patrolmen and all of the state troopers, all of the medical personnel. Wherever she was on this never-to-be–perceived-again–or-at-least–pray-God-let's-hope-not field of ice bombs, people looked to her for advice.

And she knew how to give it.

Just as she had known—at the last minute, true, but still knew—about the shields and how to use them—just so she knew what to do with the wounded, and what level of care each of them needed.

She no longer had a perception of precisely where she was on what had been the long, sloping, green lawn, or where the lake had gone to, or what had become of the park buildings. She knew only that what had once served as Starnes's headquarters was close by on her left.

And there, sitting almost motionless in a gray wicker chair that could have been perfectly in place for an afternoon summer garden party-there was Starnes himself.

He looked up at her.

She caught her breath, barely able to stutter the word:

"Sir!"

It was not a question, not a request for an order, not the announcement of a brash cadet reporting for duty.

It was more the expression of, more than concern, but rather of horror.

He had on no shield, no protective gear of any kind.

Blood trickled down several gashes and wounds on his cheeks and temples, his forehead, his neck.

"Sir!"

The same silly exclamation.

He did not really respond to it.

In fact, she was uncertain whether he really realized she was there at all.

She was just an object to which to direct his words as he stammered:

"It's the same."

"Ranger Starnes, I…"

But he just shook his head and said:

"Out of control. The same."

"Sir, you're bleeding badly!"

"I couldn't save her. And I couldn't save them."

She knelt beside him, placed her hands palm down on his knees, and said:

"Sir, no one is dead."

He looked back at her and replied:

"One is."

The wails of sirens intensified.

CHAPTER FORTY-ONE: TO BE YOUR PARTNER

It was as true to say the procession found Nina Bannister as to say that she found it. The truth is that neither could have existed without the other.

It was not a long procession as much as it was a necessary one.

In a morning of elemental forces, it stood out as, if not the most spectacular one, at least the longest in coming, and the most necessary to be fulfilled.

Pastor Tamp led it. It was he who put a hand on Nina's shoulder and looked down at her.

She was not surprised that he failed to comment on her appearance, her abrasions, her small blood-lettings here and there. He had similar blemishes. They all did.

No, he simply said:

"I believe you agreed to be one of our party."

She looked behind him.

Brother Abe.

Jack Fontenot with the guitar—a guitar scraped by hailstones but still relatively intact, its strings just as taut as they were when they were playing "Shall We Gather at the River," some hundred or so years ago. Jack, and behind him Kayla and Darius, Alanna, Cindy and Lannie, the Bennet family.

And behind all of them, smiling, bleeding, smiling still more—

Meg and Jennifer.

Nina nodded:

"Yes. I agreed."

Tamp nodded, smiled, and said:

"I believe it's time, don't you?"

She returned both the nod and the smile, but tried to spread them over the entire little group as she answered:

"It's a perfect time."

And so they set off.

The procession had grown by the time it reached the lake. There were ten to fifteen members of each church. But there were also strange faces. Members of Alt Right perhaps.

All of the faces, bleeding and bandaged though they might be, were smiling.

Nina felt a hand grab her shoulder.

Jackson Bennet.

"Are you all right?" he asked quietly.

She nodded: "Bruised up a little. But otherwise I'm fine."

"I'd like to watch this ceremony, Nina. But there's something I've got to do."

"What?"

"I've got to find Starnes and tell him what we know."

"Why? Why now? Everything is chaos!"

"That's just it. From what I know of Starnes, and from what we know he's done—he might keep trying to arrest Tamp. Or kill him."

"What are you going to tell him?"

"I'll tell him what you and I both know now to be true; that he killed Rockman with Tamp's knife, which he had stolen a short time earlier from Tamp's room. He didn't even have to pick the lock. He had a master key because of his position as head of park security. And, of course, his fingerprints, once the knife is carefully checked, will be on it."

"How do you think he'll react?"

"I don't know. But I'll be sure there are other people around in case he gets the idea to shut me up. Somehow I don't think he'll do that. I think he'll see reason. At any rate, I'll tell him we know it was his wife Tamp took down to Kentwood, and that, as far as he has known all of these years, it was Tamp who ruined his life. I'll also tell him I think he has a good insanity defense, and I'll offer to defend him—provided, of course, that he gives himself up by no later than today."

"All right, Jackson. Good luck."

He left, disappearing into what was still a growing, crying, sobbing, multi-ethnic and multi-political persuasion wedding audience.

Tamp strode to the middle to the edge of the lake, Goforth right beside him.

Jack Fontenot took his place beside Tamp, and, just to his right, Kayla.

Jack played the first chords. The wind had died almost completely by now, and the metallic wailing of sirens was muted by the thick walls of the amphitheater.

Kayla sang:
 I don't know how to love her
 What to do, how to move her
 I've been changed,
 Yes really changed,
 In these past few days
 When I've seen myself
 I seem like someone else

The guitar continued to strum softly. Kayla's singing stopped while Goforth spoke to Meg and Jennifer:

"Will you have this person to be your partner,
To live together in holy marriage?
Will you love, comfort, and keep each other,
In sickness and in health,
Forsaking all others,

Be faithful as long as you both shall live?"
Meg and Jennifer:
We will.
Back to Kayla, who sang:
Don't you think it's rather funny
I should be in this position?
I'm the one who's always been
So calm, so cool, no lover's fool
Running every show
It scares me so!
Meg and Jennifer together:
In the name of God I take you to be my partner, to have and to hold from this day forward, for better, for worse, for richer, for poorer, in sickness and in health, to love and to cherish, until we are parted by death. This is my solemn vow.
Kayla:
It scares me so!
I want you so!
Tamp and Goforth together:
"And now because Jennifer and Meg have exchanged their vows before God and these witnesses and have pledged their commitment to each other, we now pronounce them in the name of God, the Father, his Son, and the Holy Ghost, solemnly married."

CHAPTER FORTY-TWO: HER NAME WAS...

There followed a great deal of hugging and congratulating.

Among the strongest hugs came from Barbara Smallwood, who had just joined the crowd. She smiled and said:

"You made it, Nina!"

"Because of your shields. Because of Achilles' shields."

"I don't..."

"Achilles was a great warrior. Before going into his hardest battle he had made for him a special shield. The shield has pictures of battle, but also pictures of people of all races feasting and laughing together. It's a shield that says out of hatred and violence, someday peace would come."

"I love that idea. But I have to tell you, I have a note here from Ranger Starnes."

"Did he give it to you in person?"

"No, Bob—that is, Patrolman—Lee just handed it to me. He said Starnes had given it to him a few minutes earlier, and had looked very strange. Anyway, here's the note:

Nina opened the small sheet of white typing paper and read:

'To Nina Bannister:

I would like to meet you and Ranger Smallwood in the amphitheater. I want to apologize to you both. I was unfair to you.

Of course I was unfair to everyone. I realize that now. I realize that it was my child, not Tamp's. The truth is, I betrayed everyone.

Just one thing though.

Her name is Elizabeth.

I wish you could have that engraved on the stone.

That's all, until I meet you in the amphitheater.

Starnes'

"What do you think, Nina?"

"I think we should go to the amphitheater."

"What does he mean, he 'betrayed everyone?'

"It's a long story."

"Well, maybe he'll tell it to us."

Nina shook her head.

"Somehow I don't think so. But come on, let's go."

They did.

The screens on which the theatrical presentation had been played on Tuesday night had, of course, been decimated.

But their metal frames were still strong enough, and they provided a good place to tie one end of the rope.

"My God," whispered Nina, as she watched Starnes's body swinging like a pendulum in what was now a cool and increasing breeze.

Barbara simply shook her head and said:

"All our Gods."

And for a moment or so, they were silent.

Sunday Night
One Week After Returning from Camp
   Writing on my Deck
   Petting Furl
   Yes, he's back, as am I.
   I missed him.
   I think he missed me, though you wouldn't know it.

Darned cat.

The Sunday night church group met again tonight as usual.

Of course, it will never be usual again.

People tried not to talk about the things that happened at Retreat.

All of it is too painful.

But it was still like our Upper Room, our Last Supper

Pastor Tamp was there.

He told us he was leaving.

There were just too many things he had to get straight in his mind.

He said he would be back, though.

He doesn't know when.

We'll be waiting.

Solo Deo Gloria

EPILOGUE

The middle of October.

The creek drew her on, as she knew it would.

She had slipped down into it a mile or so back, at Milepost Three of the old Northern Mississippi logging trail. Now she was approaching Tombigbee Park itself, and watching for the signpost or marker that would announce her passing.

The creek itself was so different from the fir and evergreen forests that topped and surrounded it. It was a multitudinous thing, a camouflage of colors and textures, of shale rocks and speckles of iron ore and maple leaves and, here and there in the dark pools, the splash of gold and orange from perches' gills or bream flanks.

She made her way along slowly, carefully, reverently, as though she were in church.

Which, of course, she was.

She had slipped down into the creek a mile or so back, at Milepost Three of the old Northern Mississippi logging trail. Now she was approaching Tombigbee Park itself, and watching for the signpost or marker that would announce her passing.

She made her way carefully out into the middle of the creek, white limestone rocks slippery beneath her boots.

Now she could peer up between the branches of oak and pecan and fir, up into the wondrously blue October sky.

The banks closed in upon her, and she had to climb up out of the creek itself, which had become deeper.

The carpet of trees lowered themselves down over her, darkening the world.

Which became quieter too, all noises subsumed into dark-mossed green pools.

There before her in a patch of thorn and thistle sat a rabbit, deathly still, watching her as she approached, too frightened to move, almost invisible, save for its dime-shining eye that tracked her while, reflecting the sun, it gave itself away.

She would not bother it.

There before her, almost obscured by undergrowth, was a brown wooden signpost upon which, in yellow letters was carved in yellow-painted letters, the words:

YOU ARE NOW ENTERING THE TOMBIGBEE
STATE PARK

After another quarter mile, she began to hear voices, campers, parents and children hiking on the trails which surrounded the creek. She made her way up the slippery bank and out into the forest itself, tipping her hat as she met various campers, who spoke joyfully to her:

"Beautiful day, Officer!"

"It certainly is. You folks have a good time."

She walked on, the trails becoming more crowded now.

Finally Tombigbee Lake spread itself out before her.

Not a very big lake—she could easily have swum across it

She let her eye flirt across the blue surface.

A few boats out toward the center, and several fishing piers extending sixty or so feet out into the water.

A solitary young man wearing a Park Ranger's uniform met her as she neared the lake.

"Hello, Eagle Claw!" he said, laughing.

"And hello to you, Bob Lee!"

The embraced and kissed.

She still had the feeling that she could pick him up if she had wanted.

He could decidedly not pick her up, because she had become several pounds heavier.

"What did the doctor say?"

"Everything going fine."

"We still looking at March?"

"That's what he says."

"Good. Come on. Some friends of mine from Plantersville have invited us for lunch. You okay with that?"

"Whatever you say, honey."

And she walked on, her arm around him, ready to become one with her people.

THE END

ABOUT THE AUTHORS

 Pam 'T'Gracie' Reese is an assistant professor of communication sciences and disorders at Purdue University Fort Wayne (PFW). Nina Bannister was created while T'Gracie was a doctoral student at the University of Louisiana-Lafayette. She has happy memories of exploring Acadiana, dancing the Cajun waltz, catching beads at Mardi Gras and listening to French on the radio. (Geaux Cajuns!) Still, she also loves her new life in Ft. Wayne and enjoys getting to know northern Indiana. (Go Mastodons!)

Joe Reese is a writer and teacher. He's only partially responsible for the ten Nina Bannister mysteries (co-written with his wife, T'Gracie), but he has to take full blame for *Kate Dee and Katie Haw: Letters from a Texas Farm Girl* and the play *Lunacy: A Play for Our Times*.

He and his wife have three children: Kate, Matthew, and Sam. The two of them now live in Fort Wayne, Indiana, where each teaches at PFW.

Faith Change is the eleventh in the Nina Bannister mystery series. The other books are *Bed Change, Climate Change, Frame Change, Game Change, Mind Change, Oil Change, Sea Change, Set Change, Sex Change,* and *Time Change.*

www.ingramcontent.com/pod-product-compliance
Lightning Source LLC
Chambersburg PA
CBHW020226260626
47156CB00002B/551